THE
OTHER
CHEEK

The Other Cheek © 2019 Jafe Danbury
www.JafeDanbury.com

Jefe Press
P.O. Box 1714
Soledad, CA 93960-9998
www.JefePress.com

Ordering Information:
Quantity sales. Special discounts are available on quantity purchases by corporations, associations, and others. For details, contact the publisher at the address above.
Orders by U.S. trade bookstores and wholesalers. Please contact Jefe Press, or visit www.JafeDanbury.com

ISBN 978-1-7333440-0-5

First Printing, 2019
Printed in the United States of America

Cover design and formatting by Damonza.com

ACKNOWLEDGEMENTS

This book would not exist without the encouragement, support and gentle nudging provided by some key people in my life. My friends and family have been amazing, and a few specific mentions are in order.

I will always be indebted to my dear mother who years ago saw something in me that I didn't see myself, and said, "I think you should be a writer!" It only took me about twenty years to take her advice and, well, thank you, Mom! (I'm sure you're smiling down on me with pride, Mimo, and I apologize for any cuss words found herein.)

Huge thanks to my amazing wife, partner and head cheerleader, Martina, for your unwavering support as I set about telling this difficult story. I couldn't have done it without you. Thanks for believing in me, baby!

To our pack of four-legged children, I know it was a long process—like, seven times longer for you guys! Thanks for your patience while Dad did his thing. Copious amounts of turkey jerky for you all, I promise!

Ronda and Jack, thanks for your interest and enthusiasm, and for reading my early drafts. David Donovan, graphic artist and resident dream merchant at dbdonovan.com, thanks for your wizardry. Damon, and staff at damonza.com, for helping me realize my vision for the cover.

To the gifted musical artists and music publishers who kindly granted me permission to use referenced song lyrics in my work, I am very grateful. They were important to the story.

Wow...and to my nudger-in-chief: the amazing Lisl Zlitni, at Great Land Services. Your expertise, attention to detail, suggestions, and editorial services were outstanding. Thanks, "coach", for your counsel and your friendship—and helping me get off the dime to actually do something about this project. The work's better for your involvement!

Dear readers, thank you, too, for choosing to go down this dark path with me. Beyond any entertainment value *The Other Cheek* may provide, hopefully it might too—in some small way—help somebody who finds his or herself in a similar situation to Rich's.

Gratefully,

~ Jafe Danbury

Matthew 5:38-42

38 *"You have heard that it was said, 'Eye for eye, and tooth for tooth.'* **39** *But I tell you, do not resist an evil person. If anyone slaps you on the right cheek, turn to them the other cheek also.* **40** *And if anyone wants to sue you and take your shirt, hand over your coat as well.* **41** *If anyone forces you to go one mile, go with them two miles.* **42** *Give to the one who asks you, and do not turn away from the one who wants to borrow from you."*

Richie 1:1

1 *"Oy."*

◆

THE
OTHER
CHEEK

JAFE DANBURY

CHAPTER 1

Sherman Oaks-adjacent, California
Spring 1992

RICH BRYSON TUGGED at the ragged edge of his scrotum-length cutoffs, making sure he was properly tucked in, and popped the top on his frosty Meister Brau before settling into his desk. It wasn't a desk as one would think of it, but rather a silver pool raft, a cheap one at that—but he did have a cordless phone resting on his bare chest, and the deep end of the apartment complex's pool was his office. With a view and no dress code. Good work if you can get it.

Rich's buddies teased him for always wearing his trademark short shorts, even to work sometimes, but he didn't mind—who wanted a stupid tan line down by their knees? Not him. He was a trend bucker and, besides, he had the legs for them. At least the West Hollywood crowd seemed to think so when he found himself working over there.

His Revo sunglasses provided the perfect amount of "pop" to complete this Zen moment, enhancing the electric-blue sky as he took in his favorite sight: the clusters of waving palm trees that populated this little oasis. It was truly vivid and reminiscent of gazing through his favorite childhood contraption, the View-Master.

A smile crept across his face as he tuned into the mockingbird song coming from the nearest palm. It seemed this area was also the bird's place of business. Rich always found it hypnotic, and a source of marvel, that his feathered friend changed voices every few chirps, without fail. *How does he do that?!* Rich lifted his beer in a gesture of *cheers* to the bird. Life was good in this moment, floating here in this sanctuary, listening to his own personal mockingbird on this seventy-nine-degree day in March.

It'd be even better if I got a work call today.

He'd barely finished his thought when the phone rang. *Thank you!*

"Hi, this is Rich," he answered on the second ring, a mixture of cheerful and professional.

"Richie! Bob. Dude, glad I caught you. Busy?"

"Hey, Bobbie! Busy? Not for you, man. What's up?"

"Got a two-day shoot next week. Need a handheld. Full rate. Probably some overtime. You available?"

"Next week?" Rich asked, creating a pause to take a first pull on his suds and check his mental calendar. "Next week...let me check...next week...what days?"

"Thursday and Friday. Concert gig. Should be fun."

Concert gig? Woo-hoo! Hell, yes, I'm available!

"Yeah, Bob...looks like those days are good! Cool, man."

"Awesome! I'll get back to you later today with call times and location. It'll be great to see you, dude!"

"You too, Bobbie! Thanks for the call, man."

"Talk to you later, Richie! Bye."

Rich clicked off the handset and settled back into his floating cubicle. For reasons Rich never questioned, it seemed that nearly everyone in the freelance television production community—the "below the line" ones, anyway—were addressed as *dude*, and with an *ie* suffix to their name. Rich was...well, Richie. Bob, Bobbie.

Jim…and so forth. It's just the way it was. It was like their own little version of "The Name Game," a song that had been popular when he was a kid:

Richie Richie Bo Bitchie

Banana Fanna Fo Fitchie

Fee Fi Fo Fitchie…Richie!

He used to laugh when the principal at their school would come around to his fifth-grade classroom, guitar in hand, and sing that song, asking for name suggestions from the students as the song progressed. Rich's name was never chosen—for reasons he later understood, and some wiseacre would eventually yell out, "Chuck!" but Mr. Riley only fell for that once.

Rich(ie) was perfectly comfortable with the suffix dealio, really, especially when that was what his parents always called him, for as long as he could remember. They still did—without fail.

He was no longer the curly blonde toddler they still saw him as; he was a strapping, yet youthful, thirty-four-year old man now, but he was cool with it all and very much in touch with his inner child. Rich had boyish good looks that he wasn't fully aware of, and nobody ever guessed his age. He wasn't sure it was because he looked younger than his years or because his inner goofball made him seem that way. His lean, six-foot frame was a golden tan, and his sandy blonde era-appropriate mullet suggested a surfer, but that was an activity best left alone. He'd been utterly freaked-out by *Jaws*, and preferred the calm predictability of his pool/office, thank you very much.

Rich looked over toward his apartment door, a scant thirty feet away, which was ideal for this whole cordless-phone-on-the-float scenario. He'd installed a basic wood-framed screen door a while back, which helped keep the flies out of his studio apartment while still allowing his phone's base unit and handset to communicate properly.

What was also ideal was that this pool/office was essentially all his. Rich was, on average, a good fifty years younger than the geriatrics that lived in this complex, and they weren't big on going swimming in March.

Out of the corner of his eye, he spied a little orange spot bobbing on the surface nearby. A poor, helpless ladybug, far from shore, seemed in need of a rescue. Rich cupped his hand, scooped up the little critter, and slowly paddled to the edge with his free hand, placing the little guy safely atop a potted plant at the edge of the pool. "There ya go, little guy...don't forget your flotation device next time."

The phone rang again. *Susie, please hold my calls.*

"Hi, this is Rich," he answered on the fourth ring as he waved away a tenacious fly.

"Hey, honey...I got them! They're perfect!"

Richie set his beer can down carefully on the tile before responding. "Hey, you...that's great, sweetie." He wracked his brain. *Them...?*

It was Tami Matthews, his girlfriend, er, fiancée, now; they were getting married very soon.

"What—did you get?"

"The shoes, silly! They're ordered, for all the bridesmaids!" she said.

"Ah, awesome!" God. How could he forget? This had only been a three-month search for the perfect shoes to go with the seafoam green dresses she'd picked—and that the bridal party was surely going to hate.

"What are you up to today, honey?"

"Oh, you know. Catching up on stuff around here. Packed a couple more boxes. Just booked a couple days of work for next week too!" he said, perhaps a little too enthusiastically. "Thursday and Friday. Concert shoot, pretty stoked!"

"Next Thursday and Friday?"

"Yeah. Just booked it."

"You forgot about the cake tasting appointment, didn't you? And meeting with the photographer? You can't work Thursday and Friday, honey. Remember?"

"Oh, no…that's right…" *Damn!* They'd already met with this cake person twice, sampling and rejecting flavors until his taste buds couldn't distinguish between coconut cream and mashed potatoes. It was akin to going to the perfume counter when you don't know what you want—and they all start to smell the same after a while. But, apparently a third meeting with the cake lady might yield just the perfect flavor(s) that had proven so elusive. Never mind that it was like an hour and a half drive—more like two hours—each way to Orange County. *Taste buds, concert shoots and paychecks be damned! Whatever makes my baby happy, but I've got a honeymoon to pay for.*

"Listen, sweetie…any chance we might be able to reschedule those so I can take this gig? Bora Bora's going to be so expensive, and— "

"Fine. Whatever…" Tami said curtly. "I'll just call and try to reschedule another appointment with both of them—and my parents. It's just our wedding cake, and pictures."

Rich could feel the cold front developing through the receiver. "Aw, c'mon, honey. That's not fair. You know how important all of it is to me too. If we can just find a way to make both work it would be—"

Click. Dial tone. Cue mockingbird.

Rich wasn't sure if he liked the tone of voice the bird had selected, and could almost swear the thing was literally mocking him now. He swore under his breath. Why did he suddenly feel guilty for trying to enjoy this tiny window of relaxation?

It was Tami who had persisted in selecting Bora Bora as their honeymoon destination (Rich had floated suggestions of San Diego, Mexico, and Hawaii, but they were vetoed as not being exotic—*or expensive?*—enough), and Rich felt obligated to book any and all gigs possible between now and then to make it a little less hemorrhaging on his freelancer's bank account. It seemed to him Tami didn't appear to grasp the concept that he was the sole breadwinner.

He gathered his headphones and cassette Walkman from the nearby table, then tossed his nearly full beer in the trash and went back inside. His first day off in ten days, and he'd been looking forward to a day of floating, but his buzz was now killed.

◆

Tami exited the sidewalk phone booth outside of Cloud Nine Shoes, an upscale-for-this-part-of-Anaheim boutique on a busy boulevard. She was equal parts repulsed by the dirty phone receiver she'd had to endure and peeved that Rich was making her change the appointments. *Do I have to do all the work here?* Dressed down for errands, in her Daisy Mae cropped top and threadbare holes-in-the-knees Levis, she was still a 105-pound head turner. Like in the song by the Commodores, she was a "Brick House."

She didn't look pleased as she tossed her head, sending a cascade of long, shiny blonde hair past her shoulders. Had she chosen to, she probably could've enjoyed a successful career doing nothing but shampoo commercials; her hair was that healthy looking, but she was a serious actress—an *actor*, as she liked to refer to herself. *Actress* didn't have the same ring of authenticity to the profession, in her mind, so she preferred the more gender neutral—and respectful-to-the-craft—moniker. She'd definitely accept the Oscar® for Best Actress in a Leading Role, don't get her wrong, and it was something she planned on someday. She had her speech ready.

Tami was graced with the DNA of a thoroughbred. She belonged to the zero body fat club and unlike many of her peers, didn't need to rely on surgical procedures to achieve her shape. Perfect teeth, with a little help from those braces in her sophomore year, blessed her with a smile that had melted Rich the first time he'd been in its crosshairs, that day by the pool eight months ago. They were the two "youngsters" in that apartment complex, and it hadn't taken long for them to become friends, and about a month later, lovers. She was twelve years younger than Rich, on paper, but there was really no discernable age difference.

Even in her teens, Tami had never been much of a dater. A few encounters with sleazy producers and acting coaches had soured her. And she didn't have the time for that anyway, with auditions, scouring the *Hollywood Reporter* and *Variety* rags for potential gigs, and working the occasional odd job to support her ambitions.

Like everybody else, she'd done the waitressing schtick, sold office supplies over the phone, she'd even sold water softening systems door to door (a gig that she bailed on after a week). Whatever it took. But it was all beneath her.

Her pet peeve, however, was having to lower herself to take gigs as an *extra*, the very thought of which made her shudder. She was an *actor*. *Extras* were...*trees*. *Background*.

Tami was the foreground. Center frame. The *talent*.

She'd taken years of acting classes with the best coaches and had theatre experience: she could dance, and sing like an angel—making her the rare "triple-threat." It was just a matter of time before it was her turn to shine.

She had time for Rich, though. She loved him very much and took comfort in his easygoing manner and support. She was also enamored by the fact that he was a cameraman; they would make the perfect Hollywood couple. Maybe he'd be the one filming her blockbuster!

As she reached her beater Honda sedan, a couple of guys hung out the window of a passing Mustang, yelling catcalls at her.

"Whoo-hooooo! Hey, baby!"

"Dream on!" she yelled back, tossing her bowling bag of a purse onto the passenger seat. It was then that she noticed the expired meter and the parking citation on the windshield. She yanked the ticket free and tossed it toward the seat, and it cascaded onto the floor, atop the trade papers, Der Wienerschnitzel wrappers, and a few other parking violations.

"Fuck you!" she shouted, this time to the entire City of Anaheim Parking Enforcement Department, as she thrust the car into the busy boulevard traffic, eliciting a few well-deserved blares of the horn in the process.

It was going to be a long drive back to the Valley.

◆

CHAPTER 2

RICH EXITED THE shower, wrapped himself in a towel and surveyed what was left of his fading tan lines. He would've liked to add some color today, but it wasn't meant to be.

He walked across the tiny apartment to the wall calendar near his phone and looked a bit worrisome as he took inventory of the blank days for next week. He'd have to make it up somewhere, but that was the life of a freelancer: Peaks and valleys. Oh, well. He could use the time to finish packing boxes, and he prayed that Tami was using her time to do the same at her place.

As if the upcoming honeymoon costs weren't squeezing Rich enough, he'd had to tighten his belt as escrow was about to close on the townhouse he and Tami were occupying a scant few days before the wedding. The down payment had cleaned out his savings, and Tami had insisted they go furniture shopping so that everything was fresh.

He was perfectly comfortable with his garage sale furnishings—which were still in decent shape—but this was a joint step they were taking, so he agreed to the new couch with dual built-in recliners, the matching loveseat, the coffee and end table set, the designer lamps, the art, the high-end king bed and other bedroom furniture, the bigger TV, the entertainment center...

This was getting real. Real expensive! *Oy...*

The realtor had subtly mentioned to Rich that even though he was buying the townhouse as a single person, and in his name alone, it would eventually become community property. Just saying.... Rich wasn't the slightest bit concerned though because he was about to marry the love of his life and anything short of *happily ever after* wasn't even a slight possibility.

A year ago, before Veronica had broken his heart and absolutely crushed his very soul, he'd considered *her* the love of his life, but again...not meant to be.

At his lowest moment, in his darkest *poor me* period by the pool one summer day, he'd been laying there on a lounge chair, minding his own business—just him and the bird—when a shadow crept across him, blocking his personal sunshine. He'd opened his eyes to find a girl—a really pretty blonde girl—standing over him. With this game-changer smile!

She'd asked him if the neighboring lounger was taken and if he'd like to share half of her tuna fish sandwich—and she was wearing a great bikini. And he was a goner. So, it could be argued that Tami was Richie's rebound girl, but he'd have none of it. She had pulled his self-esteem out of the toilet and he jumped into this new relationship with both feet. And now he was getting married! *Too quick? Nah!*

Rich closed the blinds. It was dark, and he was half naked. Didn't want to be responsible for any old ladies going into cardiac arrest. Might even void his lease.

He took a moment to peruse the numerous framed photos that comprised his personal wall of fame. Extending the entire length of one wall, it was pretty impressive, considering all of the celebrities he was pictured with. From Milton Berle to Jimmy Stewart...

from Art Linkletter—to Mr. T., he'd seemingly worked with them all—A-list and D-list alike.

Rich plucked one of the eight-by-tens off the wall and looked at it: Rich, with Gene Simmons in full *KISS* regalia, at a concert gig he'd worked on. Gene and Rich were posing in front of a wall of Marshall amps with their tongues sticking out at full extension, and Gene clearly had Rich by a couple of inches.

He carefully placed the picture in the open packing box atop the kitchen table. He grabbed another one, this of Rich holding a monstrously heavy looking handheld camera rig, being hugged playfully by fitness guru Richard Simmons. Rich had shot pretty much all of the *Sweatin'* exercise videos over the years, and he found Mr. Simmons to be a hoot to work with, even if the flirtation felt a little awkward at times. He chuckled as he set that picture into the nearly full box, pondering the possibility of Richard Simmons and Gene Simmons being somehow related. Secret fraternal twins, separated at birth. *How twisted would that be?!*

Rich noticed the light blinking on his nearby answering machine, and he hit *play* as he continued to gather more treasures for the box. The machine's robot voice told him that he had two new messages. A moment later, a sweet older woman's voice took its place, and he paused to give his undivided attention to his favorite person in the world.

"Hi, Richie dear, it's Mom. I'm sure you're quite busy with packing, and the wedding plans, and work, and who know what else, but I just wanted to call and see if you got rid of that terrible cough yet…? Did you get those antibiotics? I hope so."

As he listened, Richie picked up the recent four-by-six framed family photo from the table: A handsome, pleasant looking family of five comprised of his late-sixty-something parents, Jeanette and Len Bryson, Rich, his forty-something sister, Ellen, and their brother, Scott, late thirties. Smiles all around, and genuine, mutual love oozed from the picture, not like that painfully posed Olan Mills schtick.

"—We're all looking forward to seeing you soon, dear, and we're praying for you, and for Tami, and we love you very much, Richie. Take care of yourself... Okay, bye bye." *BEEP.*

"Bye, Mimo," he replied with a smile, as he gently placed the picture into the box with the others.

"Next message," the robot said. When Tami's voice came on he stopped what he was doing and stared at another nearby picture on the table: Tami and Rich at "The Happiest Place On Earth"—for most anyway, standing in front of the castle, wearing the mouse ears.

"Hi, Honey..." she said. Rich braced himself; he wasn't sure which version of her he was going to get after their earlier conversation. "Miss you. Sorry we got disconnected earlier. Stupid phone booth.... Wow, I can't believe how much stuff I have...not sure where it all comes from. I'm going to be packing until late—not sure when I'll ever finish.... Hate moving—but I'm excited to be having our new place together, don't get me wrong! Moving day does suck though, huh? Oh, and the cake lady said she *can* do the Kahlua cream filling now— remember we tasted that one before and liked it! So we're set with that... And don't forget to have your brother confirm his tux. Let's see...what am I forgetting? Shit..."

Rich was now watching the little cassette reels spin inside the Panasonic machine as she continued.

"Oh, yeah! I threatened my parents and said that if they were going to be all holier-than-thou, and not allow champagne at our wedding, that we were going to change venues and elope at the last minute, even though they've already received all of the RSVPs. She must've freaked when she considered what everyone might think, because she called back later and said that she and my Dad had changed their minds about that. So, we're good with the champagne now. We're having little silver ribbons on the glasses that have sparkling cider, and gold ribbons on the ones with champagne. Or was it the other way around? Anyway..."

Rich shook his head and packed a couple of more trinkets. *Does she ever come up for air?*

"Unbelievable..." she continued, sounding more tired now that she'd had her opportunity to vent. "I want a champagne toast at our wedding, don't you? I know you do too, baby. So, that's been my day. I hope you're having a good day, sweetie. Okay, don't hurt your back. Call me later...love you."

BEEP.

The robot announced, "End of messages," much to Rich's relief at this point.

He placed the Disney picture in the box and sealed the top with packing tape. He grabbed a felt marker and wrote on the box: *UPSTAIRS—FRAGILE.*

He had no idea...

◆

CHAPTER 3

A LARGE VINYL banner reading *AMERICA'S FUNKIEST FOLKS* hung from the upper rails overlooking the food court area of the shopping mall—wherever they were this week. It was all a blur to Rich. He'd reluctantly taken the job to augment the loss of the concert gig he'd had to cancel—*and could be working on now that Tami straightened things out with the cake lady.* But Bob had already booked another handheld camera, and that was just the way it worked. Rich detested these shoots.

He'd done several of these over the past couple of years. Always set up in the food court area at some frigging nondescript mall, in some frigging nondescript town, with hundreds of frigging hillbillies auditioning to get their shameless stupidity immortalized on video tape, hoping for their thirty seconds of fame—and a shot at ten grand in prize money. *Oy. Shoot me now.*

Rich looked at the seemingly endless line of contestants waiting for their turn to step before his portable lights and share their—what the producers generously labeled—talent.

The only saving grace to these shoots, if there was one, was the fact that the "prosumer" gear was an easy schlep. Instead of the nearly forty-pound Betacam rigs he usually hoisted on his shoulder for ten hours at a shot, these shoots only called for very light duty, plastic Hi8 video cameras. Because, really, at the end of the day, how much production value do you have to throw at a bunch of toothless wonders showing you their best Steve Urkel impressions? Probably only 5% of the stuff they shot ever made it past the screening interns anyway. He was sure this was more of a publicity deal than anything else.

He shuddered to think that his six years of college had amounted to…this. But, hey, if it helps pay off the hot tub they just purchased for the new backyard, bring it. Thank God he'd be flying back tomorrow night on the red eye.

An acne-ravaged kid in his late teens stepped up to the paper-taped T-mark and handed Rich his release form. Rich scanned it and momentarily feigned just enough enthusiasm.

"So, it says here you're going to be…showing us your best arm farts! Cool." Rich looked over at Josh Goldberg, the fifty-something field producer sitting in front of a portable Sony monitor on the nearby folding table. This wasn't Josh's dream gig either, as he had once enjoyed success as one of Hollywood's go-to game show directors, but he'd signed on for the season (his and Rich's third). Josh gave Rich the thumbs up, and the twirling-finger "roll tape" signal. Rich looked over at the terminally bored nineteen-year-old goth girl standing next to him. She was seriously testing the thread count on her too-tight-for-this-gig Hooters shirt, having been hired by Josh during his shift at that fine dining establishment the night before.

Rich had always found it curious how married men, present company included, seemed to think it was okay to be flirty (and sometimes more) when working on the road. Rich knew in his heart of hearts that infidelity would never be an option for him. Call him old fashioned. Surely Josh, during his scouting for local talent, had recognized this young lady's hidden audio production skills, because she'd been hired to hold the boom microphone.

And God knows what else. He shuddered.

The poor girl looked pretty nonplussed that she had to wear

headphones during this upcoming act. She chewed her gum defiantly. Rich knew all too well that there was nothing quite like listening to squishy arm farts enhanced through a Sennheiser shotgun mic and Sony studio headphones to add sunshine to your day. Hooter Girl (Rich had forgotten her name) had signed on, and was making a hundred fifty bucks a day here, so he didn't have too much sympathy.

She reluctantly swung the six-foot boom pole into position, right above the guy's head. Rich composed the shot, chased the microphone out of frame a couple of inches, then stabbed the red record button with his thumb, telling the budding thespian to look in the camera, state his name, say what his act was and "Go!"

"Hi. My name's Billy, and I'm…I'm…gonna show you my arm farts," he blurted with a giggle. Then he tucked his palms under his sweaty pits and let loose with a half dozen beauties before stopping and smiling at the camera.

"And….CUT!" yelled Josh. "Fantastic! Thank you very much!"

Hooters Girl wasn't smiling as she yanked off the headphones and parked her butt back on the Anvil case. Josh went to shake the kid's hand but thought better of it and handed Billy an *"I'M ONE OF AMERICA'S FUNKIEST FOLKS!"* bumper sticker as he exited the makeshift stage to much applause.

"Only four more hours, Richie. Hang in there, brother."

"Yeah," he weakly replied.

Bora Bora, Richie….

◆

Rich tried to forget the day, taking relative comfort in his motel room's queen bed, which sure felt like a double; he'd requested a king, but, oh well. Propped up on one elbow, holding the phone with his free hand, he attempted to stay awake long enough for signs the conversation was coming to a close. Rich had never been one for long phone sessions, and he had met his match in Tami, who—given a bee in her bonnet—could, and would, talk for hours. The clock radio mercilessly displayed the late hour of 11:33. He was beyond exhausted, and felt like he'd been eaten by a coyote and shit off a cliff.

"Uh-huh. Okay, well you're almost all packed, right?" Rich asked, stifling a yawn. He could picture her on the other end, playing "Beat The Clock" as she packed up her chaotic hovel of an apartment. He wasn't too far off.

With her hair hiked up in a ponytail and standing amongst several empty moving boxes, Tami surveyed what looked like tornado damage. She wasn't even close, not by any stretch of the imagination.

"Almost," she lied, grabbing a tape gun, nearly dropping the phone.

"Well, maybe your mom can come over tomorrow and help you finish," Rich said.

"Not an option. She offered, but she'd just make me crazy right now."

"How about your brother? Is David available?"

Tami grabbed a framed photo from the end table and looked at it. Taken a couple of years ago, the image showed her standing next to her brother at his high school graduation. His smile and chiseled good looks rivaled Tami's.

"I'd rather eat razorblades," she replied, letting the photo drop into the box in front of her. She was unconcerned by the sound of cracking glass.

"Well, I wish I could help you, but I'm stuck here for another day and won't get home 'til o-dark-thirty," Rich said with a long, impossible-to-suppress, audible yawn. "Sorry, baby. Long day.... Couple of hours later here—got to get some sleep."

"I know you hate working on that show, sweetie, but hang in there. The money's good. And my audition yesterday went well, I think, so hopefully that'll come through too."

"Yep. Okay, baby, I'm officially destroyed and I have an early call—two hour drive to our next mall location."

"Okay...love you, sweetie. Just think: In a little over a week, we'll be married—and laying on an exotic beach drinking out of coconuts!"

"Mm, I like the sound of that..." he said, his voice trailing off. *If only we didn't have the move in between, but we'll get through it.* "It'll be great," he continued. "Good luck on the packing, honey. Love you. 'Night," he said, as he fumbled for the light switch.

"Night," Tami said, hanging up the phone and picking up her orange tabby cat, Dozer. She engaged in the requisite baby talk with him, eliciting a loud meow. "How's my baby? How's my baby boy?" If the cat could've talked, he probably would've answered something to the effect of, "How the hell do you think I am...your shit everywhere...can't even find the damn food bowl...jeezus!" But he went with *Meow.*

Tami put him down and looked at the digital clock on the counter. It read 9:36. She stared at it a moment longer as the numbers on the display seemed to be bouncing in place. Tami blinked hard, looked away, then walked into the bathroom, taking a long look in the mirror. She had dark circles under her eyes and she looked like she felt. She was usually a night owl but knew tonight was going to be a particularly long one battling those boxes.

Tami washed her hands with soap and water for the better part of a minute. They weren't especially dirty, but she washed them often and a bit obsessively. That might account for the fact that her hands looked about three decades older than the rest of her.

She reached for the light switch, her hand just resting there for a few moments. Her fingers drummed the switch for several seconds before she finally flicked off the light. In the darkened room she declared to herself, "Awesome!"

◆

CHAPTER 4

THE TOWNHOUSE WAS in the center of the cluster, with their unit sharing walls on either side. Tami had voiced, during the signing of Rich's escrow papers, that it wasn't a "unit"—it was a home, *their* home. The escrow official had politely nodded in concession as she continued pointing to the colored flags where Rich needed to sign. Tami had asked if she too could sign the documents, being as it was going to be home to both of them, but the agent explained that only Rich's signature was legally permissible.

A *SOLD* sign was still posted in the small common area out front. Located just outside the hustle bustle of the San Fernando Valley (The Pit, as Rich preferred to call it), the complex was almost on the cusp of Ventura County, and Rich had decided they had to be at least one freeway exit outside the smoggy basin. In reality, living one exit outside the smog was akin to choosing a table in a restaurant's non-smoking section when a rope stanchion was all that separated it from the toxins, but it was one of his mandates. He'd had to weigh the extra drive time that would be involved against the relative serenity of cleaner air (in his mind, anyway) and rolling hills. Even though the new Explorer's odometer would be spinning faster than a Vegas slot, this location of their first home together was deemed most important.

An enormous moving van occupied most of the parking area, and two husky moving guys were shuttling boxes and furnishings inside. They negotiated a narrow concrete path to the front door as they carried a new, plastic-wrapped couch inside. Nearby, a little boy watched the activity from his tricycle.

The couch narrowly squeezed through the door. Rich, wearing his favorite LA Dodgers cap, was standing just inside the doorway, himself holding a heavy box. He directed the movers toward the small living room. It was looking much smaller now as Rich saw it rapidly filling up with the new stuff.

"Over there, guys. Far wall. Thanks." He watched them set it down and start to remove the plastic. "It's okay, guys. I'll do that stuff." These guys were on the clock and there was still a huge truck to empty. *Ch-ching!* He was going to need to book some serious work when they got back from the islands.

Tami walked in carrying a gold-painted plaster statuette of two lovers. It was about two feet tall, and they were naked and in an embrace. "Aren't you glad we found this to go with the new stuff, honey?" she said, beaming. "It looks like us, that's why I had to have it!"

"Yeah, honey. Love it," he said with a smile. "Uh, can you supervise the guys for a second? I gotta get this upstairs."

"Sure," she said. Tami watched the movers make their way outside for another load as Rich began navigating the narrow stairs with the hefty box. She gingerly laid the figurine on the couch, hovering over it a moment like it was a newborn, her hand caressing the two lovers' heads. She closed her eyes and tilted her head back toward the ceiling. Eyes still closed, she smiled strangely and whispered to herself, "Awesome!" With that, she released her hand in a ritualistic gesture, opened her eyes, and walked out the door.

Unbeknownst to Tami, Rich had been standing there, mid stairwell when he witnessed this odd behavior. Momentarily perplexed, he shrugged it off as the movers entered with the matching love seat. He nodded to the spot near the lone living room window. "Thanks, guys. Right over there," he said as he continued upstairs with his load.

◆

CHAPTER 5

THE STERLING SILVER tray was laden with filled champagne flutes and hovered in position long enough for several guests to make their selections before continuing on its way to the next cluster of reception attendees. The caterer's assistant made a mental note that the majority of people seemed to be going for the ones with the silver ribbon attached to them, and perhaps that contributed to the merriment of the occasion. She would relay her observations to her boss so that they could throttle back on the gold ribbons and sparkling cider.

The hosts of the reception had, at the last minute, revised the catering order to include a limited amount of champagne. It wasn't a cost decision; it was because Carol and John Matthews weren't drinkers, and their Christian Science beliefs weren't completely comfortable with alcohol consumption in general.

Carol and John made a very handsome couple: well-tanned, trim, and they exuded an air of approachable sophistication. Carol's sleeveless dress was cut just above the knee and her well-defined calves were a testament to her love of the tennis courts. John had an impressive head of meticulously groomed, sandy blonde hair, and it seemed Tami had him to thank for her own mane. Tami's parents sipped from their flutes of Martinelli's and beamed with pride as they surveyed the reception site—their mini country club of a back-yard, on what seemed to be the nicest day of the year. Their property wasn't especially large at all; it was in an established Orange County neighborhood of tract houses, but John had taken particular pride in designing the backyard's layout when they'd bought the house over twenty years before. He'd envisioned that, perhaps one day, their daughter might even get married there. Thus the gazebo overlooking the sparkling pool. This was where the DJ was now stationed, spinning the customary boilerplate tunes. He could probably do it blindfolded, and with one ear tied behind his back, because the wedding playlists rarely varied.

The putting green-quality lawn area surrounding the swimming pool was just large enough to accommodate the hundred or so folding white chairs arranged in a ninety-degree L shape. The bride's side seating was along the deep end, and both groups of seats afforded a perfect view of the "altar" where Tami and Rich had been married a short while ago. Carol tried not to obsess over the fact that each of the chairs had created multiple dimples in the lawn.

The altar had been a project John Matthews had jumped at when Tami said she wanted it to look like a wedding cake, with she and Rich being life-size cake-toppers for the ceremony. He loved a design challenge, and this half-round, three-layer plywood "cake" was frosted with paint and satiny fabric and with all the embellishments (seafoam green and peach to match the bridal party outfits, per Tami, of course). To navigate the pool, a white cast iron bridge had been rented—and lowered into position by crane the day before—to allow the entire bridal party to traverse the pool and reach the altar on the other side. Fresh, peach-colored roses adorned the railings of the bridge, and scattered white rose petals still remained there courtesy of the four-year-old flower girl, who had taken her job very seriously. The two lower cake levels were designed as steps for Tami and Rich to reach the altar, which was just big enough for them and the officiant.

For a backyard wedding/reception setting, it was as close to storybook as one could expect, and equally practical since, once the ceremony was over, all the guests had to do was pivot and walk a few feet to the other half of the yard where the tables and parquet dance floor were. Only good friends of the family were in the know that under the dance floor tiles was the sand volleyball court, which had been transformed two days before. Tomorrow, when all of the rental tables and chairs—and the bridge!—were picked up, the volleyball court would be restored to its former glory. This was important, as Carol and John tried to stay physically active, and they were in quite good shape for their early fifties.

"Just look at her," Carol said as she squeezed her husband. "Absolutely beautiful," she added, wiping away a tear.

It was true. Tami looked radiant in her form-fitting designer wedding gown, for which they'd spared no expense. After the honeymoon it would be cleaned and vacuum-sealed in a display box—probably stuck up in the rafters for eternity, but for now Tami was, as Carol overheard Rich say earlier, rocking it. And that's all that mattered on one's wedding day.

As Tami and Rich made the rounds at the guest tables, Carol also took note of how spiffy her new son-in-law looked in his tuxedo. She had a fleeting thought: Had she ever seen Rich in long pants?

"She's all grown up, honey. I've pictured this day a thousand times, and—" Michael said, trying not to choke up, "—it's exactly like I imagined it back when she was our little four-year-old princess…." His voice trailed off, and they hugged each other tighter.

Tami and Rich thanked the group at another table and turned to leave when a raucous laugh got their attention and most of the other guests' as well. It was one of Rich's work buddies, Mike, and his laugh was legendary and impossible to miss in a crowd. He was seated with a couple of other camera guys Rich worked with, Dave and Tim.

"Okay," Mike said to his tablemates, "Baseball trivia quiz."

"No, dude. I suck at that," Dave said.

"Bring it, dude," said Tim.

"Okay. Reaching back: Decade of the 1970s.... Who hit the most home runs?" Mike asked.

"Reggie Jackson!" Dave blurted out.

"Dude, you said you weren't playing. And besides, you're wrong," Mike said.

"Decade of the seventies? I was gonna go with Reggie too. Who was it?" Tim asked.

"Okay, I'll give you the first one: Willie Stargell. All right, same decade: 1970s. Who struck out the most times?"

"Same guy—Willie Stargell, right?!" Tim replied.

"Very good. Okay, same decade, 1970s. Who got hit in the face by balls the most times?"

"Stargell!" Dave offered confidently.

"Nope! Give up?" Mike said with a mischievous grin.

They both shrugged. "Yeah," Tim said.

"Liberace!!" Mike said too loudly for the occasion and doubled over laughing.

"Gawd..." Dave said, throwing back the remains of his champagne.

Tami and Rich had arrived at this point, and his three buds jumped up to greet the couple. They'd each made an effort and had at least worn neckties for the occasion, but they remained the most casually dressed of the guests there. Mike's ever-present beard was neatly trimmed today, Rich noted as they embraced.

"Hi, guys! Sounds like you all found the right glasses!" Tami said with a laugh.

"Mikey!"

"Richie…. Dude!"

"Thanks for coming, guys," Rich said as he joined in bear hugs with the three.

"Wouldn't have missed it, Richie," Tim said.

"Yeah, Richie. Congratulations, man!" Dave added.

Rich turned to his bride and made introductions. "Tami, I'd like you to meet Mike."

"Charmed," Mike said as he hugged Tami. He turned to Rich long enough to mouth the word "Wow!" then turn back and say, "Very nice to finally meet you, Tami. Richie, where have you been hiding this one? Jeezus…."

Richie laughed. "And Dave, and Tim. Guys, this is Tami—*my wife!*" he said incredulously, since this was the first time he'd verbalized it since the vows.

"Ooh, I like the sound of that!" Tami said with a laugh. "I've heard a lot about you guys, and it's great to meet you. Thanks so much for being a part of our wedding day."

"Do you have a sister?" Mike asked, perhaps a little too lasciviously for comfort. Tim gave him a little course-correction thump on the head. "What?" Mike said to Tim. "Perfectly legit question." He grabbed another silver ribbon flute of bubbly from the passing tray and turned back to the groom.

"Okay, Richie. So, now that Tami's made an honest man out of you 'n' all, I need assurances you won't just go 'n' forget all about your friends and become one of those…" he said, his voice trailing off as he switched to a wussy voice before continuing, "'I-can't-come-out-and-hang-with-you-guys-anymore-'cause-I'm-a-married-man-now' kind of guys. Okay? Promise."

"You don't have to worry about that, man," Rich said, chuckling awkwardly.

"Seen it happen, man. Pinky swear. C'mon," Mike said, holding out his little finger.

"No worries. I promise. Pinky swear." Rich relented, locking digits with him.

"Good man," Mike said.

"Boys…" Tami joined in, shaking her head and laughing as the four guys shared another round of bro hugs. Just then, the microphone crackled to life, and the DJ faded down "Vision Of Love" by Mariah Carey. Everybody turned to the gazebo.

"If I could have your attention, please…" the DJ began, tweaking a knob and bringing the mic closer. "Thank you, everyone. It's time now for the traditional First Dance, so if we could please get the lovely couple, *Mr. and Mrs. Bryson*, out here to the dance floor…."

"*Mr. and Mrs. Bryson!* That's us, honey!" Tami squealed as she led Rich to the parquet surface. Rich smiled as they took their positions to a smattering of applause and a few whistles. He had never really enjoyed dancing, with the possible exception of dancing naked, alone, in the privacy of his apartment after a restorative shower on a day off. Besides looking forward to taking off these half-size-too-small rental clown shoes when they were done, the nearby pool looked pretty inviting, and he was secretly jonesing for his pool raft right about now. But he really was in the moment, and all of their preparation—and the awesome wedding planner's efforts—allowed them to fully enjoy it.

As the music began, he took Tami in his arms. Sinatra's "I Get A Kick Out Of You" had been cued past the intro, commencing with the verse, *I get no kick from champagne.*

John and Carol exchanged a bemused look at this song choice, then beamed with pride as they—and everybody—watched the dance. As Frankie wound down the song with *I get a kick out of you*, Tami pantomimed kicking Rich in the behind, which got several laughs, then came into his arms for a hug and kiss. Several guests clinked their glasses, prompting a longer kiss, and the couple happily obliged.

Standing by the corner of the gazebo, David Matthews

applauded and made his way through the guests to join his parents. John gave David a proud slap on the shoulder. Scott Bryson was watching the festivities from his family table, seated next to his sister, Ellen, as well as Len and Jeanette, their parents. Ellen had wisely left her two children at home, as they were a bit squirmy at adult gatherings, and her soon-to-be ex-husband was all too willing to stay home with them. Plus, there was that rare, televised Giants/Dodgers game on.

The siblings from both families had been invited to be in the bridal party, and the women dutifully wore the seafoam green dresses with the squared neckline and dyed-to-match low-heeled shoes. It was a virtual guarantee that none of these outfits would ever see the light of day again after this shindig. It did make for a pleasant enough blended family portrait, however, and it was a joint relief that the requisite photo sessions were behind them.

The Sinatra-thon segued to "The Way You Look Tonight" as the DJ nodded to John. "Now, if we could please get Tami's father out on the dance floor to join his lovely daughter for the traditional father/daughter dance."

"Hold this, Sport," John said as he handed his flute to David and strutted over to meet the bride. He smiled broadly and exuded an air of royal host as he crossed the dance floor. Tami followed her father's lead and they flowed well together. John looked into his little girl's eyes, which were sparkling, and she looked every bit the princess she felt.

"Thanks for a beautiful day, Dad," she said with a wide grin.

"Of course, honey. I love you, and you look absolutely beautiful. Take it all in, Tami," he said, looking around, "this is your day."

While Tami did that very thing, John thought back to his own wedding day and, for a fleeting moment, second-guessed his and Carol's decision to elope versus having a traditional affair of their own, twenty-five years before. He didn't really regret anything, and theirs had been a very happy marriage all of these years. They couldn't have asked for a more picture-perfect family, at least from a visual standpoint.

Rich was taking in these moments as well, a heartfelt smile on his face as he escorted his mother to the dance floor. Jeanette smiled warmly at her son as they did the box step. Hers was the most genuine kind of smile because you noticed it in the eyes first, and it exuded the warmest, purest form of love.

Rich held her gaze for several moments, then had to look away briefly. He was atypically sensitive for a man, and despite his best efforts to stifle that side of himself, certain moments could trigger tears. This was one of those, and he did his best to blink it away before meeting her gaze again.

"I'm very proud of you, and so happy for you, Richie."

"Thanks, Mom," Rich replied with a smile, mindful of the tears threatening to expose him. He took that as a cue to sneak a peek over at the father/daughter dance a few feet away.

"I'm pretty sure this is the first time we've ever danced together, Dad," Tami said.

"No way. Really?" he replied, thinking about it. "Well, that's unacceptable, isn't it?" he added with a smile.

"Yeah… What's up with that?" Tami grinned.

John laughed and gave his daughter a perfectly executed dip.

Len and Tami had enjoyed their brief dance, as had Carol and Rich, all to polite applause before the DJ switched gears and invited everybody out to the dance floor. You could've bet the farm, and won, that Sister Sledge's "We Are Family" would be followed by Kool & The Gang's "Celebration." The videographer took his camera off the tripod for this and tried not to bump into dancers as he navigated the crowd with his gear, which was awkwardly tethered to a video record deck hanging from his shoulder.

During this, Rich ducked away for a long overdue restroom break. As he exited the bathroom, he was shaking water off his hands and could hear the B52s' "Love Shack" booming from the patio. He bumped into Tami in the hallway.

"Well…hello, Mrs. Bryson."

"Fancy meeting you here, Mr. Bryson," Tami answered with a laugh.

Rich wiped his hands on his tuxedo trousers. "Um, they're out of guest towels in there. Did you need…?"

"No," Tami said, grabbing his hand. "C'mon, I want to show you something." She led Rich down the hall to the next room and opened the door: a perfectly preserved teenage time capsule of a bedroom and a shrine of sports trophies, ribbons and testosterone.

"Wow, David's old room, huh?"

"Yep. C'mon," she said as she grabbed Rich's hand and led him further down the hallway. She opened another door and stepped back so that Rich could see: a fitness room, complete with treadmill, rowing machine, free weights, and other gym trappings.

"Great workout room," Rich said.

"*My* bedroom," she corrected. "They apparently couldn't wait to convert it. Typical. David's room hasn't been touched—probably never will be. Mine? I never existed."

Rich took a second to process this, then replied simply, "Huh…."

Tami pulled his hand again, escorting him around the corner and opened a set of French doors leading into her parents' master bedroom. It was bright, stylishly-furnished in dark woods, bathed in a happy shade of light yellow paint, and finished with beautiful crown moldings. A few small family photographs sat atop the dresser by the door. Seemingly out of place was a larger framed photo of David in his football uniform.

"Uh, should we be in here?" Rich asked, a little uncomfortable.

"Don't worry!" she laughed. She walked him further into the room, over to her dad's closet and opened it. "Check this out," she said, flicking on the closet light.

Rich took in the almost surreal site. All of the clothes were hung in gradated, color-coded groupings, but that wasn't the weird part. It was the hangers—they were all precisely and equally spaced from each other, as if painstakingly measured by a team of minions with a micrometer. John's shoes were highly buffed and also symmetrically arranged, with the laces tucked inside. The neckties' patterns were aligned. Organized, sure. Maybe a slight bit *Stepford*, Rich thought.

"Did I mention my Dad's a little anal," Tami said.

"Wow. That's…impressive," he replied.

"Not exactly the word I'd use to describe it," Tami said, as she reached into the closet and mussed up all the hangers. She stood back, admiring her handiwork. "C'mon, let's get back to our party," she said, shutting the closet door.

"Great idea," Rich said uneasily. "You like to live on the edge, don't you?" he added, mostly to himself.

"Sometimes," Tami said. She grabbed him by the hand as they made a hasty exit outside.

"Here they are!" the DJ announced as Tami and Rich rejoined the crowd on the patio. "How about another round of applause for our newlyweds…Mr. and Mrs. Richard Bryson!"

Rich's facial muscles were still recovering from hours of smiling for the photographers, but he mustered his best one now for the crowd. Tami did too, but her smile faded once she noticed David and his girlfriend, Tiffany, posing for pictures at the center of the bridge. *Her bridge.*

◆

CHAPTER 6

Fade in:

ELLEN HANDED HER champagne flute to an unseen person as she looked straight into the video camera, which had framed her in a medium shot in front of the star jasmine bushes, which were in full fragrant bloom in the front yard.

"Tami and Rich.... Where to begin? Wow. Well, I'm sure everybody's said this already, but you guys make the most beautiful couple. Really. Okay.... Okay, Richie. Rich, you're my favorite brother," she said.

"Hey! What am I, chopped liver?!" Scott interjected from out of frame.

"Sorry! You're my favorite *married* brother," she said, looking off at Scott before returning her gaze directly into the lens. "And I love you very much. Okay, sorry to embarrass you, but it's true: Richie, you haven't had a lot of girlfriends, I know, but I'm glad that you and Tami found each other and that you make each other happy. Tami, I'm sure you will, but please take good care of my little brother. Rich, take good care of Tami, I'm sure you will." Ellen took a deep breath before continuing. "Treat each other like gold, you guys, and you'll be very happy together! Love you!"

The video frame widened slowly to become a two-shot, as Scott stepped into the shot next to his sister. "Pardon my intrusion, but Ellen's right, guys. Love and respect each other, always."

"And *honor* each other!" Ellen added, sounding just slightly tipsy at this point.

"Honor. Absolutely. Rich, I'm happy for you, little bro. Tami, I'm happy to have you as my new sister, and I love you. You looked beautiful today. I wish you both every happiness, and thanks for letting me be a part of your special day. Congratulations!"

"Love you guys!" Ellen added.

"Love you like family!" Scott said jokingly as they exited frame.

"Still rolling?" David's voice could be heard now.

"Absolutely," replied the unseen videographer.

David immediately came into view, cleared his throat, and flashed his megawatt smile to the camera. "Hey, guys. It's David. But you already knew that…. Hey! It was a beautiful ceremony, wonderful reception, and a great celebration. It was an honor to be a part of it. I've got to say that I was blown away when I first heard you guys were getting married, and I'm very stoked for you guys. Tami, I never thought you'd get married before me! I'm glad you finally found someone, and Rich…well, you're a lucky guy. Congratulations, Tami and Rich. Love you guys!" he said with a wink before the picture faded to black, then dissolved to another shot—this one in slow motion, black and white video as Tami and Rich popped their heads out of the moon roof of their limousine and waved to the wedding crowd in the street. It was unintentionally a little reminiscent of the Zapruder film of JFK in Dallas, but not as grainy and nobody's melon explodes. Music swelled over this: "When You Wish Upon A Star," as performed by Linda Ronstadt, singing with the Nelson Riddle Orchestra. This version was beyond emotionally charged when coupled with the imagery, and in the song's final verse Linda reassures us that every hope will be realized, if we just do as the song suggests. As she masterfully held that final note, the music faded down in sync with a freeze-frame image of

the bridal couple smiling broadly. A graphic came up over the shot:
And they lived happily ever after.

Fade to black.

Rich set down the remote control and dabbed away a tear. Tami put the empty popcorn bowl down on the end table, next to a beautifully framed eleven-by-fourteen-inch wedding photo of them. They sat silently for several moments, on the loveseat in their now-established living room.

"Wow.... They nailed it!" Rich said, stifling a sniff. "I love it, don't you, honey?"

Tami got up and walked over to turn off the TV and returned to the loveseat next to Rich, but sitting cross-legged now. She folded her arms.

"What do you think your sister meant?" Tami asked.

Rich was still caught up in the emotion of the video.

"What?"

"Ellen."

"Right...? And?"

"When she said, 'Tami, please take good care of my brother' like I *wouldn't* take good care of you."

"She was just wishing us both well. Those are the things you say when you want to wish a couple well," Rich replied, not sure why he was having to explain this.

"Really? I don't know.... Didn't sound that way to me. And my brother. What was with his snide remark about, 'Glad you finally found someone...Can't believe you got married before me!'" she said in a mocking, nasally voice. "I want to edit him out of the video," she added. Rich's initial reaction was to laugh, because she couldn't be serious. One look at her expression told him he was wrong.

"Honey, c'mon...don't be ridiculous. They spent the past three months editing that video. It's perfect as it is, and what your brother said was just fine."

Tami stood up in a huff, then walked back over to the entertainment center and ejected the tape, waving it in the air as she spoke. "Well, I don't think so, and I want them to re-do it," she said, dropping the tape onto the coffee table glass. "Without him in it." Rich stood. "Please listen to yourself, Tami. You're being unreasonable and not making any—" Rich managed, before Tami's open palm met his face with a resounding *SLAP!*

This stopped him in his tracks. His face reddened, both from the sting of her hand and the shock of the moment. Rich slowly brought his hand to his cheek and looked at Tami, searching her through moist eyes.

"I—I'm sorry, baby... I didn't mean to do that," Tami said.

It took a moment before Rich could reply. "I'm sorry too.... I didn't mean to upset you," he said softly. If he'd had a tail, it would be between his legs now.

Tami reached up and cradled his face in her hands. "I would never—I just...love you so much," she said, pulling him into a hug.

Rich blinked away a tear before he spoke. "I know. It was my fault."

They stood that way for several moments. Rich glanced over Tami's shoulder to the gold lover's statuette across the room. It had its own halogen light on it now, and it glowed from its perch in the semi-dark room.

"I guess we can re-edit the video if you feel that strongly about it," he conceded weakly.

Tami started to cry as she replied, "Thank you, honey. I do."

It was dusk, and from the common area outside, just the faintest amount of room light was evident through the closed vertical blinds of the Brysons' townhouse. The last remaining leaves of their sycamore tree were dropping more rapidly now as the wind began picking up, and their neighbor ushered her son—and his tricycle—inside.

◆

CHAPTER 7

QUIET AS A church mouse, Rich opened the front door and surveyed the deserted common courtyard area, then set his well-used travel coffee mug on the metal porch railing, and relocked the deadbolt. He carefully closed the screen door with an almost imperceptible *click*. It was 4:20, after all. The only other sound at this unholiest of hours was in the distance: the almost subliminal whir of fellow worker bees' cars making their way down the nearby Ventura freeway, only to jockey for position onto the dreaded 405 South. Rich hoped to God that he wasn't getting too late a start. His call time was 6:00 in Santa Monica today, and he'd hoped to be wheels-up by 4:00, just to be sure, but Tami had eaten up much of the clock playing 20 Questions about where he was working, who he was working with today, what time he'd be home…. All legitimate questions, to be sure, but he'd wished she'd asked last night and not when he was desperately trying to get out the door.

Rich stepped down the few steps from the landing and proceeded toward the carport. He paused for a brief moment to glance up at the couple's second story bedroom window. The blinds were closed, naturally, but he could see them move, just a little, as he thought he saw Tami's fingers slip back inside them.

He turned, let out a private sigh and proceeded towards his awaiting chariot, a months-old Ford Explorer, the Eddie Bauer edition. *Only sixty-nine more payments and she's mine!*

Rich settled into the cool leather, started up the Explorer, kicked the heater into high gear, and studied his dog-eared Thomas Guide map book and the notes he'd scribbled on a Post-It. He slowly backed out of the carport space, turned onto his dark, desolate street and proceeded toward the nearby freeway on-ramp to do battle with his fellow gladiators. *Gawd.*

Rich's work locations varied greatly, and daily, and he might be called to work anywhere, from Santa Barbara to San Diego, from Tehachapi to San Bernardino and anywhere in between. Long commutes came with the territory, he knew, and he had no one to blame but himself for his choice to be a freelancer in the television industry. And he had compounded this situation further with his move out of the valley, for sure. As the crow flies, Santa Monica shouldn't be an issue, as it was only…like…eighteen miles away. As the car creeps, thirty-two miles didn't seem like it'd be problematic either, but there was this monstrosity called *the 405* in between. There was the rub.

For anyone who ever doubted the very existence of Hell, all one has to do is jump in their car and take a trip down that multi-laned parking lot of a roadway, that especially evil stretch of pavement where, if you spent enough years navigating its surfaces, it would consume your very soul. Rich had been at this freelance schtick for a decade now, and he wondered how long he had left.

As he crept along, he couldn't help but people watch: There was invariably some woman doing her makeup as she drove, or the one who decided to spend that hour of drive time perfecting her hair. Oh, and don't forget the guys who liked to read the *Los Angeles Times* while they steered with their knees. Never a dull moment, yet always a dull moment.

If Rich had a questionable driving habit, it was a benign one.

He was a closet drummer, and his steering wheel—and surrounding dashboard—was equipped with an imaginary drum set that would make Neil Peart envious.

Music was Rich's escape from this commuting madness, and he finally switched on the radio, stabbing at presets until he found a jam he could get into: the opening riff of LTD's "Every Time I Turn Around (Back In Love Again)." *Yes!! Thank you!!* He cranked it up.

Rich channeled his funky white boy and jumped aboard the *Soul Train* now, taking his hands off the wheel to clap along with the beat, and sliding his hand up the neck of the invisible bass guitar when the moment called for it.

He belted out the verse as he switched lanes, inching along and doing his level best Jeffrey Osbourne and the *Da-da-da-da-da-da* from the brass section.

<insert bass guitar riff here>

Thank God for car audio. And nine Bose speakers!

Rich had always thought that if his life were ever made into a movie, it would at least have a wicked soundtrack. Yep!

Next thing he knew—and with lots of help from the Commodores, Bill Withers, and Luther Vandross—an hour and a half had passed, and he pulled into the parking lot outside a building with enormous satellite dishes atop the roof. Westside Studios.

He pulled into an end space, next to a huge Class A Winnebago, and away from other vehicles. His was the Eddie Bauer edition, after all, and he liked to keep his stuff perfect for as long as possible. Rich checked his watch, took the last sip of caffeinated nectar from his travel mug, and proceeded inside for another exciting—and long—infomercial shoot. *Whoo-hoo!*

◆

CHAPTER 8

I T WAS LATE morning, and Tami set down a bowl of dry cat chow next to the bowl of wet Friskies. She threw the empty can in the trash and proceeded over to the kitchen table, littered with dozens of Post-It notes, circled casting notices, and trade papers. The cordless phone was wedged under her chin as she stapled her resume to a stack of headshots.

"No, Mother, I didn't get it," she said, a bit irritated.

Carol Matthews stood at the built-in, fold-down ironing board in her sunny home office. Carol's phone was tucked under her chin as well, as she expertly smoothed the wrinkles from her designer jeans. Behind her, several headshots of Tami were stapled to the wall in a linear row—ranging from her mid-teens to the present. A portable TV sat atop a VCR nearby and was playing the soap "All My Children" at a low volume.

"Well, I'm sure you'll get the next one, honey. Did you feel like you had a good audition?" she asked.

"I nailed the audition, Mom," Tami replied as she stapled another resume.

"I'm sure you did. What were you wearing, honey?" Carol asked, multitasking with the iron, the phone, and her soap.

"What's that have to do with it?" Tami said.

Carol flipped over the jeans and continued. "Did you wear those new slacks I got you? You weren't wearing those awful jeans—the ones with the holes—were you?"

Tami slammed down the stapler and got a firm grip on the phone as she barked, "I *know* what to wear and how to dress for an audition, Mother!"

Carol shot a blast of the iron's steam into her jeans. She probably could've just placed the phone receiver against the denim and gotten the requisite amount of steam coming through it from Tami. "I know you do, honey. You don't have to get angry with me. I'm just asking so we can maybe figure out why you didn't get the part."

"It has *nothing* to do with what I was wearing, and you have no idea what you're talking about!" Tami snapped.

"Well, did you bring that nice new headshot—that one I liked, the smiling one?" Carol asked, leaning in for a closer look at her show.

"I *told* you! I'm going with the other headshot—the *serious* one," Tami replied, holding one in her hand and trying not to shake. She got up and angrily strutted over to the living room, the phone still to her ear. She peeked out the blinds: a beautiful autumn day. A couple of kids were playing hopscotch on the common-area sidewalk. The little boy with the trike was watching them.

"I'm a serious actor and I know what I'm doing, Mother!" she yelled, apparently loud enough to make the kids look her way.

Tami snapped the blinds shut, darkening the room considerably as she did. She was seething as she turned and stared at the muted TV. Some infomercial was on.

"There's no reason to raise your voice, Tami. I'm just trying to help. Of *course* you're a serious actress, honey."

"Actor."

"What?" Carol asked.

"I'm an *ac-tor*. A serious actor!"

"Of course you are, Tami," Carol replied, dripping a little too much sweetness. "I'm sorry if I upset you. I just—"

"It's my career, and my decision!" Tami interrupted as she walked back over to the table and grabbed her headshot.

Carol picked up her remote control and paused the VCR. She smiled as she talked now, as if her daughter could see her expression. "I know it's your career, honey. But as long as your Dad and I are paying for things like your pictures, I think we should have a say-so on which ones we think are—"

Tami clicked off the handset, hurling it into the couch.

"*Bitch!*"

◆

CHAPTER 9

A LARGE FLOOR monitor stood atop a rolling cart, located between Camera 1 and Camera 2, a few feet from the kitchen set at Westside Studios. The red tally light on Camera 1 went out just as the tally light on Camera 2 lit up, indicating the past-her-prime blonde hostess was no longer in a close-up shot and was now sharing a two-shot with her co-host. She noticed the tally switch, then glanced at the monitor out of the corner of her eye as she smiled so broadly she could almost be mistaken for Jack Nicholson's Joker. A meticulously trimmed, bearded pitchman stood next to her and gestured to the gleaming pasta machine on the counter as if he were David Copperfield and, through some unexplainable wizardry, he was about to produce a troupe of monkeys flying out of it. The pitchman flashed his perfect implanted choppers.

"It's really that easy now, Susan, with the PastaMaster 5000! Give it a try for yourself!" he said like it was Christmas morning and he was jacked up on cocaine.

"Really? I thought you'd never ask!" she giggled, a little too giddy for the real world. She pushed the button on the machine and started to feed the prepared dough into it.

"Wow...this is fantastic—and fun!" she said, as she continued to extrude the noodles. "Just look at that beautiful spaghetti!" she added, looking up at the camera.

"Absolutely beautiful, Susan," the pitchman added, noting with a quick glance that Camera 4's jib shot had taken over for a beauty shot close-up as the pasta started coming out. After a couple of moments, the strands of pasta began to jam as the machine groaned and regurgitated a mangled clump of doughy crap that spewed messily about the counter.

"Shit!" Susan said.

"Dammit!" added the pitchman.

"And...cut!" said the "voice of God" from the studio's P.A. system. It was Stu, the prematurely bald director, who now appeared on set nervously rubbing the top of his shiny, sleestack-shaped head. Stu was well known in the LA production scene as the Infomercial King, and he and his crew had shot infomercials for just about every product known to man, all of which seemed to earn that coveted, red *As Seen on TV* logo on the box, for what that was worth.

"I'm sorry, Stu... I fed it in exactly like we rehearsed. I don't understand—"

"I know. Don't worry. We'll go again, and it'll work this time," Stu reassured her.

The amiable stage manager, Phil, was in his early seventies and had enjoyed a long career in 'real' television, from which he had retired on his terms. He'd been married for fifty years to his sweetheart, a former make-up artist whom he'd met on their first day working together at KTLA, and they were both now enjoying a simpler life as fulltime RVers. He still took the occasional gig for Stu, but that was all he cared to do anymore. He was allowed to park his 40-footer in the lot here when he was working, while his wife happily stayed in the coach, crocheting things for craft fairs.

Phil was always cool under pressure, and Stu relied on his calm nature and professionalism to keep things going smoothly on the set.

Like now.

He joined Stu and the hosts at the "kitchen" counter.

Stu turned to him, "Can we please get another machine? Quickly? We're in overtime here."

Phil spoke softly into his headset's mic, requesting the prop department bring in a new unit. He relayed to Stu that a new one was flying in, then asked the director, "Do you want to break for second meal?"

Stu looked at his watch, polished his noggin further, then nodded.

"That's a crew *thirty*. Back on headsets in thirty minutes, everybody," Phil said into his mic. Rich removed his headset and hung it on his studio camera's pedestal. He was *Cam 1*—host cam—today, which was fine with him, because doing handheld on these gigs could be brutal. He'd worked countless informercials, as well as several cooking shows for the Food Network over the years and was almost invariably pressed into service as the handheld guy because he was such a steady shot. With the newer jib camera technology being utilized more on these gigs, he found it was freeing him up a little from being The Human Tripod, a moniker that had stuck long ago.

Rich gave a sarcastic thumbs-up to the Cam 2—wide shot—guy, who shook his head and returned to his crossword puzzle. He wasn't hungry, as he'd seen the unpalatable delivery boxes arrive moments before.

Suit yourself, Rich shrugged, as he negotiated the line and joined the gang assembling at the lunch tables backstage. *Mmm... Pizza! (Again!)* He sat down and deployed several napkins to mop the grease from his flimsy pepperoni slice. Seated across from him was his buddy, Mike, who was assigned Cam 3 today.

"Yummy!" Rich said, fooling no one.

"It's bullshit," Mike said, barely understandable with his mouth full. He wiped the grease from his beard, which—since the wedding—had returned to its previous, scraggly glory.

"Cheap bastards," he managed before huffing down another bite.

"Any port in the storm. This *almost* looks good right now," Rich replied, removing the onions from his piece.

Mike took a long pull on his Dr. Pepper, belching softly. "Wanna go for beers after?"

Rich looked at his watch, shaking his head. "Sorry, man. It's gonna be after eleven before we get outta here, right?"

"I know. But, dude, we've hardly seen you since the wedding. Been forever—"

"What are you talking about?" Rich laughed. "I've seen you— what—three times this week alone, right?"

Mike gave Rich a piercing look. "Pizza doesn't constitute a meal, Richie—just like hangin' at work doesn't constitute hangin' out," he said, gesturing with his pinky.

"Yeah, I know, man. I'm just trying to pay off Tami's ring, the furniture, the hot tub, our honeymoon.... Plus the Explorer. Oh, and I've got a mortgage now."

"So do I—the mortgage part anyway. I admire your ethic, dude, but that's beside the point. What I'm saying is, all work and no play makes Richie a very dull boy. Your friends miss you. Just sayin'." Mike suddenly lit up. "Dude...there's an *unbelievable* new chick dancing at Thirsty's tonight. Insane set of knockers, man! We—"

"I'll try to do something about that, Mikie," Rich said, not really listening.

"Uh-huh...right," Mike replied, furrowing his brow as he got up to grab himself another slice of the foul offering that had been delivered by the lowest bidder.

A faint buzz and jolt got Rich's attention as he grabbed the vibrating pager from his belt. He'd forgotten he even had it and had sworn he'd never get one—he figured only doctors needed them— but Tami had worn him down and insisted he embrace carrying one now, "for good business." He looked at the pager's display. Next to his home phone number, the message: *911.*

"Shit."

"Everything cool?" Bob asked as he returned to his seat with two pieces.

"Um, yeah...excuse me. The little lady," Rich said apologetically. Mike raised his eyebrows knowingly and let out a long, thunderous belch—deliberately loud punctuation. As Rich stood up, Mike made the pinky swear gesture, just as the "voice of God" boomed from the PA speaker, reminding the crew: "We're back in five, everybody."

"Great," Rich muttered to himself as he exited the stage to the dimly lit parking lot. With his other new appendage, a Nokia cellular phone (Tami had insisted they get matching ones), Rich nervously stabbed in the numbers, praying everything was all right at home. He listened for a moment, smiling at Phil, who was gesturing for him from the doorway.

"I know I did, honey. Might be another hour or two, I don't know. So, what's the emergency? I got a *911*—", he managed, before Tami cut him off.

"The *emergency* is that it's almost ten o'clock and you're still not home, and I haven't heard from you since you broke for what-was-supposed-to-be-lunch—oh, I don't know—five *hours* ago!"

Rich nervously paced, knowing he was supposed to be back on headsets now, and he also had a snake by the tail. "Honey—look, I'm sorry. We haven't had much in the way of opportunities to call here, and we're back up in just a second," he said, looking at his watch. "Look, I've gotta go, honey. Is it okay if—?"

CLICK.

"Perfect," Rich sighed as he stuffed the phone in his pocket and went back inside. It was going to be an already-long night made longer.

◆

CHAPTER 10

THE EXPLORER STEALTHILY inched into its designated carport spot, and Rich looked at the dash clock, wishing that the 12:22 it displayed was wrong. But he knew it wasn't. He turned off the engine and sat there for a long moment, psyching himself to get out of the car and head inside. Hopefully Tami would be fast asleep, and he could get a few hours himself, before he had to arise at the *crack o'*, and repeat the cycle.

Jackson Browne's "The Pretender" came to mind for a fleeting moment. After a silent Hail Mary, he got out.

The thirty yards from the carport to the front door felt like a death march. The common area was pitch dark and quiet as a tomb. People were actually sleeping at this hour...what a concept!

Rich squinted from the blinding porch light as he fumbled for his keys. He then noticed a faint flickering light from the TV, sneaking between the closed vertical blinds.

He took a deep breath, quietly unlocked the deadbolt, and proceeded inside.

Tami was seated cross-legged on the loveseat, staring vacantly at a sitcom rerun. The living room was bathed in a bluish light, coming solely from the new 25" TV. Rich took off his coat and walked over to the couch, leaning over to give her a kiss. "Hey, honey...."

Tami avoided his gesture and continued to stare at the screen.

Rich took the hint. He walked over to the kitchen, turned on the light, and hung his keys on the wooden key rack. Tami's keys hung from an adjacent peg. The two-pegged key rack had been a wedding gift from his brother, who had handcrafted it in his shop, and the wooden base was wood-burned, then painted, with the words *Home Sweet Home.* Yeah.

Rich turned out the kitchen light, ran his fingers through his tousled hair, and returned to the living room.

"What a day.... What a *week*," he said weakly, taking a seat next to the ice queen.

"Sorry it's so late, honey," he continued. She was offering him nothing. "How was *your* day?"

Tami now turned from the TV to face Rich. He didn't know how much to attribute to the cathode ray lighting, but she looked like warmed-over hell: dark circles under her eyes, her hair half hiked up in a chip clip, pasty complexion, and lounging in her holey socks and mismatched sweats. If she were going as zombie girl to a Halloween costume contest, this would be the look. And she would've won.

This can't be good.

"Oh, I'm glad that you're finally interested in something other than yourself! *My* day?! Hmm, thanks for asking. Let's see.... Well, I got in another fight with my fucking bitch of a mother, for one thing. Then my holier-than-thou asshole father called back and told me never to speak to my mother in *that tone of voice*." Tami stood hovering over Rich now, who had sunk low into the loveseat's cushions. "You know what else he said to me today?"

"No, honey," Rich said, way beyond exhausted. "What's that?" he dared.

"After my Mom said that they should have a say-so in my headshots, just because they helped pay for them—*fuck* them, by the way—I reminded my Dad that it's *my* career...."

Tami paused and rubbed her eyes in exasperation, which completed the Alice Cooper effect.

"And you know what he said next?"

Rich shook his head, trying to follow what she was saying and wondering how long this was going to play out tonight. He had another early one tomorrow. He chanced a peek at the VCR's time display through strained eyes that felt like two burn holes in a blanket. 12:37. He had nothing left and had to get to bed.

Tami made no notice of Rich's condition; she'd waited all day to vent this, and she was on a roll now.

"He says,"—she switched into a mocking-Dad voice now—'What career?' and I reply, 'My *acting* career, of course!'"

"Of course," Rich responded softly.

"And he says, '*Tami, when you're Meryl Streep, then you'll have a career.*'—Like that!"

"He said that? Jeez," Rich replied.

Tami began storming around the room. "That fucking *ASS-HOLE!*" she yelled, too loud for these walls and for this hour. Dozer, the cat, scampered upstairs to safety. Rich stood and attempted to comfort Tami, resting his hands on her shoulders, but she shrugged him off.

"I'm sorry, honey. That was wrong."

"I HATE HIS FUCKING GUTS!" she screamed.

"Shhh.... Please.... Keep it down, honey. The neighbors might—"

"Don't you '*Shhh*' me—ever!! You're just like them!"

"No, I'm not. You know that, Tami. C'mon. It's late. You're tired. I'm tired. It's been a rough day and—"

"I wish they were both dead."

"Don't say that, Tami."

"Don't tell me what to say! I wish they would both die—in a fucking car wreck!" she yelled, gesturing to the coffee table where the mangled remains of their cordless phone sat.

"And look what they made me do," she said, sounding oddly calm.

"Jeez, Tami. That's the second one! We can't afford to just keep buying phones every time you get upset—"

"It's not my fault! Fuck *you!*" she bellowed, giving Rich a sudden and forceful punch to the stomach. Rich, unprepared, and too weak to react, fell to one knee, and Tami grabbed him by the hair.

"Take it back! Apologize!" she shrieked, a glob of white spittle erupting from the corner of her mouth.

"Ow! Let go! Take what back? For what? Let *go!*" Rich groaned, with a little less wind, and a burning scalp. Tami had an iron grip on his mane and gave it another tug, pulling out an impressive handful, like Velcro.

"Take it back…"

Rich grabbed at her wrist, but Tami was relentless. His hand fumbled about as he tried to brace himself on the coffee table. All he managed to do was accidently trigger the VCR remote, which in turn cued up the perfect moment from their wedding video. Memories of dancing at their reception flickered on the screen, as Sinatra crooned to "Just The Way You Look Tonight." Even in this moment, the irony wasn't lost on Rich. He would've laughed if he weren't in so much pain, and currently under siege.

"I—I take it—back," he managed between clenched teeth. "Let… go!!"

Tami released his hair and Rich collapsed to the floor. "It doesn't go with that!" she said, ejecting the video.

She walked over to the stairwell, flicked on the light, and stormed upstairs. "You can sleep down there tonight!"

Rich just lay there on the floor, massaging his scalp and his ribs. A tuft of his own hair was clumped on the floor near his face. Moments later, a tiny throw pillow landed on him.

"And not on the couch," Tami barked, flicking off the light as she went back upstairs, leaving Rich to lie there in the soft blue glow of the TV, too tired to argue or move.

◆

CHAPTER 11

RICH GROANED AS he opened his eyes in the darkened room, his cheek buried in the low pile carpeting. It took him a few seconds to remember he was in the living room, still in the fetal position and in the clothes he'd spent the past twenty fours in. He was freezing, and he strained to read the blinking green numbers on the VCR's display: *3:48. Three hours. Christ.*

The muted TV was airing an infomercial for some kind of miracle kitchen product. Something he'd worked on.

He was achy, and he hadn't really noticed the carpet's substandard padding until now. With considerable effort, he sat up, turned off the set, and quietly made it upstairs where he drew a hotter-than-usual shower. He was going to need a good soak to wash away last night. He carefully folded his shirt and pants because he was going to have to wear them again today. It was either that, or enter the viper's nest and risk waking Tami right now. *Um.... No.*

After his shower, Rich grabbed a new triple-bladed disposable and went about a shave. The face looking back at him in the mirror was one he didn't recognize, as there was a discernable sadness about the downturned corners of his mouth. How long had those been there? He opened his mouth extra wide for a long moment, in an effort to clear the frown lines from becoming muscle memory. He put the razor down on the corner of the sink next to the small, framed picture of the newlyweds, all smiles, on a beach in Bora Bora, nearly three years—a lifetime—ago.

Rich retreated to the adjacent second bedroom—his office—and returned with a Post-It note he'd written in Sharpie. He placed it in the middle of the mirror:

SORRY ABOUT LAST NIGHT.

HAVE A GOOD DAY.

LOVE YOU.

◆

The Explorer crept along slowly and Rich wished he'd taken the time to make some coffee before he left. It was bad enough to wear the same clothes two days in a row, but not having any coffee on top of that was nothing short of inhumane. Pretty sure there was something in the Geneva Convention about that.

He rolled down his window in hopes the brisk air would help wake him up, while his heater's blower tried to compensate.

It was going to be a monster day, and a mind-numbing schlep to Pomona, so he stabbed at his presets until he landed on "Sing A Song" by Earth, Wind & Fire. They tried to convince him that all he had to do was simply belt out a tune, daily, and things would magically improve. But he was having none of it.

He switched the radio off and drove in silence for a while until he noticed what sounded like a Tijuana Brass tune, coming from outside the car. Glancing to his left, Rich found the source: the driver in the next car was steering with his knees and busting out a respectable solo version of "Lonely Bull" on the trumpet. *Only in LA....* Rich nodded and rolled up the window. He was dreading the day ahead.

◆

CHAPTER 12

HIS BONES SHOOK violently upon launch. The two top fuel dragsters screamed away from the starting line, mere feet from Rich's position, leaving a huge cloud of putrid smoke, nitro and burning rubber in their wake.

The bleachers were full of screaming fans, but Rich couldn't hear them; the rubberized plugs were wedged so far up his ear canals he thought they might have to be surgically removed. Mere foam inserts didn't even begin to diminish the brain-rattling noise, nor the icepick-to-the-eardrum pain once the vehicles roared off, but he'd opted not to wear the dual-ear industrial plastic earmuffs today because they were too obtrusive, and they interfered with his hand-held camera.

As the braking chutes opened at the far end of the drag strip, Rich lowered his camera and stepped over to the sidelines. He took inventory of all his senses that'd been destroyed today: *sight... sound...hearing...taste—yes, even taste—*as he hocked a nitro-infused loogie onto the ground. His face looked like a chimney sweep's— covered in a black layer of burnt rubber and nitro mist—save the perfectly round clean spot where his Ikigami HL79 camera's eye-piece had been.

This was the final heat on what felt like the longest day of his life, and he was beyond thankful he'd made it through. He'd been running on adrenaline all day, and for the first time since arriving at the racetrack, Rich had a moment to decompress as he began stowing his gear.

For the next hour and a half, his thoughts intermittently went to Tami, and the previous night, as he and rest of the crew set about wrapping out of the location. There were eight cameras, long lenses, tripods, a jib arm, and riser scaffolding to disassemble, not to mention the seemingly endless miles of camera cable to be coiled and stowed back to the production truck. It was grueling work but, in a way, he was thankful for the distraction.

Amazingly, it was still daylight when Rich found his vehicle in the parking lot and, once inside, he pulled out his phone. He was a bit surprised—and relieved—to get the home machine. He looked at his watch.

"Hey, it's me, sorry I missed you. It's about 4:30, and we've just finished here," Rich said, pausing long enough to cover one nostril and shoot a black rubber-coated booger from the other. "Listen, I'll be home probably around 6:00—6:30 maybe, depending on traffic, and I'll make dinner when I get there, okay? I hope you're having a good day…. Love you."

On the way home, Rich made two stops, first to Target to buy a new two-station cordless phone and then to the grocery store. He rang the bell for the meat guy. The middle-aged butcher, an amiable black guy Rich hadn't seen there before, arrived at the counter, wiped his bloody hands on his smock, smiled and gave Rich a long look before asking how he could be of assistance. He didn't know what to make of Rich in blackface, and he didn't feel like asking.

"Those two rib eyes, please," Rich said, not sure why he was getting the odd stare back.

When he got back to the car, he caught a glimpse of himself in the rearview, and then it dawned on him. As tired as he was, he still found humor in the situation.

"Damn," he muttered, laughing.

◆

CHAPTER 13

IT HAD TAKEN a bit of effort, and a couple of Tami's special exfoliating facial scrubs, to get himself back to looking (almost) normal. His face was a considerably more pink now, and Rich wondered how many layers of dermis he'd scrubbed off in the process. After cleaning the gunk out of the sink, and throwing the disgusting towel in the hamper, he grabbed a fresh pair of jeans and a comfy tee shirt. And fresh skivvies!

Rich found his way downstairs and got to work. He shooed Dozer off the kitchen counter, away from the expertly seasoned steaks. "Not for you!" he said as the cat scurried away, a bit pissed. There was a pan in the oven sporting a couple of baked potatoes—really big ones—and a couple of enormous steamed artichokes on the stove.

He turned when he heard the key in the front door. Tami entered, draping a garment bag across the stair railing. The cat rubbed against her leg.

"Hi, honey. Glad you're home," Rich said cautiously.

"Hi," Tami managed. She reached down and picked up the cat.

"Hello, baby...how's my baby boy?" she said to Dozer. Rich walked over and gave her a peck on the cheek, which she accepted this time.

"How was your day, honey? Did you get my message?"

She put down the cat before replying. "No. I didn't. I was at work."

Rich tried not to overreact to that bit of news. "Really? Great! I didn't know you had a gig today," he said, smiling, then gestured to the kitchen. "Excuse me, I'm right in the middle of dinner; I want to hear about it, though." He walked back to the tiny kitchen and began futzing with the artichokes. "So, how did it go? Was it a movie, or—?"

"M-O-W," Tami said softly as she entered the kitchen and leaned against the counter, kicking off her black high heels.

"Sorry, I don't know what that is," Rich said as he opened the oven door to check the potatoes.

"Movie of the Week. Nothing too exciting."

"Hey, well, it's something, right?" he offered encouragingly, closing the oven door. "It's great, honey! It all helps the cause."

"I guess," Tami replied. "Working tomorrow too. Different location, but same show."

"Cool. Hope you're hungry!"

"I am," she said with something resembling a weak smile.

"Okay, why don't you go put your feet up; I'll put the steaks on right now."

"Okay…" she said through a sigh.

Dozer jumped up, making another run for the steak platter, but Rich snatched it away. "Dream on," he said as he headed out to the propane Weber awaiting him on the patio. As he passed by, he turned on the spa's heater.

Just in case.

◆

With her last little bite of steak still on the fork, Tami scooped up the final dollop of potato, and sour cream along with it, before savoring it all. She had always enjoyed saving a perfect last bite, whenever possible, combining the tastes she loved. The artichoke was long finished and an impressive mountain of discarded leaves—plus mere remnants of what had been a sea of mayonnaise—was all that remained on the TV tray.

It was like the previous night had never happened.

"Thanks for making dinner, honey. I love your steaks," she said. She set the TV tray off to the side and reclined her side of the loveseat. An episode of *Friends* was starting, and Rich took that as a cue to go and turn off the spa. They'd used it maybe twice since it had been installed—Tami had lobbied for it—and there was no use in running the heater on that thing tonight. *Sigh.* Rich took pride in maintaining the spa's perfect pH balance, as he knew Tami couldn't be bothered. One of these days he'd get to enjoy it.

"Sure," Rich said as he got up to attend to the dishes. "Glad you enjoyed it, honey," he added as he made his way to the kitchen. A man's work is never done. For a guy, Rich was quite domestic in every sense of the word. In addition to being the breadwinner, he was resigned to his unofficial roles as cook, bottle washer and keeping on top of the dusting and vacuuming duties.

He let the dishes soak in sudsy water while he scraped the charred remnants off the now-cool grill surface and flavor bars, then replaced the BBQ cover and looked up at the very full moon. Scurrying across the wood fence was a mama possum and three offspring. She flashed her teeth and hissed at Rich, and he returned the sentiment before heading back inside.

Once the dishes were washed and dried, he quietly put them away and finished wiping down the counters. He couldn't hear the TV but could see the light flickering in the next room, so he walked in to see what Tami was watching: an infomercial for a juicer.

Ah, yes…some of his finest work.

Tami wasn't watching any longer; she was completely crashed out. Rich saw a note pad on the TV tray next to her and noticed she'd jotted down a few details about the *Three Easy Payments* and a phone number to call for ordering the thing. He shook his head and moved the tray away. After a deep, silent yawn and a moment's hesitation, Rich knelt down next to Tami, kissing her gently on the forehead.

"Honey," he whispered. There was no reaction, so he tried again. "Honey…time for bed," he said softly. He brushed a hair away from her cheek and very gently nudged her shoulder. "Sweetie…."

Tami scowled and jerked her shoulder away. Her eyes remained closed, a look of disorientation and agitation skewing her features. "No!" she blurted, as if at someone other than Rich. He regarded her with tired, now-stinging eyes as he contemplated another tack. He had to get her—*and himself*—to bed.

"C'mon, honey. It's getting late—"

Still in Lala Land, Tami hissed, "No! Fuck you!" Rich looked around helplessly. The cat looked back at him from the comfort of his carpeted cat tower as if to say, *You're on your own, pal.*

Rich put on his imaginary kid gloves and gently slid his hands under her. "Honey, it's me. C'mon, I'm gonna carry you upstairs." She squirmed, completely disoriented and a million miles away. "Hey, Sweetie. It's Rich…. I'm taking you to bed."

"No! Don't! What? What—are you doing?" she said, her eyes blinking open with a wild look. "Don't ever do that!" Tami sat up, looked blankly at the flickering images on the TV, then got up and slowly ascended the stairs.

"Sorry, honey—I was just…." Rich said, mostly to himself at this point.

He turned off the TV, flipped off the cat, and slowly made his way upstairs as well. After spending several minutes on his oral hygiene—he still had one baby tooth that required careful flossing—Rich eased himself into bed as gingerly as possible. Tami was fast asleep and had left him with only about a foot of space on his side of the king bed. He was used to it and, being a side sleeper, it wasn't too much of a hardship.

As his back gently made contact with hers, he looked across the dark room to the framed black and white school portrait sitting atop the dresser, illuminated by a single shaft of moonlight sneaking through the vertical blinds. In the photo, six-year-old Richie was smiling innocently. Not a care in the world.

He stared at the picture until his eyes got heavy, which didn't take long at all, then surrendered to a deep, and long overdue, sleep.

◆

CHAPTER 14

GAFFERS AND SET crew were scurrying around making adjustments to gear while the prop department tweaked the tables, chairs, and various accoutrements on the sound stage's bar set. At a nearby craft service table, Tami was spreading a generous layer of cream cheese on a bagel and topping it with a thick slab of beefsteak tomato. As she was about to take a bite a very familiar, but most unexpected, voice called out to her.

"Hey, Tami!"

When she turned around, the last person in the world she would expect to see on a film set was standing there with a big grin. "David!" she said incredulously.

"What's up, sis?" David said as he initiated an awkward hug. Tami wiped the cream cheese from her finger onto a napkin and looked at him quizzically.

"What are you doing here? Are you delivering something, or—?" Tami asked, genuinely curious why her brother would find himself on a film set—her turf.

"Me? Delivery gig?" he replied with a laugh. "No."

"Well, what brings you to a sound stage? Mom told you where I was working, right?" she said. "I can't believe you came here just to see me work. I wish you'd told me—"

"Not exactly," he said. "I'm here to work too."

Tami's brow began to furrow as David elaborated.

"I signed up with a casting agency and I'm here to do some extra work today. This will be my third gig," he beamed, then added, "this time with you!"

As if it were suddenly crawling with maggots, Tami tossed her bagel into the trashcan and stared at him, an awkward half-smile on her face. "*What?*"

"Yep! I know, I'm just starting out and all, but you gotta start somewhere, right?" he said, his enthusiasm not appreciated by his sibling.

"David.... Since when did you become interested in—*extra* work?"

"Actually, I've been looking into acting for a little while. I was waiting on my headshots, and—"

"Wait—your *what!?*" Tami said loud enough to get a look from the craft services guy. She smiled at the guy across the table, grabbed a granola bar, and ripped it open. She spoke with a mouthful; she was starved. "David.... David.... Listen...," she said, a condescending smile forming as she continued. "You know that I'm the actor in the family and that I've been studying my craft since I was fifteen."

"Yeah," he replied.

"And you probably know that acting's a craft, right?"

"Of course," David said, not appreciating her tone.

"You don't just walk in, right off the turnip truck, and say, 'I'm an actor'—you know that, don't you?"

David grabbed an apple, nodded to the guy, then turned to his sister, with a newfound resolve. "Look, Tami. I respect you and what you're doing—always have. But please don't insult me and pretend to have a lock on the acting profession. Because you don't."

Tami tried to tamp down the slow burn, but her button had been pushed, and it couldn't be undone. She grabbed her garment bag from a nearby chair as she responded.

"I can't believe this. I've got to get ready," she added as she began to walk off. David followed her until she spun around on her heel and gave him a wild glare he hadn't ever seen before. She leaned into him.

"Look, little brother. I don't need any distractions, and I sure don't have time to have you following me around like a little lost puppy on the set!"

They stared at each other for several moments before David weighed in.

"You don't have to worry, Tami. I'll stay out of your way. I know what to do. I'll be fine."

"David," Tami said slowly and in a very hushed tone. "Understand this: You're not an actor. You're—an *extra*. You're *background....* You're a *fucking tree*, okay?" she added, slamming her granola bar into the trash as she stormed away, letting out a loud sigh.

"Whatever," David said softly.

◆

The first assistant director was placing extras at tables as the camera crew rehearsed a dolly move, and the director scribbled a note in the margin of his script. The first AD motioned for Tami, and a male extra in his late twenties, to sit at a designated table in the middle of the set.

The remaining cluster of extras was standing in their designated place just off set, and David positioned himself in the front of the group, smiling widely, hungrily. Tami watched as the AD walked over to the group, then selected David and the blonde bimbo next to him—the one with the short skirt and an impressive store-bought rack—and had them follow him.

He placed David and the blonde at the front table, nearest the camera position, and gave them a bit of "business" to do for the shot. After a quick laugh, the AD walked back over to the rest of the group and began making more selections.

Tami was seething, and her obviously-gay table mate tried to chat her up.

"I think the camera will be able to see us really well!" he said, like he was going to piddle.

Tami rolled her eyes, ignoring him as she watched the other table.

"Tomorrow I'm in a concert crowd scene for a Mariah Carey video!" he added.

Tami turned to him, no longer trying to hide her annoyance. "What?"

"A Mariah Carey video!"

"Wow—that's fabulous," she replied, dripping sarcasm.

"I know!" he giggled.

The first AD's voice boomed, "Okay, background! Attention. Listen up for instructions, please!" All got very quiet, and the camera/dolly crew made it back to their "one"—their starting position.

"Thank you," he continued. "Now, in this scene you are all quietly chatting amongst yourselves—and by quietly, I mean *silently*, just smiling and pretending to chat while our lead actors do their scene here at the bar. You are to ignore the couple at the bar until after he throws his drink in her face, okay? Any questions?"

There weren't any.

"Okay, then." He paused, kneeling down to talk with David and the blonde at their table. "Now, you will react to this because some of the drink has splashed onto your dress, okay?" he said to the bimbo. She smiled at this, this role of a lifetime. "And you," he said, turning to David, "You're going to react to this because you're upset that your girlfriend has had her beautiful cocktail dress splashed on by this guy at the bar, okay?"

David looked over at the two sickeningly attractive leads standing at the bar, momentarily wondering what he'd seen them in before, then turned back to the AD and smiled confidently.

"Absolutely. Hey, do you want me to say anything to him? Maybe I—"

The AD. nipped this in the bud with a quick, "Uh, no. Just give him the stern look. Let me see it."

David scrunched his brow, giving his best version of pissed off. "How's that?"

"Perfect," replied the AD as he exited the set. *Extras....*

"Picture's up!" the second AD yelled out, loud enough for everybody in the sound stage to hear.

A revolving red light, like those found on police cars, began flashing and Tami tightly balled her fists under the table. The boom mic was lowered into position.

"Roll camera!" said the first AD.

"Rolling," replied the camera operator. "Speed!"

"And...*action!*" said the director.

◆

CHAPTER 15

RICH SORTED THROUGH the day's fistful of mail as he made his way toward the front door. *No checks today. Damn.* It was a flawless afternoon, and he couldn't help but think how odd—and, who was he kidding: *great*—it felt for him to be home, alone, while Tami was out making a buck for a change. As he neared the front steps, his next-door neighbor, Karen, looked up from her broom and brushed away her bangs.

"Hi, Rich," she said in her rather mousy voice. With her Dorothy Hamill-esque brunette bob, she was cute as a button, but, wow. Rich wondered if it was that voice that had driven her husband away a year before. God only knew.

"Hey, Karen, didn't notice you there."

"Beautiful day."

"Spectacular," Rich said, letting the sun hit his face. "First daylight I've been able to enjoy in—forever, it seems."

"Busy, huh?"

"Yeah, you might say that." He laughed, waving his stack of bills. "As long as these keep coming in!"

"Mail came early?"

"If you can call this mail," he said with a smile.

"I know…. So, is Tami working today?"

"Yeah. Actually, she is," he said, sounding a bit more surprised than he'd intended.

"That's great," Karen said. She studied her shoes for a second, then looked back at Rich. "Everything all right with her?"

"Sure. Why do you ask?" Rich inquired, searching her face.

"Oh, I dunno. It's none of my business. I just thought I heard her screaming at someone the other day. Your car wasn't here, so I figured you weren't home," she said meekly.

Rich glanced around the common area before he replied. "Yeah, everything's fine. Maybe it was the TV you heard." He gestured to the common wall he and Karen shared. "They probably could've sprung for some beefier drywall," he added. "But, seriously, sorry if it bothered you, Karen; we'll keep an eye on the TV volume."

"No problem, Rich. Just thought I'd mention it."

Karen's ten-year-old clone/daughter walked up the path and immediately jettisoned her very cumbersome school backpack when she reached the porch.

"Hi, Rich, hi, Mom," she said, relieved to have lightened her load.

"Hi, Melissa," Rich said.

"How was school, honey?"

"Fine."

Karen gave Melissa a hug, then looked at Rich and shrugged. "It doesn't matter how many times I ask that question, the answer's always the same. 'Fine.'"

Rich winked at Karen, then turned to her mini-me. "So, did you make the team?"

Melissa turned excitedly back to her mom, a huge smile revealing her new braces." Oh, yeah! Mom, I start softball next week! I'm going to need cleats!"

"That's great, honey! Okay, we'll go shopping."

"Okay! Yay! When?"

"Maybe tonight, after dinner."

The unmistakable sound of an approaching ice cream truck punctuated the celebratory moment. Karen had always thought it odd that this ice cream guy played Christmas jingles year-round. Melissa interrupted "Rudolph the Red Nosed Reindeer" with a squeal of delight.

"Ooh! Can I have some quarters!?"

"*May* I have some quarters?" Karen corrected.

"Mom! May I have some quarters? Please?"

"On the counter," Karen replied, laughing as Melissa streaked inside, the screen door slamming loudly.

"Ah, the simpler pleasures. I kind of miss those days sometimes," Rich said.

"Yep. Me too. You're so good at remembering things, Rich!"

"Oh?"

"Melissa's softball tryouts, for example."

"She'd mentioned it in passing a couple of weeks ago. I'm happy she made the cut. I was sure she would."

As the odd playlist switched to a torturous version of "Jingle Bells," the screen door flew back open, and Melissa streaked past, down to the curbside truck. "Can I buy you an ice cream, Rich?"

"*May* you?" Rich laughed. He patted his tummy and said, "I'm good. Watching my girlish figure, thanks."

"Yeah, right," Karen laughed. She paused at the door, then said, "So you're still wanting Melissa to feed your cat this weekend?"

"Yes, if that's still okay?"

"It's fine. Melissa's been looking forward to it. Anniversary, right?"

"Yep, three years! Time flies…. Just a little surprise getaway. We've been needing one."

"Mum's the word. Sounds nice," she said, trying to remember when she last enjoyed such a getaway.

"Almost forgot," he said, reaching into his pocket. "Here's the spare key for Melissa. Cat food's in the pantry, along with a note," Rich added.

"Great, thanks. See you later, Rich."

"See you, Karen. And thanks."

They exchanged waves, and Karen returned to her broom as Rich proceeded inside.

◆

CHAPTER 16

UPSTAIRS, IN THE spare bedroom, Rich sat at his cheap, particleboard desk, one of those wood-grained veneer monstrosities that comes in a box and you had to piece together for hours with a bunch of tiny dowels, some glue, those goofy locking hub thingies, and a gazillion screws, all with little help from the completely inadequate instructions. Rich had always wondered why fake wood weighed so much more, and was so less sturdy, than the real deal, and he'd decided whenever it came time to move again, this expendable piece of faux furniture would stay behind as his gift to the new homeowner.

Not unlike his old apartment, Rich's office showcased his framed photos and memorabilia, and he kept track of his work assignments on an oversized wall calendar—it had to have squares big enough to scrawl his notes into.

As he sorted through the day's mail, which seemed to be entirely comprised of bills these days, he noticed a few that he didn't recognize, and upon closer inspection saw that they were addressed to Tami. *What the heck? Since when does Tami have three Visas?* Yikes. He'd have to ask her.

He set hers aside and pressed one of the many speed dial buttons on his office phone. It was a corded phone he'd bought a few years before, and he'd been enamored by the fact that it had sixty preset buttons, all of which he'd programmed and neatly labeled with his clients' names. A lot less hassle than the Rolodex he used to keep on his desk. He put the phone on speaker.

"Richie!"

"Jimmie! Hey, man. Just wanted to confirm: same call time on Monday?"

"Yeah. Nothing's changed. Looking forward to seeing you, buddy," Jim replied.

"Perfect. Yeah, you too. Gracias, mi amigo. See you then!"

"You bet, Richie. Later."

Rich hung up, circled the Monday date in red Sharpie, and wrote the client info, and 5:30 in the square. He stepped back and surveyed all the red. Red was good. He flicked off the light and bounded downstairs.

He had chores to do.

◆

Rich was taking guilty pleasure in being home alone today, as it was a rarity to say the least. Dusting, vacuuming, straightening up on his day off was no big deal because he did not enjoy living in chaos. And if he didn't do it, it wouldn't ever get done.

He set down the can of lemon Pledge and a dust rag atop his oak rack stereo system, his pride and joy. He had embraced the newer CD technology a few years prior and had begrudgingly duplicated much of his LP album collection in the new format, but he was still fond of the vinyl—not only for its arguably richer sound, but the artwork and sleeves were so much cooler than those little CD liner notes.

He perused his alphabetized collection, stopped in the middle of the C section, and selected one of his all-time favorites, a double-album gatefold masterpiece: *FM/Live* by the Climax Blues Band. *Yes!!*

Music to vacuum by! (And music that doesn't suck.) This was, by Rich's estimation, the definitive live album *ever* recorded—by any Earth humans—and he'd long ago decided that if he were ever stranded on a deserted island (one that happened to have power and a working turntable, of course), this would be his "desert island album" to listen to for eternity.

He found Record 1, Side A, placed it on the turntable, and gently lowered the tone arm until the stylus just kissed the disc's surface. Like many old school audiophiles, he found odd enjoyment in that initial sound of diamond needle meeting vinyl groove—that almost-like-bacon-frying sound that let you know you were in for a tasty bit of ear candy. He lowered the lid, and cranked the volume knob.

After introductory remarks by the emcee, a very raucous New York crowd welcomed the band as the gifted lead guitarist, Peter Haycock, launched into "All The Time In The World," joined by the powerful rhythm section of the band's saxophonist, Colin Cooper—pulling rhythm guitar duty here, John Cuffley behind the drum kit, and powerhouse bassist, Derek Holt, providing the thunderous bottom end. The combination was potent, filling the townhouse (and undoubtedly his neighbor Karen's as well, but she was cool) with their incendiary blues/rock licks. Even though he'd nearly worn the grooves off this album, it still gave Rich goosebumps. *Okay, now we can get to work.* Newly energized, Rich began on the stairs.

About half way through the third song, a tour de force instrumental called "Flight," Rich stopped dancing with the vacuum as he noticed the front door slowly open and Tami enter. She had a drawn look and held her heels in one hand and garment bag in the other.

Rich switched off the vacuum, then the stereo and closed the door behind her. "Welcome home, honey. Here, let me take that," he said, relieving her of the garment bag and hanging it from the cat tower. He kissed her forehead, and she tossed her purse and shoes onto the loveseat before plopping her deflated self down onto it like a lead balloon. The cat found her lap and cranked up his motor, earning some absentminded scratches on the head. After several moments, Tami began sobbing.

"I hate my brother!" she wailed, sending the cat upstairs to safer ground. Rich moved her shoes and sat down next to her, his arm around her shoulder.

"Hey! Tell me, what happened?"

She continued sobbing, pausing only to belt out a response. "He's such a *fucking asshole!*"

Rich's kneejerk reaction was to glance over to the shared wall by the stairwell. Was Karen hearing this? *Gawd*, he hoped not. He couldn't explain this away on the TV again, not believably anyway.

"It's okay, honey—relax…. C'mon, let me get you something to eat. You've had a long—"

Tami sprung up, jerked the cordless phone from its cradle, and fervently stabbed at the keypad. "I don't want to relax! And I'm not hungry!" she snapped before rechanneling her anger where it belonged. Rich began slowly pacing as he braced for the fireworks.

"How long have you known about this, Mom?"

"Tami? Hi, honey. Wait. Slow down—what?"

"David! He showed up on the set today!"

Carol tucked the phone under her chin as she glided her iron along the hem of a flowery skirt. On the wall behind her there were two new headshots—these ones of David in cheesy actor poses—displayed alongside Tami's.

"Tami. What is the problem? Why are you upset?"

Tami laughed to herself, then replied, "*Why*—? Did you just ask me *why* I'm…upset?"

Rich began stealthily winding the vacuum cleaner cord, briefly entertaining the thought of hanging himself with it as the silent alarm switch activated in his head.

"Honey, I don't understand," Carol replied, genuinely puzzled.

"My so-called *brother,* your *son*—the *asshole*—is trying to be *me* now! *That's* why I'm... *upset!*"

"Tami, please don't talk about your brother that way, and you know I hate when you use that kind of lang—"

"He's an asshole, Mother! Ass-*hole!*"

Carol parked the iron and ran a hand through her hair. "David is your brother, Tami. He is not trying to be you. Your brother loves and respects you, honey! We all do."

"If he respected me, Mother, he wouldn't be trying to *be* me! He can't be me!" Tami said, astonished that this wasn't painfully obvious to everyone else.

Rich quietly stashed the vacuum in the hall closet. He looked over at Tami, who was pacing like a caged tiger.

"Of course he can't be you, Tami! Nobody can be you!"

Tami lowered her voice a notch but made up for it with intensity as she continued. "I have been studying my craft since I was fifteen years old. Who does he think he is—saying he does what I do now?! Do you really not get it, Mom?"

Carol smiled into the phone and tried to summon up a non-offensive response. What she came up with failed. "Honey. Look, there's no rule that says there can't be two actors in a fam—"

"Hel-lo! He's not a fucking actor!" Tami yelled, cutting her off.

"Tami—I'm going to hang up if you're going to—"

"Yeah? Well, *FUCK YOU* too, *bitch!*" Tami clicked off the phone and slammed it into its wall cradle. She let out a primal scream and lifelessly flopped onto the loveseat. As she began sobbing quietly, Rich emerged from the kitchen, drying his hands on a towel. He took a deep breath, and smiled.

"Honey, I have an idea."

◆

CHAPTER 17

TAMI WAS SULKING in the passenger seat as Rich backed the Explorer out of the carport and proceeded down the street. After a few minutes she turned to Rich.

"I told you I wasn't hungry."

"Yeah, well you might be later," he replied.

She looked out the window as they rode in silence.

"I'm sorry you had a rough day, honey."

Tami turned from the window as she noticed they were passing by the normal eating establishments.

"Where are we going?"

"Away," Rich replied.

"What do you mean, away—where?"

"You'll see."

"We can't go *away*. I didn't pack anything. And we can't just leave Dozer—"

"Not to worry. Got it handled," Rich said calmly. "Why don't you just recline your seat, close your eyes a little while."

"Not tired," Tami muttered, barely audible. Her head rested against the window, her eyes closed now.

Rich looked over at her and let out a small sigh. It was like he was dealing with somebody going through their "terrible twos," but an involuntary smile crept across his face as he drove in blissful silence, drinking in the early stages of what was sure to be a spectacular sunset. The kind of colors Lennon & McCartney described in "Lucy In The Sky With Diamonds."

◆

Tami had been lights out the entire way—a nearly three-hour drive—and only awoke once the tires crunched on the noisy gravel driveway of the quaint Victorian B&B. As it was now too late to even think about going out for dinner, Rich had taken the liberty of driving through one of Tami's favorite fast food haunts, Der Wienerschnitzel, a few miles back and picked up her usual trio of kraut, mustard, and chili dogs—plus fries and a chocolate shake. Not exactly fine dining, nor the best thing right before bed, but it was the only port in the storm, other than the sketchy-looking burger joint they'd passed coming in. He'd wolfed down his food as they drove, and he took the last noisy sip of his shake.

"Where are we?" she asked groggily. "I smell chili."

"I'll be right back, honey," he whispered, exiting the vehicle and popping the rear hatch as Tami explored the contents of the food bag.

Rich got the room key from the kindly proprietor and carried in the suitcase he'd hidden in the Explorer's cargo area. By the time he came back out for Tami, she was finishing the tail end of the kraut dog, the one she'd saved for last. He helped her from the car and guided her up the path to what would be their home-away-from-home for a couple of nights.

Rich lit the faux log in the gas fireplace and got their things organized as he told Tami all about how he'd had this little surprise jaunt planned for some time. Several minutes went by with no response, so he turned around, only to find her fast asleep in her clothes. Not worth waking her up. He tucked her in, put on his own pajamas, brushed his teeth, and sat on the edge of the poofy, king-sized, four-post bed for a brief moment. Resistance was futile as he surrendered to the pillow-top Venus flytrap, which instantly swallowed him whole.

◆

CHAPTER 18

THE NEXT MORNING, Tami awoke to the sound of a key rattling around in the door lock. She blinked several times as she took in the surroundings of their beautiful, period-decorated room bathed in soft rays of sunlight coming through the wooden blinds.

"Housekeeping," Rich said in a deep voice as he entered with a large tray laden with breakfast goodies. He was wearing shorts and a polo shirt and was freshly showered. He closed the door with his foot and set the tray on the bed for Tami's approval. Amongst the food offerings, a small vase held a beautiful yellow rose.

"Wow…" she managed.

"Fresh squeezed orange juice, very hot coffee—for me, hot chocolate with marshmallows for you, eggs over medium, the way you like 'em, sausage links, crispy bacon, sourdough with strawberry jam, seasonal fruit, and…oh, yeah: Happy Anniversary!"

"Aww. Happy Anniversary to you, too, Honey. You thought of everything."

"You have no idea," he said, laughing, as he went over to the suitcase and extracted her make-up case and jewelry box.

"There are a couple of outfits for you to choose from for dinner tonight, and I brought your matching shoes, purse, and accessories. Turns out I forgot the Q-Tips though. Rookie mistake."

"Thank you, Richie." Tami took a bite of bacon and smiled up at him. It was a relaxed, contented smile, one that Rich honestly couldn't remember seeing in a very long while. So far, based on this one early indicator anyway, it seemed that his plan was working. They'd needed this, and it'd been hard to carve out the opportunity, but this was the most important thing right now. Away from the hustle, away from the smog, from the job(s), and a respite from the family drama that had been consuming Tami of late.

"Hey, save me some bacon!" He laughed as he sat on the bed and joined in on the bounty.

◆

After breakfast, Rich placed the tray atop the wicker trunk on the porch, as instructed by the innkeeper. "Be right back, Honey. Take a shower if you want; I already did."

"Okay," she said, from behind the bathroom door.

Tami took her time shaving her legs before stepping into the inviting stream of piping hot water and enjoyed the coconut shampoo and luxurious body gels while she replicated Streisand's "Memory."

Perfectly.

Rich smiled at the beautiful sound wafting from their little cottage as he wheeled the second of two rental beach cruiser bicycles onto the porch. Her voice was pretty incredible, really, and he remembered how she used to sing so joyfully when they were first married. He made a mental note to not wait so long for their next spontaneous getaway.

Tami would be a while, so Rich plopped down onto the wooden porch rocker and entertained himself by watching a family of quail navigating the garden like they were on their way to church. A distant woodpecker was hammering away, and a couple of Monarch butterflies flittered amongst the flowers. He closed his eyes as the morning sun caressed his face.

He quietly whispered to himself, maybe to God, "Thank you."

◆

CHAPTER 19

THEY HAD ENJOYED a leisurely bike ride down the lightly traveled country road into the sleepy little town a couple of miles from their inn. The highlight might've been the game-changer waffle cone with double scoops of artisan ice cream. Peanut butter/fudge with a hefty scoop of pistachio hit the spot for Rich, while Tami enjoyed every lick of her towering mint-chocolate chip and butter toffee creation.

Back at the ranch, what started out as "nap time" morphed into some tender lovemaking, with Tami initiating. Rich really missed this version of Tami, and he made a secret vow to do whatever it takes to get her back.

A brief, but restorative, nap followed.

At dinner, Tami looked radiant in her perfectly accessorized ensemble as they dined at the highly recommended, rustic-but-elegant, steakhouse down the road. Following a brilliant meal of New York steaks and scallops, they followed their server's suggestion and polished off an insane Bananas Foster, prepared in dramatic fashion tableside.

On the short drive back, Rich reflected on how it had been— start to finish—a perfect day, and he couldn't remember the last time they'd had anything close to that. Tami was back to her old self it seemed, and an irrepressible smile formed on his face.

They slept like the dead.

◆

With no real agenda and nothing to distract from their blissful country weekend, the second day and evening were…even better. It was kind of like *Godfather II*, where the rare sequel surpasses the first one, and then goes on to win Best Picture as well.

They slept until almost ten before Rich bed-headed his way over to the main house to retrieve another tray of delicious B&B room service breakfast. The inn's hospitality continued to border on the unreal. This morning it was Belgian waffles with real Vermont maple syrup—none of that Aunt Jemima jive, yogurt with fresh-picked blackberries, an egg scramble consisting of ground beef, spinach, mushrooms, cheese and country potatoes, plus a side of crispy bacon for the win!

Rich knew this was going to be a tough act to follow, so he'd have to up his game when he got home.

After a return bike ride into town to explore uncharted ice cream flavors, they returned to the room and found a couple of board games in the bookcase. Tami absolutely mopped the floor with Rich in *Monopoly*, while he returned the favor in his specialty, *Scrabble*.

An afternoon hike amongst the evergreens led to much-needed showers, more lovemaking, and another dress-up opportunity at dinner. It was prime rib night and the cuts were generous.

◆

The day's activities had laid the groundwork for a streak of sorts, as this was the second consecutive day, in God knows how long, where they had actually enjoyed each other's company in a consistent state of peace, harmony, relaxation and—sanity.

Had it been since their honeymoon in Bora Bora? All Rich knew was he'd take this little personal-best streak of theirs, and he prayed to the heavens they could build on that.

◆

CHAPTER 20

A FTER A LATE checkout and stops at several antique stores on the way out of town, they made their way back toward The Pit. It was a quiet drive home, as neither did much talking.

No need to kill the buzz.

It was dark when they pulled into their carport, and light rain was beginning to fall.

Tami wheeled the small suitcase and cradled the foil swan leftovers with her free arm, as Rich carried a cumbersome load of stuff toward the front door.

"That was a great two days, but I can't wait to see my baby," Tami said as Rich fumbled for the key.

"Mm, yep," he said.

Rich pushed the door open and set his load down by the loveseat as Tami walked inside. She left the leftovers atop the suitcase on the porch and switched to kitty talk. "Where's my baby? Where's my baby boy!"

Rich wheeled the damp luggage into the house and closed the door.

"We're home, baby!" Tami called, looking around. She walked over to the kitchen, then turned to Rich. "You see him?"

"Not yet…probably upstairs," he replied as he placed the swan in the fridge. Tami immediately retrieved it.

"Come here, Dozer," she said, waving it in the air. "We've got a special treat for you, buddy! Prime rib!"

Rich took the small suitcase and made his way upstairs. Tami paced the tiny dining room, then the living room again.

At the landing, Rich froze in his tracks. Tami walked around toward the staircase and could see Rich's feet, stopped short of the top step.

"You see him, Rich?"

He did. Sprawled there on the landing, the cat laid still, stiff, and obviously dead. His eyes were wide open, and his tongue protruded a mile from the open mouth. The expression on his face suggested an excruciatingly painful death, and the shock of seeing him this way was as viscerally jolting as anything he could remember from any horror movie.

"Is he there?! What is it?"

He truly didn't know how to answer; he'd lost his air, and the resulting silence was deafening.

"Say something!"

Rich turned away and slowly stepped down a few steps to where he could see Tami. "Honey," he answered, numbly, not believing it himself. "He's…he's dead."

"What?!!!" Tami bounded up the stairs, past Rich, wide-eyed in panic and disbelief. "What?!!!!"

Rich tried to hug her, to shield her, but she tore herself away. She could only manage a brief glance at her worst nightmare. Her poor baby stared back at her in a silent scream. "NOOOOOOOOOOOOO!!!!!" she bellowed, heaving and flailing at Rich. She pounded on Rich's chest with her fists, then redirected her energy toward the wall, punching a hole into the drywall of their common stairway wall. Instantaneously, a glacial chunk of her remaining sanity had cleaved away and was ripped to smithereens, and what was left of her fragile world crumpled like a house of cards in a hurricane.

Again, Rich tried to comfort her, but she channeled her rage and adrenaline, conjuring considerable strength as she pushed him backward into the bathroom.

"No! God!! God, no!!" she screamed as she shoved him again, this time sending Rich back hard against the wall, crushing the cheap aluminum towel rack in the process. The hardware fell noisily to the floor as he rebounded, grabbing Tami in a tight, protective hug. He held her in his arms as her body heaved violently, like a raging rodeo bull trying to launch its cowboy. Her bellowing sobs sounded decidedly non-human—more like those of a mortally wounded beast— and emanated from the absolute deepest chasms of a very troubled soul.

Rich kissed the top of her head as she rocked. "I'm so sorry, honey... So sorry..."

◆

CHAPTER 21

THE RAIN WAS coming down harder now as Rich stomped onto the rusty shovel, removing more dirt/mud from the small strip of garden surrounding their back patio slab. The soil was crappy clay, mixed with random rocks and cement chunks, which made it more difficult, and he was getting soaked in the process. But he didn't care about that.

He had to get the cat in the ground.

He pushed a shock of wet hair from his eyes and looked over at the bath towel-wrapped carcass, resting near his feet.

How could this have happened? They were only gone a couple of days! He shook his head. He'd have some questions in the morning.

He'd managed to get Tami settled in on the loveseat and asked if she wanted him to take the cat to the vet for an autopsy in the morning. But she'd have none of it.

"No," she'd replied absently. "Doctors won't know anything. They won't know what happened to my perfect boy…" she said, her voice trailing off.

"Maybe they can tell us—"

"No doctors!" she said, cutting him off.

"Okay…" was all Rich could muster before she continued.

"My baby boy!" she cried softly.

That's when he'd made the executive decision—the backyard—and she'd weakly nodded in agreement, fully numbed at this point.

Rich leaned into the spade again, scooped out the load, and surveyed his handiwork. He'd lost track of time but guessed he'd been at it for close to an hour. He hoped the hole was deep enough now, and that coyotes wouldn't scale their modest fence later and dig it up. Several cats had been reported missing since they moved into this hilly neighborhood, and it was no mystery that they were a favorite food source for these predators.

Rich gently laid the towel and its rigid contents into the hole. It would have to do. He tilted his head back and let the rain wash over him for several minutes, then began refilling the muddy grave.

"Goodbye, buddy."

◆

CHAPTER 22

MELISSA WAS STILL in her Scooby pajamas, tucked in extra close to her mom on the sofa, as she wiped the tears from her eyes. She stared at the floor, fearing judgment by Rich, who sat in a nearby chair. He set down his coffee and flashed a smile before he spoke. "Sometimes things just happen, Melissa. Nobody's saying it was your fault, honey. It wasn't, okay?"

She looked up at Rich for the first time now. "He seemed okay, Mr. Bryson. I fed him in the morning, like I was supposed to. He was kind of meowing loudly when I left, but he…seemed fine."

"I know. It's okay, sweetheart. And please call me Rich. Nobody's blaming you for anything. Okay?"

Melissa slowly nodded and wiped away another tear as Karen kissed her on the head. "Why don't you go upstairs and get dressed, honey? I'll make you French toast, okay?"

Melissa got up and stood closer to Rich as she spoke. "I'm sorry, Rich. Please tell Tami I'm sorry…."

Rich nodded and gave her a reassuring smile. "I will. Hey, good luck with your softball game today, sweetie. You'll be great. I want to come to a game one of these days, okay?"

Melissa half smiled and headed up the stairs as Karen carried the coffee mugs to the kitchen. Rich followed.

"How's Tami handling it, Rich?"

"Not well—that's an understatement. That cat was her world."

Karen poured two fresh cups, adding cream to both and handed Rich his mug. "Such a shame…. Are you going to have them do an autopsy?"

"Too late for that. I buried him last night. I hope I didn't keep anybody awake with my shoveling."

"The shoveling…no." Karen shook her head.

"Besides, Tami wouldn't want vets involved."

"Oh? How come?"

"Tami was raised Christian Scientist."

"Really? Don't they believe in space ships and alien volcanoes?"

"No. You're confusing them with Scientologists," he said with a tired chuckle. "Many Christian Scientists, Tami included, don't believe in disease, or going to doctors for that matter."

"Really…" she said, pausing for a sip before continuing. "What about if they get really sick—like cancer, or something?"

"Prayer. Mind over matter, that kind of thing. What we—you and I—would call disease, they call 'error.'"

"Hmm. Wow. So you're not Christian Scientist then, Rich?"

"Me? No. I was raised Presbyterian, actually. Not that I'm a big churchgoer or anything, but I respect her beliefs." He took a sip of his coffee.

"Does she respect yours?" Karen asked, a little too directly.

Rich carefully set his nearly full mug down in the sink and gave it a lengthy rinse before answering.

"Yeah—pretty much…" he replied, taking a moment to chew on that before continuing. "Hey, thanks for the coffee, Karen. I should be getting back."

"Don't mention it, Rich. I'm so sorry for what happened and for your loss."

"Thanks."

"If there's anything I can do, please don't hesitate to ask, okay?"

"Okay… I'm no expert, but I'll bet it was a urinary tract infection—a crystal, or something. My sister took some veterinary classes and that's her opinion at least. Pretty common with male cats, supposedly, and it can manifest quickly. A painful way to go, but it would've happened anyway. So…anyway, this is for Melissa."

Rich reached into his wallet, extracted a crisp fifty-dollar bill and held it out it to her.

"Honestly, Rich, I—"

"She did a great job, and a deal's a deal. Maybe she can buy a new glove or something. I insist."

Karen took the bill and smiled at Rich.

"That's very generous. Thanks for being so understanding with Melissa, Rich. That means a lot."

"Of course," he said, and initiated a hug at the door, then smiled and walked away.

"Bye, Rich," she said as she closed the screen door behind him.

Karen couldn't help but feel a triple dose of sadness as she continued to watch her next-door neighbor make the short—yet very long—journey back home.

◆

CHAPTER 23

THE BLISS FROM their anniversary getaway had evaporated instantaneously, as if it had never happened, and it was a complete reset.

Only worse.

Several weeks passed, then months, with Tami's behavior morphing more toward bizarre. Shortly after Dozer's death, she'd spent that one overnight with her parents, at their insistence, and Rich knew better than to ask her how that went. There was still the occasional flare up with her folks on the phone, but this seemed to be the new normal, and it was increasingly poisonous. In her last heated conversation with them she had forbidden her parents from calling their house ever again.

◆

Holidays seemed to come and go with little or no fanfare, as Tami continued to drive the wedge deeper with her family, and her slight-of-hand puppet master grip was getting stronger as she now almost imperceptibly controlled Rich—and his access to his own family.

Each night, when Rich dragged himself in the door from an exhausting day, she felt the need to sit him down and rant for hours, which he obliged out of some twisted sense of marital duty, but it was often at the expense of sleep and at times even food. It was a diet he wouldn't recommend to his worst enemy.

◆

The vertical blinds in their bedroom were drawn and the room was still in relative darkness as Rich lay on his side, his eyes open and face a blank canvas. Tami's back was to his. He had lain there as long as he could on this rare day off, and he slowly sat up, swinging his feet out of bed and unkinking his neck with a head tilt and a resultant pop.

Tami stirred and turned over to Rich, her eyes half open. "What time is it?"

"Mornin'. Didn't mean to wake you."

"You didn't."

"Almost 10:00, if you can believe it," he said, smiling. "You needed that. Guess we both did," he added.

"Ten," she replied with a yawn.

Rich got up, walked over to the blinds, and parted them with his fingers as he peeked out. "It's an unbelievable day out," he said, very upbeat, as he gave the blinds control wand a full twist, instantly bathing the bedroom in warm sunshine.

"Isn't it gorgeous, honey? Nice day for—"

"Would you please close the blinds for a second?" she interjected, looking away from the light.

"Close them? Why?" Rich asked.

"Could you just close them?"

"Okay." Rich's euphoria faded as he complied, sending the room back into its cave state.

"Thanks," Tami said, that strange, unnatural smile on her face now. Her eyes were closed tight, with her head tilted back toward the ceiling, as her bizarre smile broadened to include all of her teeth.

A few moments went by as he watched, the control wand in his hand, silently wishing he had an exorcist on speed dial.

"It doesn't go with that!" she whispered, her eyes still shut.

"What?"

She ignored him. Another seemingly eternal moment went by before she continued. "Okay...Ready...? GO!"

Rich was regarding her closely as he went about twisting the control in his hand. The shafts of sun slowly marched across her face.

"Back a little...."

Rich took in a slow, careful, deep breath as he dialed it back a little more. Still more, in search of some elusive mini-blinds G-spot he didn't know existed. It didn't matter; his buzz was killed, and the day was going to be impossible to salvage.

"Right there." She broke out of her odd trance and looked out at the day, now that she was ready. Her eyes were beyond wide. Ready, Go! "Gorgeous!" she said, flashing her version of a smile, but it was forced now, and not based in reality. That train had already left the station.

"Yeah...it's...nice," Rich replied weakly, no longer the slightest bit enthused. He gave her a peck on the forehead before heading downstairs. If he was sure of one thing in this world, he thought, it was that this day was going to completely and utterly suck. Perhaps he could at least postpone the inevitable with a nice, death row breakfast. He couldn't deal with full-on crazy on an empty stomach.

He paused a moment as he looked at the empty cat tower, then opened the living room blinds, painting the room in the desired glow, and went to the kitchen.

After grabbing some eggs, milk, juice, and the applewood bacon from the fridge, he fired up the day's half pot of coffee. His stomach growled as he watched the slow drip process commence, then he retrieved the tube of Pillsbury biscuits, peeled the wrapper back a ways, and smacked it open on the edge of the counter. Pop! That's when he heard, from the next room, "Would you come in here, please?"

Rich gently set down the tube of oozing dough and counted to three before answering her. "Sure," he said, trying to disguise his sense of foreboding.

For months now, Tami had felt the need to share (to rant, more like it) what she was feeling—mostly variations on a theme about how screwed up her family was, how toxic they were to their marriage, and how they were trying to steal her identity, etc. Same old dance, over and over, and Rich tried to be there for her, no matter what. Her wanting to share was fine, even encouraged—in a sane and productive dialog setting—but the sermonettes were many, and seemed to drone on longer and with more frequency and repetition. This day was shaping up to be no different, and he was tired. Emotionally, physically, spiritually—exhausted.

He dried his hands, then proceeded to the now-darkened living room. Tami was seated on the loveseat, and she'd closed the blinds.

"Jeez—it's like a tomb in here," Rich risked.

She tapped the cushion next to her. "Would you sit for just a minute?"

"I was just getting breakfast started—"

"Just for a minute," she said, cutting him off.

Just for a minute.

"Can we at least open the blinds?"

"In a minute."

Rich sat down next to her. He didn't like where this was going. "Thanks."

"Sure," he said, just short of curtly. "What's up?"

"Would you lean forward a little?"

"Lean forward?" he asked, looking around before complying. "Okay...."

"A little more." Then she whispered to herself, "It doesn't go with that!" with the head tilt/eyes-closed deal.

Rich leaned forward a little more, not sure why. His neck was stretched out an uncomfortable angle now, like a turkey in the guillotine.

Unbeknownst to Rich, when he leaned forward, from Tami's point of view, his head now fully blocked her view of their framed honeymoon photo on the side table behind him, which was the desired effect, since the crazy didn't go with that.

"Right there," she said, her creepy smile directed toward the ceiling now.

Also unbeknownst to Rich, the voices in Tami's head were now speaking to her, both of them taking turns.

"He's not going to love you anymore," Carol's voice cautioned Tami.

"It doesn't go with that!" Tami whispered in response.

"What?" Rich asked, his stomach growling again. "What did you want to talk about?"

The unnatural strain was too much and he leaned back.

"Forward!" Tami barked. Then she whispered, "It doesn't go with that!"

Rich leaned slightly forward again, his neck crimping. "Okay. What doesn't go with what?"

"Just tell him!" Michael's voice chimed in now, but only for Tami.

"Shut up!" Tami yelled in response to the voice. Then to Rich, she blurted out, "I don't want to go to your parents' next weekend!"

"What?" he said, leaning back into the loveseat, a bit defiant. "Where's that coming from? We've—"

"I don't want to go there. I don't think it would be good for us," she interjected.

Rich took a deep breath before speaking. "Look, Tami. We've had this planned for over two months. I haven't seen my family in—forever. Why are you all of a sudden changing your mind?" He stood and turned to her. "Can you give me one good reason?"

"Sit down, please."

"I don't feel like sitting down, Tami. I'm hungry. It's a great day out—and I don't want to miss it, okay?"

Tami rose off the loveseat and entered Rich's space. Her hair was hastily hiked up in a clip and the dark circles under her eyes were blacker than usual, like she'd just emerged from a crypt. "Your parents aren't healthy for you to be around right now, Rich." Her foul, morning crypt breath pushed him a step back.

"What are you talking about?" he said incredulously.

"Rich, your parents are coddling you and that's not good for you—or our marriage," she said, bridging the gap again. Rich didn't recognize the person speaking.

"Your mom and dad are always calling you 'Richie'—like you're a little boy or something. Ever notice that?"

When he didn't respond, she continued. "The Bible says that a man should leave his parents and hold fast to his wife, and—"

"Whoa! Wait a minute! For your information, my parents have called me by that nickname ever since I can remember, and there's nothing wrong with that. A lot of my friends call me that too. So?" he said, an impossible-to-repress edge creeping in. "What the hell are you talking about?"

Tami reached over to brush a hair out of Rich's face, causing him to reflexively flinch. "Did you just flinch?"

"No," Rich said, his brow furrowed.

"Did you just fucking flinch from me?" she demanded with a curious laugh.

"I said, NO."

"You did! Are you making me out to be somebody I'm not?"

Rich just looked at her. The wild look in her eyes was worse than he'd seen it, and the white cottage cheese-like spittle was forming in the corner of her mouth again. *Fuck.* "I'm not making you out to be anything," he said as he turned away and walked toward the kitchen. "Look," he said over his shoulder, "if this where you're gonna take the conversation, and if this is what you have planned for the day—" He opened the long cabinet and reached for his keys. But they weren't on the hook.

He returned to the living room.

"Tami, where are my keys?"

She looked at him resolutely. "Why? Where'd you think you were going? We're not done with this conversation yet."

"Oh, is that what you call this—a conversation?" He ran his hand through his Flock of Seagulls bedhead. "I'm going to go out for a while and give you a chance to cool your jets a little," he said, his hand outstretched. "Where are my keys?"

"You aren't going anywhere. You can't just walk out on me."

"He doesn't love you," Carol's voice said to Tami.

"Shut up," Tami whispered in response.

"Just tell me where my keys are, please."

"He's going to leave you!" the voice said, this time Michael's.

"No!" she whispered to the voices, then turned to Rich, building up steam before leaning in for emphasis. He tried to ready himself the best he could.

Rich was beginning to wonder if there just might be some unseen others joining in the conversation. *Yeah...*

"If you left, I'd find you, you know. I'd track you down. Wherever you went... You couldn't hide from me."

"Who's talking about—"

There was a new menace in her twisted smile, and it sent a chill down Rich's spine, a subliminal shiver, which didn't go unnoticed by Tami. "Oh, is Richie afraid of Tami now?" she jumped in mockingly.

"Stop it."

"Little Richie gonna go cry to Mommy?" she mocked as she laughed.

"I said—stop it, Tami."

"Or what?!" she yelled, striking Rich's face with a violent, stinging SLAP!

Rich's eyes started to water slightly as she laughed at the

powerless man standing in front of her. His hands slowly clenched into fists but they remained by his side. He wasn't aware of it, but in real time his subconscious playlist had cued up some sage advice, sung by Roger Daltrey now, reminding him to unclench that fist before...y'know....

His Mom had trained him right, and if there was one unbreakable, universal rule in this world it was surely this: Boys Don't Hit Girls. Ever. He blinked quickly and slacked his fingers. He looked back at his wife—if this was even still her—and was repulsed by what he saw and felt. She taunted him with her grin.

"Richie gonna cry? Poor Richie!" she said, laughing loudly.

He turned to walk away but Tami grabbed a hank of his hair and yanked him to a stop. He groaned loudly.

"Don't you—ever—walk away from me!" she said, as she yanked harder. He dropped to his knees, his mane still firmly in her grasp as he grabbed at her wrist to wrest himself free.

"Let—go!" he groaned, and after several moments she finally did.

He got back to his feet just in time for Tami's jackhammer fists to begin their assault on his head and neck. He raised his arms defensively in an effort to ward off the blows, but he was largely unsuccessful. She landed several punches on her intended target areas, with her forearm occasionally making violent contact with Rich's blocks.

"You—are—out—of—control!! Stop!" Rich said between blows. He ducked down, covering his head with his arms to the best of his ability, but she ratcheted up her delivery.

"You—are—a—piece—of—shit!!" she yelled, switching out her armaments to fingernails. She dug her claws into the fleshy part of Rich's neck, then his ears and scalp, before aiming her ten mini daggers at his forearms, producing a series of bloody gashes. She came in closer, biting Rich's ears, his neck, and sinking her teeth into his forehead. Rich felt—and heard—the sickening crunch. He was in survival mode as he summoned the strength to grab her wrists firmly. She tried to shake herself from his grip, but couldn't.

"Afraid of a woman, Richie? Huh?" She laughed again. "I weigh a hundred five pounds!"

Rich held her wrists at a safe distance. "Gonna hit me now? Huh, Richie? Huh, Mama's Boy?" Tami was covered in sweat, and she stared back at Rich like a rabid wolf in a trap, with nothing to lose. He didn't dare let her go.

"No."

"No, what?"

"No. I'm not going to hit you."

"Oh, you think you're better than me, is that it? Does Richie think he's better, huh?"

"Nobody's better than anybody" he said rather calmly. "I was taught not to hit girls, and I'm not going to start now."

Tami stared back at Rich, an insane smile returned to her face.

"Now, Richie, you go out and play and don't let the girls beat you up, okay? Be a good little boy, Richie!" she said, in her best mocking, sing-songy voice.

He stared back at her, trying not to let hate enter the equation, but it was in the on-deck circle. "You done?"

"Let go of my arms."

"Not until you get yourself under control."

"Let go."

"I will. Are you done?"

Tami's knee came up swiftly between Rich's legs, delivering a devastating blow to his manhood, and doubling him over. She rubbed her liberated wrists. "Yeah... I'm done!" A series of stomps from her bare heel landed on Rich's head, then she kicked him in the back repeatedly. He groaned as he rolled over, prompting her to stomp his ribs, cracking a couple. Rich managed to grab her nearest leg and pull her—carefully—to the ground, guiding her onto her back, and making sure she didn't hit her head in the process. A gentleman, even under assault. *Mom would be proud.* Tami let out a shriek as Rich straddled her midsection, her arms again in his grip at the sides of her head.

"Get off of me, you asshole!" she said, gritting her not-recently-brushed teeth at Rich.

"He doesn't care about you," Carol's voice chimed in, pouring fuel on the inferno.

"I'm not—going to let you up—until you're under control," Rich said with his remaining wind.

"Fuck you! You're just like them!" Tami screamed.

Rich looked down at her and couldn't believe he was holding down his wife, sprawled out on the living room floor, the two of them like a couple of wrestlers waiting for the slap on the mat from the referee.

"You need help, Tami—"

"You need help, you son of a bitch!" she replied, still struggling. They remained in this Mexican standoff for several moments, while Rich tried to think of a way to diffuse the situation. What he said next didn't help, but it was all he had. And it was the truth.

"I think you need medication, Tami."

With that, Tami hocked the mother of all loogies onto Rich's face. He grimaced, shocked and disgusted, but ever mindful not to release his grip on this out-of-control beast. The thick spittle slowly made its way down his cheek, starting at the inside of his left eye. He could smell it, and taste it when it reached the corner of his mouth. It was all he could do to not heave on her.

They remained in that configuration, and the spit reached his chin now. It began to dangle, like a stalactite, hovering over Tami's face. Their sparring match was interrupted by the sound of the phone ringing, a scant few feet away. It rang several times, until the machine picked up, and their giddy-sounding outgoing message from much happier times played through the speaker.

Recorded on that blissful day they'd moved in together, it now sounded so sad, so surreal under these circumstances:

(Rich's voice) "Hi, this is Rich…"

(Tami's voice) "And this is Tami…"

(Both together) "Sorry we missed your call…"

(Tami laughs) "Please leave a message at the tone, and we'll call you back…"

(Both laugh) "Bye!"

BEEP!

"It doesn't go with that," Tami whispered to herself when the recording concluded.

"Hi, Richie dear… It's your mom." Tami looked up at Rich defiantly, a rabid, possessed, petulant demon child. "And, hi, Tami," the message continued. "I hope you're both out enjoying this beautiful Sunday, doing something fun. I'm sure you are."

"Is this fun, Richie?" Tami taunted, letting loose a bellow of insane laughter as she struggled again to free her wrists. This only caused the dangling spittle to drop down onto her face, despite her best efforts to elude it. "Fuck!"

"Richie, I was just calling to find out what time you both were coming next weekend?"

Tami smiled at Rich and shrugged.

"We can't wait to see you both. Richie, I was thinking of making the lamb roast you like so much, so I just need to know what time to expect you two."

They were both perspiring profusely at this point, and Rich could barely see through the burning cocktail of spit and sweat. And blood.

"Call me when you can, dear. Look forward to seeing you both. Love you. Bye bye…."

BEEP!

Meanwhile, just outside their front door, in the townhouse's common area—out in the real world—on this nicest day of the year, a couple of youngsters were riding their tricycles, and another one chased his playful puppy through the flower beds. Butterflies were flitting about, and a hummingbird joyfully hopped from flower to flower. The sun was shining. Life was good. Just outside their front door. *In the real world.*

A few feet away, Karen's door opened, and she and Melissa stepped out. Melissa was carrying her new glove and a bat and as they made their way toward the carport. Karen glanced over at Rich and Tami's door with a concerned look, then back to her daughter.

"C'mon, we're going to be late, honey," she said, with a sigh.

◆

CHAPTER 24

S EVERAL HOURS PASSED, and the happy squeals of the neighbor children at play subsided, signaling it was probably dinnertime. Or was it breakfast?

Rich couldn't tell anymore. He didn't even know what day it was right now. As he sat there, slumped on the loveseat in the darkened living room, his head hung low as his neck was barely strong enough to support its weight any longer. His disheveled hair and various battle scars were indicative of how tortuous a day it had been—and continued to be—with his captor. His bride.

His empty stomach complained loudly as it sputtered on the fumes of yesterday's lunch. They'd skipped dinner again last night, and the kitchen now smelled of the raw, room temperature bacon that sat on the counter, next to the dead doughboy.

Tami sat—more like hovered—next to Rich, and he had no memory of how or when they'd made their transition from the floor to where they were now seated. He stared ahead vacuously, through dead eyes, the left one now blackened and swollen. The VCR's clock blinked 5:50.

Tami's voice droned on, though it almost seemed a distant echo now, and he had no idea how long they'd been sitting here. It was only slightly less painful to sit here and endure her propaganda than to continue with the full-on fisticuffs, though this was promising to be more damaging. He surrendered to it. And to her. Every particle of his power was slowly being drained from him, as if by liposuction, and Tami was the beneficiary of the transfer. It emboldened her mania.

Just make it end soon, he probably would've thought, but he had nothing left in the tank.

"—and your sister is also coddling you. Your whole family isn't healthy for you…." This continued for quite some time, as Rich drifted in and out of consciousness while she continued her diatribe. He heard her, and he made his best efforts to discern what she was saying, but he was too exhausted to process the situation now.

Trapped in this darkened room, with only the tiny table lamp offering its dimmest glow, and being fed a steady diet of Tami's bullshit, Rich was essentially becoming a human mushroom. And he was no longer a fun guy.

Caught in his wife's powerful riptide, he had now lost his mental footing and was being swept under…down into the depths…further, further…into the blackness, the absolute void where only those freakish, bioluminescent anglerfish—the ones with the built-in headlights and horrific underbite—dwelled. This murky place made the Marianas Trench seem like a kiddie pool, and was devoid of light and sound—save the sound of Tami's distant voice pinging him, indoctrinating him without pause, and to the exclusion of any other sensory awareness. That's where and when her programming was most effective and penetrative. To the exclusion of all else.

She didn't need to turn a queen of hearts playing card with him; he was all in, though he didn't know it. Hell, he didn't even know his own name right now. He wasn't aware of the process, as nobody ever is. But these couch sessions were adding up, and taking their toll, to the point where he was slowly slipping down the rabbit hole and was now, officially, a card-carrying member of the Stockholm Syndrome club.

Another menacing anglerfish began circling him.

"—and that's been going on for years, and you couldn't see it. It's not your fault," she said, pausing just long enough for a weak nod from Rich. "So now you're beginning to see how unhealthy they all are for you, right?"

His stomach screamed, and he nodded again. Tami wiped away the small bit of drool escaping from Rich's open mouth. She rubbed her own eyes and looked over at the VCR clock which now read 1:27.

"We'd better get you to bed. What time did you say you had to get up, 4:30?"

An almost-imperceptible nod confirmed it. "Okay," she said, helping him stand, "c'mon...."

◆

CHAPTER 25

O DARK THIRTY. Technically 5:15, and sunrise issued in another day in Hell. Rich's Explorer crept along, stuck in the sticky molasses flow of the 405 South.

They weren't needed for this time of day, but he was wearing his dark Ray-Bans, and as he waited for somebody to let him over a lane, he tugged at the long sleeves of his flannel shirt, also unnecessary on what was forecast to be a ninety-nine-degree day in the pit. The long sleeves would hopefully help cover the scratches and bite marks though.

Rich's deep frown only hinted at his even deeper despair, and his expression slowly took on the look of a tribal death mask. Madness, hopelessness, and prolonged sleep deprivation were chipping away and working in concert to carve their tracks into his features.

Traffic wasn't moving, and he hadn't had time for a scrap of breakfast before he rushed out. Small flashes of yesterday's madness were replaying now, but they still made no sense to him, and he wondered how much of it had been a bad dream.

For the first time in his life, he wondered if he might be completely losing it.

Somebody flipped him off for no apparent reason. A nearby traffic helicopter noisily thumped the air, and he was surely going to be late. And Rich was never late. He hastily exited onto a frontage road few others were on. His knuckles went white as he gripped the wheel tightly, and he felt he was about to blow a gasket. The drone of the copter grew louder, as did the drone of Tami's voice in his head. It was all too much.

"Fuck it!" Rich muttered between clenched teeth as he suddenly stomped down hard on the gas pedal. He yanked the wheel hard to the right as he did, and the Explorer launched, careening off the road wildly and obliterating a wooden railing in its path. As he sailed off the embankment, there was a momentary feeling of freedom, of flying—not unlike that Thunderbird scene at the end of one of his favorite movies, *Thelma & Louise*, but without the freeze-frame and without the awesome Pete Haycock slide guitar accompaniment.

The Explorer's right wheels made purchase with the hillside first, at an awkward angle, and it rolled violently, flipping several times before coming to an abrupt stop at its final resting place, wrapped around an enormous, unforgiving oak tree. Smoke billowed from the mangled wreckage. Rich's bloody torso was one with the steering column, and the twisted, crumpled cabin had invaded him mercilessly.

Survivable? Not a chance in hell.

The loud blaring of the horn went on forever as the engine compartment's smoke turned to fire.

After several moments, an entire chorus of blaring horns joined in. That and somebody yelling, "Move it, asshole!!"

Rich was suddenly jarred back to reality, only to find that he was still in the middle lane, intact and alive, but only technically. More horns and gestures, and he gasped for breath. He tried to collect himself by turning on his radio, stabbing at radio stations—anything to keep himself together.

The first song that came up was Dave Edmunds' "Crawling From The Wreckage." Rich quickly hit another stereo button, only to find Pat Benatar challenging him with "Hit Me With Your Best Shot"—*FUCK!*

His thumb found another button, but it offered no relief, as Karen Carpenter sang of the despair of "Hurting Each Other," only to segue into 'Til Tuesday's warning: "Voices Carry"....

It didn't matter how many buttons he jabbed; he couldn't escape this especially cruel DJ in the Sky's medley from hell this morning, and Ann Wilson screamed maniacally now, repeatedly begging for permission to go stark raving "Crazy On You"!

"Jeezus!" Rich yelled, finally—mercifully—landing on something slightly more palatable, by George Harrison and the rest of the Traveling Wilburys: "Handle With Care."

◆

CHAPTER 26

THE STUDIO DOOR flung open and Rich rushed inside, still wearing his shades and carrying a small leather satchel. Mike walked up, nursing a Mountain Dew.

"Dude...glad you could join us," he said with more sarcasm than Rich needed—or could handle—right now. He nodded in the direction of the female stage manager, who was scurrying around, talking into her headset. "Might wanna check in with Ashley. She was just about to send out a search party for you."

Rich sighed as he dropped his satchel next to a camera pedestal.

"Took the 405, didn't you?" Mike continued, shaking his head in disbelief. Rich didn't answer and instead made a beeline toward the craft service table. He didn't need this right now. He needed sustenance.

"Richie, I'm tellin' ya. From your place, it's Malibu Canyon, dude. Every time. Seriously, saves you—"

"I know, I know, Mike...okay?" Rich said, waving him off as he grabbed an apple fritter and shoved it in his mouth. It had been nearly two days since he'd eaten anything, and this was perhaps the finest thing he'd ever tasted. He savored the apple-y/sugary/bumpy, life-giving goodness and inhaled it in a few bites. Without thinking, he pocketed his shades. Mike was staring at him.

"What?", Rich said, having forgotten all about his monster shiner.

"Jeezus!" Mike said, leaning in for a closer look, then, "Dude! What the fuck?"

"Oh…that," Rich said, shifting into his best recovery mode. "Bumped it on a friggin' C-Stand yesterday, like a dork," he said, hoping to end further inquiry.

"Want me to get something for it? Block of ice? A porterhouse?"

"Nah. It's not as bad as it looks," Rich replied, just as the sublimely sexy Ashley walked up. She was wearing her usual painted-on jeans, the ones that were the eye candy of seemingly every guy in the freelance community and the fodder for much lascivious conversation between crew guys. She did a double-take when she saw Rich.

"What—?"

"Morning, Ashley. Fear not, I'm here," Rich said.

"Oh my God, Richie," she said. "Were you in an accident? I was—"

"No. No…nothing as exciting as that. Clumsy is all. Wish I had a better story for you," Rich lied.

"Well, glad you're here. And glad you're okay," Ashley said, then to her headset, "Okay, Stu, yes, he's here. Yes, okay." She looked at Rich again then turned to walk back to the kitchen set. She looked over her shoulder and said to them both, "Stay close, we're up in five," flashing her killer smile as she walked away, seemingly in slo-mo. There should've been her own walk-on (or walk-away) music playing, her strut was that fine. Some classic Bob Seger would've worked.

Another very lanky crew guy, a grip, named Doug, walked up and the three of them watched her walk away for longer than was appropriate. Mike was clearly still hypnotized.

"So. Smokin'. Hot," he said in a dirty whisper.

"Yeah," Doug chimed in, "I'd tap that."

Mike turned toward Doug and howled in laughter.

"Dougie, you're so full of shit, man. Even if you were the last man on this earth, you would never—and I mean *ever*—score with something as fine as that. Few mortal men could."

"Man, I'd *punish* that!" he replied, confidently.

Rich took a deep swig of his coffee and decided to stay out of this schoolyard chat. He felt a junkie's rush as the caffeine slipped into his bloodstream, joining up with the sugar bomb he'd just consumed.

"Okay, dude. Let me put it to you this way," Mike said, surveying his beanpole friend for emphasis. "You. And Ashley." He laughed again, then, "That'd be like, like throwing a hot dog down a hallway!"

This got a spit-take from Rich, who managed to spray the front of his flannel shirt.

"Fuck off, Mike," Doug muttered as he walked away. Mike watched Rich dab the coffee from his chest.

"So, Richie...what's with the friggin' Paul Bunyan shirt anyway, dude? You auditioning for a Brawny commercial, or is Tami dressing you now?" When Rich didn't answer, he added, "Guess you didn't get the memo: It's only s'posed to be, like, a hundred fifty degrees in Santa Monica today."

"Yeah, well. Laundry day," Rich offered.

Mike gave him a sharp slap on the shoulder, and Rich tried not to wince. There were bloody gashes, a few bruises, and several teeth marks imbedded in that shoulder. He hoped that the red and black pattern of the shirt would camouflage any oozing blood.

"Oh, I forgot to tell you: You're handheld cam today. Have fun with that."

The technical director's voice boomed loudly through the stage's loudspeaker, "Crew to headsets!"

"Perfect," Rich mumbled, knowing this was likely going to be the *new* longest day of his life.

◆

CHAPTER 27

RICH WAVED GOODBYE to Ashley as he emerged from the studio door. He strapped on his Ray-Bans once he got to the parking lot. Still some daylight! It had been a brutal day, mostly because he was still running on vapors, and he was thankful it was still light outside. Infomercial shoots were always guaranteed to be long days, often with overtime, but a product malfunction had saved the day.

Plus, rescheduling the shoot meant another day of work, which was a bonus.

Rich slunk into the Explorer's leather seat and sat there with his eyes closed for several minutes, the engine's idling drowned out by the air conditioner, which was blowing on the blizzard setting. Only on the Eddie Bauer edition.

Eventually, he began his slow rollout from the lot.

As Rich cruised the surface streets of Santa Monica, it took a little time to reorient himself. It might as well have been the surface of the moon he was navigating. After he got his bearings, he remembered there was a new book megastore nearby. Tami wouldn't be expecting him home this early, and he sure wasn't going to dial her so she could begin prepping another indoctrination script, so he decided to kill some time. He switched on the stereo: Pink Floyd's "Comfortably Numb." He went with it. The DJ must've dedicated this set to Rich, because he followed with a perfect segue into Floyd's "Run Like Hell."

Rich entered the massive book outlet and wandered around until he found the Psychology/Self Help section. It might have been a faster process navigating the miles of aisles without his dark shades on, but he didn't need any more stares right now.

The amount of subtopics within this one section, and the volume of books crowding the aisles were a bit overwhelming. In a perfect world, there would be an end cap display, or a table stacked high with the latest bestselling book he needed, if one even existed, but he couldn't find one. With no convenient titles like, *So, Your Psycho Wife's Kicking the Living Shit Out of You, Now What?* Rich could only reach the conclusion that perhaps he really *was* the only able-bodied man on this planet who was getting beat to a pulp by his adoring spouse. Besides, who would believe him if he were to tell someone?

He was browsing through another book, *The Bipolar Express*, when a very cute girl clerk startled him. "Anything in particular I can help you find?" she asked with a broad smile. Rich shelved the book a little too hastily.

"Me? Uh, no…just…looking. Term paper research."

"If you change your mind, let me know" she offered.

He thanked her. Then he left the store, empty-handed.

A couple of exits before his, Rich stopped at the local hardware store. He stood there at the counter while the teenaged guy grinded away at a key. Rich looked at his phone and couldn't read the display, so he took off his sunglasses. The screeching of the grinder came to a halt and the clerk turned to Rich, holding two keys. The kid had no business being in customer service as he was now staring impo-litely—taking excessive interest in Rich's black eye, as if regarding a deadly scorpion. Rich might've been reading into things but he thought he detected a hint of a smirk.

"Okay. One—house key, one car key. Want a bag?"

"Yes," Rich replied, trying not to be too annoyed as he reinstalled his shades, ending the show. "Thanks."

Rich opened the rear hatch of the Explorer. Lifting up the carpeted false floor of the cargo area, Rich tucked the small bag containing the new keys inside a larger Walgreens bag containing several toiletries and grooming items. He secured the bag alongside the spare tire in the well and slammed the hatch.

◆

CHAPTER 28

PUNCH-DRUNK TIRED, AND still wearing his shades, Rich slowly walked the gauntlet toward his front door. He paused briefly when he got to the porch. By all rights, there probably should've been an embossed sign affixed to the door that read, Please Leave Your Shoes—and Your Sanity—at the Door. He glanced around the quiet common area and put his key in the door, breathing deeply before turning the knob to enter his cell.

Tami was at the door and she pulled it open, greeting him with a kiss and an unusually cheery demeanor—as if the previous night had never happened. She was like that now, up and down, back and forth, sane then insane, and with seemingly no pattern. Rich was also continuing to question his own sanity, and he was only vaguely aware enough to know that it was slipping through his fingers like quicksilver.

Tami took Rich's keys and relieved him of his leatherette satchel. "Welcome, home, honey," she said, beaming a smile.

Rich never knew what to expect anymore, and was more than slightly disarmed, especially since she had put on light makeup and to good effect. She'd also shampooed and styled her hair, and he thought he picked up a trace of her White Shoulders cologne. His favorite. What was up?

He was so tired he could only manage slightly more than a grunt in response. "Hi.... Thanks," he muttered, pocketing his shades.

Tami responded to the visual of Rich's black eye by looking away, then her quick head tilt back to the ceiling and, whispering to herself, "It doesn't go with that!" She turned back to Rich with a grin that was too big and too weird to process. Rich noticed two TV trays set up with place settings.

"Honey, I'm too tired to cook tonight. Maybe we—" he managed before she put a finger to his lips.

"*I'm* cooking dinner tonight, silly!" she exclaimed happily.

"You're...cooking?" Rich replied cautiously. That was literally a first in all the time they'd been together.

"Yes! And guess what we're having!" she said, putting her hands over his eyes as she guided him to the kitchen.

"I'm too tired to guess right now, honey," he replied, his right hand waving the air like a blind man.

"Come on now. Don't be a party pooper! Okay...are you ready?" she asked, as they reached the kitchen.

"Yes, I'm ready."

"Ready, GO!" she squealed, removing her hands for the big reveal. Rich stared in disbelief: A gleaming PastaMaster 5000 sat on the countertop next to its box, which featured a red logo saying, "As Seen On TV." Next to that were two opened jars of pasta sauce and a shaker can of Parmesan cheese.

"Tada! We're having homemade pasta!" She gushed like a pitchwoman.

"Honey—wow...." He tried to muster the requisite smile, but failed. "Look, I appreciate what you're trying to do here, but that pasta machine—"

"What about it?!" She cut him off, annoyed that he was dampening her enthusiasm. He knew that tone and expression: he had to tread lightly.

"Well, we can't really afford to be buying another appliance right now, and—"

Tami waved three fingers, interrupting him. "It was only three easy payments of $34.99— and they included a free recipe book, a video, and the free ladle!" she said, sounding eerily like a spokesperson.

"Honey," he proceeded cautiously, "I worked on that infomercial."

"And..." she began,, not trying to hide her irritation now.

"And, I hate to say it, but that machine is a piece of junk. Okay?"

"No, it isn't! I've seen the infomercial! It's great! I'm gonna use it, and I want it! And I'm keeping it!"

"I'm just saying—"

"You're just trying to kill my excitement!" she yelled, grabbing a jar of sauce and hurling it against the dining room wall. The loud crash sent glass shrapnel and tomatoey crap spewing everywhere.

Rich watched, slack-jawed, as the red sauce crept down the wall that now looked like a Manson Family crime scene.

"Jeezus, Tami—what the hell!" he bellowed.

Tami gave him a hard slap across the jaw and stormed out of the room, his key ring still in her hand.

"Fine! Cook your own fucking dinner! You *try* to do something nice," she continued, under her breath, then screamed, "Asshole!"

Rich followed her into the living room where she was pacing furiously. "I'm not going to do this again tonight, Tami."

"Fuck you!"

"Please keep your voice down."

Tami stuck her tongue out at him, like they were in the second grade. Then she flipped him off.

"You know what? I'm too tired for this bullshit—and I am definitely not cleaning up your mess in there."

Tami brushed Rich's shoulder as she flew back into the kitchen and grabbed an enormous butcher knife from the knife block, a wedding present from his parents. As she reentered the living room, Rich's eyes went wide when he saw her brandishing what almost amounted to a sword. He was fully awake now.

The room felt like the walls had all suddenly and silently crept inward, reducing its size to half, then to the size of a phone booth, as Tami gripped the knife handle tightly. She paced, looking at Rich.

"You all try to kill my excitement!" she yelled, slashing the air.

"Whoa! Wait, Tami!" he exclaimed, never taking his eyes off the blade. "What are you talking about? Please...put that down before somebody gets hurt."

"My parents don't care about me!" she said, swinging the knife randomly, wildly, with her eyes closed now. Rich took a step backward, his back finding the stairwell's railing, finding himself with no real estate left. "Tami...."

"How would *you* like it if somebody stabbed *you* in the back?! Huh?" she said, thrusting the knife forward in a series of jabbing motions, her eyes still clamped shut. "How would *you* feel?!" she said in a sinister voice he didn't recognize.

Rich risked looking away just long enough to choose his path. She was still a few feet from him when he bolted for the stairs, Tami in hot pursuit.

"You're just like them! You don't care about me either!" she said menacingly as he tried to backpedal up the stairs. At the landing, Rich was trapped, his back now up against the linen closet door. Tami made the landing, her eyes still closed, as she closed the short gap, thrusting the knife out in little jabs, at gut level.

"Huh! How do *you* think it feels? Being constantly stabbed?" she said quietly now, thrusting the knife forward. A very panicky Rich sucked in his stomach, narrowly avoiding the tip of the blade.

"Tami! Stop!"

"...and stabbed!" she continued, with another thrust for emphasis.

Rich again evaded the blade, which made contact with the closet door, as he barely managed to get around and past Tami. With his life on the line, he blazed down the stairs, three at a time and threw open the front door. An unknown, untapped reserve of energy—a raging river of adrenaline—pumped through his exhausted limbs now as he traversed the common area with surprising speed, and gazelle-like agility, as he escaped into the cool, dark void.

"Don't you run away from me, you son of a bitch!" she yelled, dropping the knife and heading down the stairs after him. She stood in the open door and looked out at the darkness that had fallen. She held up his key ring and shook it furiously in the air.

"Where do you think you're going? I've got your keys, you idiot!" She laughed maniacally as she continued toward the carport. As she turned the corner she stopped, half out of breath, and dumbfounded as Rich punched the gas, and the Explorer roared from the carport, out the driveway, and down the pitch dark street.

Like a bat out of frigging hell.

◆

CHAPTER 29

A SCANT FEW streetlights barely illuminated the dark residential street, and only a few houses dotted this quiet neighborhood on the southern edge of town. He wasn't sure where he was, or how he'd arrived here, but it was perfect. The Explorer slowly pulled up into a dark, open space between two streetlights. He turned off the engine and began breathing. He sat there for a minute, listening to the deafening orchestra of crickets. Then a few coyotes joined in, howling in the not-too-distant hills.

He yawned, bigger and longer than any human being had ever yawned before and climbed out of the car. He extinguished the dome light as he did. Rich had no strength left, but he dug deep and began the necessary task of removing headrests, folding down seats, and extending the retractable cargo cover in the back. He had no bedding to speak of, but he was more than grateful for the furniture blanket he kept there to keep the interior nice. After he made himself a makeshift bed, and carefully closed the rear hatch as quietly as possible, he walked around to the far side of the car, away from the houses, and released a long-overdue urine stream into the gravel. To him, it sounded like Niagara Falls, but he didn't see any lights come on.

Holy Mother of God.

Another howl from a coyote, closer this time, prompted Rich to zip up and get inside. He locked the doors out of habit.

Aided by his unwieldy four-cell Maglite flashlight, Rich set the alarm on his wristwatch, then tried to find a reasonably comfortable sleeping position on the hard surface of the cargo area. Yeah, right.

It wasn't happening, but it'd have to do. As sleep deprived as he was, even a bed of nails would've been most welcome. He extinguished the flashlight, and the world was again steeped in pitch darkness.

*Chirp...chirp...chirp...*went the crickets.

◆

CHAPTER 30

*BEEP...BEEP...BEEP...*WENT THE ALARM.
Rich's watch rudely alerted him to the fact that it was
5:00, and time to rise and shine. At least rise; there'd be no
shining today.

He tried to sit up but was reminded of the outstretched cargo
cover a few inches above him. He blinked his crusty eyes open,
groaned in all-over pain, and retracted the cargo cover. He sat there
and stretched, then remembered how he got here.

And why.

He awkwardly climbed into the driver's seat and dared a look
in the illuminated visor mirror. *Gawd!* He surveyed his red eyes, the
carpet impressions on his good cheek, and the rest. He'd definitely
have to do something about that Gumby shock of hair!

And there'd be no shower today....

Down the street, Rich could see a flurry of headlights as several
people began to pull out of their driveways.

They would be his competition, jockeying for position on the
freeway momentarily—plus, he had a stop to make, so he joined
the fray and drove back out the way he came in.

On the way to the freeway, Rich saw a last chance gas station opportunity and pulled in adjacent to the restrooms. The place was a dump: run down, with litter everywhere, and a homeless guy asleep on the ground near the door. The guy in the booth with the turban was busy stocking cigarettes and gave Rich no mind, so he retrieved his toiletries from the wheel well and went inside.

The place was a study in Disgusting. Graffiti was everywhere—scribbled on the walls, scratched into the paint of the stall, and etched into the cracked glass mirror. The florescent bulb was flickering and in need of replacement. He'd have to make this quick.

Rich held his breath.

He pushed open the door of the lone bathroom stall and it was a test of his gag reflex. The toilet was a fecal spin art catastrophe, and it looked like a pottery class for the blind had just vacated the space.

"Jeezus," he said, stepping back out. He ran some water in the rust-stained sink and hastily shaved, then wet his hair enough to tame it into a combable helmet, before locking it in with enough hairspray to kill all the dinosaurs. He brushed his teeth, grimacing at the sketchy, nasty-tasting water coming from the faucet, and prayed he wouldn't get lockjaw.

After a couple of swipes of his deodorant stick, he stuffed his things back into the bag and stared at his reflection in what was left of the mirror.

Rich looked like a slightly spruced-up, but recently beat-up, homeless person.

Fuggit.

He put on his shades, spread his arms wide, and smiled sarcastically, and in his best Roy Scheider impression from *All That Jazz,* summed up the day ahead.

Show time, indeed.

◆

CHAPTER 31

TAMI SAT ON the bottom step of the stairs. Her hair was straining under the flimsy chip clip, and she had charcoal circles under her eyes. Wearing a ratty tank top and an old pair of sweat bottoms, she didn't look much better than Rich did this morning. She had on her well-worn bunny slippers, and the exposed part of her calves revealed a forest of unshaved hair.

On the floor in front of her lay several framed photos of her family. Tami's expression was blank as she gently and methodically tapped the glass on each one with a hammer until they cracked into pieces.

She liberated an eight-by-ten from its shattered frame and stared at the posed family portrait in her hand. Her parents and brother all had that forced, cheesy Sears portrait studio smile, which repulsed her to no end.

Tami switched implements, opting for a Bic lighter now. She spun the wheel with her thumb until it produced a tiny flame and began the process of systematically burning her ex-family's faces away, like the Ponderosa map in the opening credits of *Bonanza*.

The corners of her mouth slowly took the form of a twisted smile—especially eerie when paired with her expressionless eyes, which reflected the growing flame. Her trance was interrupted slightly by the ringing of the phone, but she ignored it, waiting for the machine to pick up.

"Hey, are you there?" Rich's voice asked. "If you are, pick up." David's face finished its slow burn, leaving a charred black hole, which she took particular delight in watching. She put down the lighter, blew out the smoldering picture, and sidestepped the glass shards as she walked to the phone.

"Hello? Listen, Tami, I—," Rich said, just before she picked up.

"Hi. Are you guys done for the day?" she asked.

"Hey, you're there…. Um, no, we're not—probably looking at a coupla more hours here," he replied.

Rich braced himself for what he anticipated to be a painfully awkward conversation. A few silent moments went by before the smoke alarm began emitting an ear-piercing series of shrill beeps.

"Fuck," Tami muttered.

"What's the matter? What's that sound?" Rich asked.

"Nothing…baking cookies," she said as she made her way to the kitchen and thrust open the patio door. She glanced at the dining room wall she'd wiped down, but it would definitely need repainting. A couple of coats. She closed her eyes and tilted her head back as she whispered her mantra, "It doesn't go with that."

"Cookies?" Rich asked incredulously. The alarm beeps were shrill, even through the receiver.

Tami waved a kitchen towel, forcing some fresh air inside. The shrieks stopped several agonizing seconds later.

"Never mind. What were you saying?" Tami asked.

"I, uh, was just gonna say, about last night, I—"

"I'm sorry," Tami said, beating him to it.

"What?"

"I'm sorry about last night," she said. A moment of silence passed, then she added, "I want you to come home."

On the other end of the line, Rich pressed the wall-mounted

studio phone closer to his ear, an index finger stuffed in his other ear to block the commotion of the nearby cooking show set.

"Yeah… I'm sorry too. That's the main reason I called, really," Rich said, waving at Ashley as she gave him the "wrap" sign. Mike also walked by, sticking out his tongue as he passed. Rich shook his head.

"You had me scared," he whispered.

"I know," Tami sighed. "Let's put it behind us."

"What?" Rich said, still processing. "Listen, honey, you've got to figure out this stuff with your parents—"

"You don't have to worry about that," she said, cutting him off. "It's over with my whole side of the family."

"What do you mean *over*?"

"They're all dead to me now, and we won't have any contact with them ever again," Tami added, with an eerie calm in her voice.

The line was silent as Rich processed this.

"Did you hear me?" she asked.

"Yeah…I did…. Look, you've got me really concerned now, Tami, and I don't—"

"I had an epiphany this morning," Tami blurted.

"A what?" he asked, rubbing his burning eyes.

"Epiphany. It came to me so strongly! It was from God!"

"Yeah?" Rich replied, looking over at the set.

She launched into it: "Only Life, Truth, Love, Good, over all, and all. It's the only thing that exists, it's the only thing that's real…."

"Wait…what?" Rich replied.

"Only Life, Truth—" she began.

"No, I mean, what is that?" he asked.

"That was my epiphany!" she said excitedly. "We won't be having these problems any longer!"

Ashley gave Rich "the look," which he acknowledged with an apologetic smile and a thumbs-up.

"Good, honey. Look, I'm sorry; I've gotta get back to work, but I think—"

"We should go this weekend," Tami blurted out.

"Excuse me?"

"This weekend. I've been thinking about it. It's your Dad's birthday. We should go."

Rich stared at the handset, sure he'd heard incorrectly. "I'm sorry, did you just say—?"

"Uh-huh," she replied.

Rich honestly didn't know how to respond.

"You still there?" she asked after a long silence.

"Wow," Rich said quietly, completely floored. It was like somebody had just flipped a breaker in her brain. "Really? Yeah—great, honey. I'm—I'm glad you—changed your mind," he added, fumbling for words.

"Crew to headsets," the director's voice interrupted through the PA system.

"Sorry, we're back up here. I'll call you later.... You okay?"

"Yeah. I'm good. Bye."

"Bye, honey."

"Love you," she added, but Rich had already hung up.

Tami retrieved a whiskbroom and dustpan from the closet and began sweeping up the glass and ashes. She paused for her mantra. "Only Life, Truth, Love, Good...over all and all," she said, then her head tilt/smile. "Awesome!"

◆

CHAPTER 32

I T WAS LATE afternoon when the Explorer pulled in, joining
the three other cars that populated the Brysons' semicircular
driveway. It was an attractive, one-story ranch home in a pleasant neighborhood with lots of mature trees.

Rich took a moment to assess his left eye in the rearview before
putting on his sunglasses. He shook his head. As he got out and
walked around toward the passenger side, Tami prepared herself.

"It doesn't go with that!" she whispered.

Rich opened her door.

"Ready, GO!" she said to herself.

"Yep," Rich sighed, closing the door and retrieving the pies
from the backseat.

Jeanette Bryson was removing a large lamb roast from the oven
when the doorbell rang.

"Oh! That must be Richie and Tami!" she chirped.

Scott pinched off a crusty corner bite of the steaming roast as
he passed the counter. "I'll get it, Mom," he said, licking his fingers.
"Wow, that's awesome."

"Good, now keep your mitts off of it until we sit down," she
replied playfully.

Scott opened the front door. Rich smiled as he straightened his shades, while Tami stood slightly behind, holding the two pie boxes.

"Hey!" Rich said, giving his brother a 'bro' hug.

"Hey!" Scott said, before turning to Tami. She was wearing a blouse and skirt, and her hair and makeup were dialed. She'd even shaved her legs for the occasion. Tami handed Scott the pies.

"Hello, beautiful," Scott said, leaning in for a one-armed hug, while balancing the pies in the other.

"Hi, Scott," Tami smiled nervously, returning the hug.

"Lamb!" Rich said, inhaling deeply. "Oh my goodness, I smell lamb!"

"Well, get in here then," Scott laughed, as he stepped aside.

Jeanette came to the door, wiping her hands on a towel and smiling softly. Her eyes sparkled. "Well, bless your hearts! Hi, Tami! Hi, Richie! Come on in, you two," she said, pausing for warm hugs.

"Hi, Mimo," Rich said affectionately.

"Hi, Jeanette," Tami offered.

"Hi, dear," Jeanette replied. "Just look at you, Tami! It's so nice to see you two!"

Tami smiled as Scott squeezed past them to retrieve the bags from the car. "Nice to see you too, Jeanette," Tami said.

"You two must be exhausted from the long drive."

"It wasn't too bad," Rich lied, kissing the top of her head as they all made their way inside to the kitchen. Rich followed his nose and approached the object of his obsession. He grabbed a tiny piece with his fingers.

"What's with the boys in this house?" Jeanette laughed. It brought her such joy to have the family together.

"Oh—my—God!" Rich said blissfully.

"Did you at least wash your hands first?" Ellen said as she entered from the other room. Rich licked his fingers then gave her a hug.

"Hey, sis! Good to see you."

"You too, Richie. Seems like forever."

"Yeah," Rich said, then kiddingly, "You remember Tami." The girls hugged.

"Didn't you marry my brother a few years ago? I think I remember," she laughed. "Been a while...great to see you, Tami," she said, kissing her cheek.

"How are you, Ellen? Tami responded politely.

"Good, good."

"Just the one suitcase and the bag?" Scott asked, joining them.

"Yes, thank you," Tami said.

"I put 'em in the second room down the hall—your room," Scott said.

Tami smiled. Rich nodded.

"You won't be needing these in here," Ellen said, as she reached over and pulled off Rich's sunglasses.

Time stood still as everyone individually took in the sight of Rich's burgundy-colored eye socket.

"Wow, Richie," Scott laughed. "Tami been smackin' you around again?"

"Ha! Funny...." Tami said with an awkward smile.

Scott punctuated his remark with an uppercut motion. "Kapow!!" he added with a laugh.

"Yeah...*not*," Rich said, defensively.

"Richie, dear, what on earth happened to your eye?" Jeanette asked with motherly concern.

"Whoa, Richie! Yeah, really, what happened?" Ellen chimed in.

"What's all the commotion?" Len Bryson said, entering the kitchen with a book in his hand.

"Hey, Dad...." Rich said.

"Richie! And Tami! Good to see—wow!" Len stopped abruptly and lowered his readers as he took a long hard look at Rich's eye.

"You're just in time, Dad. I was just about to tell everybody how I—I bumped my eye on a light stand at work a few days ago."

Tami's eyes darted around from face to face, assessing their reactions, while straining to keep her composure.

"Sure you did...." Ellen said kiddingly.

"True story," Rich replied with a shrug, avoiding eye contact with his wife.

"We should put some ice on that right now, Richie," Jeanette advised.

"Really. It's okay," he said to her, then to everyone, "Nothing to see here, folks."

Ellen's two children, Kailee, seven, and Adam, five, entered noisily from the backyard, through the patio slider.

"Kailee! Adam!" Rich smiled.

"Uncle Rich! Uncle Rich!" they said in unison, running up for their hugs, then pausing to stare.

"Wow. What happened, Uncle Rich?" Kailee asked.

"Were you in a fight? Cool!" Adam said with a smile.

Rich gave them both a quick hug. "No, your Uncle Rich just hurt it at work," he said. He hated lying to anyone—and most of all to his family. He quickly offered some redirection. "Hey, you remember Aunt Tami, right?"

They looked at her, unsure.

"Give your Aunt Tami a hug, guys."

"Hi, Kailee. Hi, Adam. Look how big you're both getting!" Tami smiled. The kids gave this stranger an obligatory hug.

"Hi, Aunt Tami," they managed before scampering off.

"Don't go too far off. We're eating in a few minutes," Ellen called after them.

"Okay, Mom," Kailee said, slamming the screen slider.

The family stood there for an awkward moment, looking at each other, before Len broke the silence.

"Well, when do we eat?"

◆

CHAPTER 33

EVERYONE WAS SEATED, with Rich sitting to Len's left. In full patriarch mode, Len sat at the far end of the table and sunk the electric carving knife into the roast. It cut effortlessly, like a chain saw through butter. He placed a generous slab of perfectly prepared meat on a plate.

"This end piece is for you, Richie," he said, smiling. "I remember how much you always liked that," he continued, handing the plate to his son.

"Mmm…thanks, Dad."

"Glad you have a good appetite, Richie," Jeannette chimed in. "You look like you've lost weight, dear."

She turned to Scott. "Would you please pass the mashed potatoes to your brother?"

Len carved a smaller piece for himself. His appetite wasn't what it used to be, and he knew where he could find more if he wanted seconds. The roast was ample.

Now everyone had been served, and you could almost hear the roaring tsunami of saliva.

Scott enjoyed several bites in nirvana before looking up from his plate. That's when he noticed a series of cuts on Rich's wrists, where they protruded from his long sleeves. "Jeez, Rich," Scott said between bites. "You been working with a wood chipper too? What happened to your wrists there, bro?"

Tami's eyes darted around nervously, her fingernails digging into Rich's thigh under the table as he tugged at his sleeves.

"Huh? Um, no…just…pruning the rose bushes," he said, taking a bite and turning to his mom. "Delicious!"

"Thank you, dear. You have to be more careful, Richie. I didn't know you had roses. Your dad could teach you a thing or two about roses, you know."

"I'm sure he could," Rich said, taking another bite. He and Tami exchanged peripheral glances as everyone continued eating. The only sounds were those of busy utensils, with the occasional hums of pleasure.

Rich looked over at his father and noticed that his left wrist was naked, and sporting a "farmer's tan" where his watch used to be.

"Hey, Dad," Rich said, changing the subject none too soon. "What happened to the Timex we gave you for Christmas? Didn't break, I hope."

Len took a bite of lamb, took his time chewing it, and set his fork down. "Well, son, I'm afraid I lost it."

"Really? Do you know where you last had it?" Rich asked.

Len wiped his mouth with a napkin and nodded. "Know exactly where," Len said, looking at his wrist, then back up at Rich. "You see, son, I was sitting on the bowl, doing my business the other day…"

"Oy," Ellen said as she set down the gravy boat.

"Now, Len, that's not dinner table talk," Jeanette reminded him. He paid no attention.

"…and after I finished, I got up, and reached over, and flushed the darn thing…" he continued, pantomiming with his left hand.

"You paint a great picture, Dad." Scott groaned.

"…and when I did, well, I'll be damned if that nice watch didn't pop right off my wrist and fall down into the toilet!"

"Oh, no," Ellen said.

"Yep, 'fraid so," Len said.

"Were you able to get it, Dad?" Rich asked.

"Well, Richie...the water was spinning, and I reached in and—" he said, pausing to look at Tami, then Rich, with a huge grin on his face, "—I got everything but the watch!" Len crowed.

Jeanette tried to suppress a smile and Tami snickered, grateful for the comic relief. Rich shared in his father's laugh, while Ellen groaned, and Scott set his fork down.

"I'm done," he said, pushing his plate away.

"Wait—what? What's so funny?" Adam asked.

"Nothing, honey. Your grandpa's just being silly, and a little gross. Finish your dinner," Ellen said.

"Grampa picked up poop!" Kailee sang out as she giggled.

"Grampa picked up poop!" Adam parroted with a snort, which generated a reluctant snicker from his mom, then from Scott. Len crowed again.

Jeanette shook her head in mock disapproval, but the little curl of her smile was testament to how much she loved hearing the sound of family assembled around the dinner table again. And it was heartwarming to see Richie here, and so happy, with his beautiful bride.

◆

CHAPTER 34

THE ENTIRE FAMILY, minus Ellen, had retired to the living room, slouched in their chairs, in full food coma mode. The pies had done them in.

Len was in his well-worn recliner, surrounded by several golf-related gifts and crumpled wrapping paper littering the floor. He admired the shiny Ping putter in his hand. "Well, nice people, thank you for a wonderful birthday," he said, looking around at each of them.

"Happy Birthday, Dad," they called out happily in unison.

"Happy Birthday, Grampa," Kailee and Adam added, climbing onto his lap and kissing him.

"Thank you, my beauties," Len said, returning kisses to the little squirmers before they jumped off and headed to the kitchen. "Whew! I'm beat," he managed through a yawn as he extracted himself from his trusty throne. He pantomimed using his Ping as a prop cane, adding, "and I'm old." This got a few laughs.

"I'll see you all in the morning," he added, gesturing with his new toy. "Can't wait to try my new putter!"

"'Night, Dad," Ellen said, folding a dishtowel and giving him a peck as he passed her.

"'Night, all," Len said as he shuffled down the hall.

"'Night," everyone replied.

"Me too, I've had it. 'Night," Scott said, laboriously getting up from the couch.

As if on cue, everybody else started to get up as well.

"You might want to grab first dibs on the bathroom," Scott said to Tami.

"Thanks. I'll be quick," she replied.

"'Cause you don't even want to go in there after me," he laughed.

"That's the truth," Ellen said, rolling her eyes.

The group began picking up the room as Tami exited down the hall. They all exchanged hugs. Rich had missed them all more than he realized. As he helped Ellen carry dessert plates and glasses to the kitchen, he made a mental promissory note to increase the frequency of visits.

Somehow.

He was next in the bathroom. Wearing only his pajama bottoms, Rich stood at the sink, absently brushing his teeth when the door cracked open.

"You almost done?" Scott asked, peeking his head in. "We're dying out here," he whispered. Then he got a glimpse of the full extent of the arm cuts, several bite marks, and various bruises and welts on Rich's torso. Rich's twenty-pound weight loss was also more pronounced without his pajama top.

"Doesn't anybody knock anymore?" Rich muttered as he grabbed his pajama top and began hastily slipping it on, like a teenaged girl whose parents had caught her making out.

"Jeezus," Scott said as he touched Rich's arm, stopping the process and getting a closer look. He closed the door behind them and surveyed the carnage, looking up from the bruises, to the bite marks on his shoulders, then up to Rich's face, to his purplish eye. "Bro. Tell me what happened here. And no bullshit."

Rich tried to avoid eye contact but Scott kept shifting positions to be directly in front of his little brother.

"Talk to me, Richie. You didn't get all this from trimming the damned roses." His face was grim, and the look in his eyes was laser-focused.

Rich's shoulders went slack, and Scott gave him a moment to finish buttoning his PJ top.

Rich tried with all his might to stop the flow of moisture he could feel welling in his eyes. It made his vision blurry, like he was looking through a melting glacier. Despite his best efforts, a couple of tears found their way down his cheeks and he silently cursed them for giving him up.

"Rich…it's okay…talk to me."

The best Rich could muster was an involuntary whimper. He was finally being called on his demons, and the hellish secrets he'd managed to keep tamped down all of these years. Fully exposed now, he'd never felt so utterly naked.

"It's me, Rich. Your brother," he said, his hands gently but firmly placed on Rich's shoulders.

He wasn't going away, and Rich knew it.

"C'mon, man. Tell me what happened," Scott said very quietly. He took a deep breath before continuing his line of questioning. "Did—did *Tami* do this, Richie? Did Tami hurt you?"

Rich's lip quivered uncontrollably. He wiped away a tear and didn't say anything for several moments. "She didn't mean to…it was my fault…" Rich stammered as Scott held him in a brotherly hug. He was afraid to let his brother go, because he could feel that all of the strength had left Rich's body, as if some body-snatcher had stolen his skeletal system and just left this limp bag of fleshy matter. What remained of Rich just rocked there in Scott's arms.

"We love each other," Rich said, almost breathlessly.

"I know you do, bro," Scott said.

They stood there for a few moments. Rocking silently.

"Look, Rich. I know you love Tami."

"And she loves me," Rich replied softly, automatically.

"I know…" Scott glanced over to the mirror, where the image of him holding up his broken brother began reshaping his feelings—from disbelief, to sadness, and then anger. "I know. And I love you…we all love you, Richie," Scott said, pausing to let that sink in. "You know that, right?"

Rich nodded slightly.

Scott ended the bear hug and made sure Rich could stand on his own two feet. He looked him in the eye now. "But, Rich, if Tami hurt you—if she *beat* you—that's not…" Scott said, softly, barely stifling his anger before continuing, "…that's not acceptable, bro. You know that, right, Rich?"

A nod from Rich.

Scott started processing the situation. "That's not cool. Has this happened before? Does it happen a lot?" Scott wanted to give him all the time he needed. Rich nodded again. "How long, Richie? How long have you been keeping this a secret, huh? Who knows? Does anybody know?" he asked.

Rich shook his head, an empty, naked, broken and defeated warrior.

"Tell me, Rich. How often?" Scott persisted.

"Three…four…five, maybe…I dunno…maybe more…I'm not sure. I've lost track," Rich managed under his breath.

"*Times*, Rich? Four or five times?" Scott asked, seeking clarification.

Rich shook his head before answering. His eyes found Scott's. "Years…"

"Jeezus," Scott muttered to himself, his closed fist striking the counter.

There was a quiet tapping on the door. Rich spun around out of reflex, terror written on his face.

"You almost done in there?" Ellen said quietly.

Scott pushed in the lock on the doorknob.

"Be right out," Scott said to the door, then back to his brother. "Look at me, Rich. Look at me!" he said firmly, yet in a hushed tone.

Rich's eyes came around to meet Scott's again.

"Get some sleep, bro. We'll talk about this in the morning, okay? Just you and me, Richie," he affirmed.

Scott started to slip back out through the door but paused long enough to ask, "You okay?"

Rich nodded weakly and Scott closed the door behind him.

Ellen was standing there, holding her toiletries. "Some kind of party I wasn't invited to?" she asked, slightly annoyed.

"Nah. Let's just use the other bathroom," he said, putting his arm around her shoulder.

"No, Scott. The light's better in—"

"C'mon, we need to talk."

"Now? It's late, I'm tired, Scott. Whatever it is can—"

His look silenced her. "We need to talk. Right. Now."

◆

CHAPTER 35

RICH CRAWLED INTO bed, foggy, depleted, and with no expectation of sleep whatsoever. Doing his best not to disturb Tami, he folded his arms behind his head, his still-moist eyes staring at the ceiling.

The encounter with Scott had blindsided him—an unexpected and to-be-avoided-at-all-costs moment. The facade, the charade, had come crashing down, and all he could feel was an overwhelming sense of shame. He cursed himself for not locking the bathroom door.

He rolled over on his side, away from Tami and settled into the small sliver of the mattress space she'd left him. On his nightstand, a black and white picture stared back at him, another of a six-year-old version of himself, a favorite of his mother's. He wondered whatever happened to that happy little guy, that seemingly confident version of himself with the innocent eyes, the not-a-care-in-the-world smile.

He closed his eyes, and within seconds, completely surrendered into a deep, coma-like sleep. And, it began.

◆

Though he'd have no way of knowing, this seemingly long-lost dream had long been tucked away for decades, in a secret place. It had always been cued up; it was just waiting for its intended audience of one and the right moment.

And that right moment was now.

So the "on" switch had been flipped.

As this premier would now be allowed to play in its entirety, it was particularly vivid this time; it was the director's cut, re-mastered, in widescreen Technicolor, with some glorious black and white thrown in. As the curtain opened, he was pulled in, powerless to escape its gravitational pull. He didn't even try.

Fade In:

It appeared murky at first, but the image cleared to reveal a late fifties-era school's multipurpose room, with a raised stage area. Perhaps a hundred or more—it might've been a million—six year olds were silently filing into the large space and were being corralled by a handful of teachers, whose silent gestures directed them to sit at the many lunch tables set up there.

A very stern, decidedly unfriendly-looking vulture of a man, the principal, watched the children file in from his vantage point center stage. The man was lanky, like Ichabod Crane, but more threatening, like his evil twin.

"Enter and take a seat, quietly. No talking," he said into the stand-mounted microphone, his voice booming across the auditorium.

There was complete compliance, without so much as a single utterance being made, as the tables filled. Next to where the principal was standing, there was a small wooden table with a portable record player sitting atop it. Behind him, a framed presidential portrait of John F. Kennedy hung on the wall.

Little Richie, the version from the photo, smiled as he took his seat; he recognized the portrait of the president, having seen him on television. He wondered what this first assembly was going to be about.

"Quietly...take your seats. There shall be no talking," the unsmiling principal reiterated. Other than the soft shuffling of little feet and the occasional creak of a bench, it was oddly, surreally quiet.

When the last of the first graders had taken their seats, the principal stood there menacingly, surveying the group, looking at each table carefully, checking for compliance. Maybe something else too, but Richie had no clue what. Satisfied, and without any further word or explanation, the tall man turned toward the phonograph and rotated a knob.

If someone had dropped a pin at that moment, the sound would have been deafening. The man swung the tone arm into position and gently lowered it to the 45 RPM record until the stylus made contact with the vinyl, producing a series of pops.

Little Richie watched with rapt attention, not knowing what to expect, but he absolutely loved music, and he listened to it often at home, for hours on end.

This was going to be exciting!

The music began, and Richie immediately recognized the instrumental lead-in to "Sugar Shack" by Jimmie Gilmer & the Fireballs. As the song continued, the principal closely scrutinized the students' faces, looking for reactions perhaps, like it was some kind of weird scientific experiment or something. All Richie knew was that he recognized the song, and a few kids at his table exchanged glances. A few started bobbing their heads, ever so slightly, not sure if it was allowed.

The principal watched, and the students listened.

About forty seconds in, Jimmy Gilmer was singing about something Richie didn't quite understand, but he liked it just the same, and from what he could gather, it seemed very important that the singer make a return trip to some place called the Sugar Shack.

Oh, well, it still had a good beat.

By this time, there was no doubt in Little Richie's mind. Ellen had played this record at home, for her friends, on the record player she got for Christmas! He smiled at this, turning to the boy seated next to him and whispered, "My sister has this record!" Little Richie's whisper, as innocent and soft as a mouse's fart, might as well have been a lion's roar, through a megaphone and broadcast from the rim of the Grand Canyon.

Of course, this did not go unnoticed by the principal, and as his brow furrowed, his lips pursed like he'd just bitten into a dirt clod. The classmate seated next to Richie looked up at the stage in horror as the principal was now staring at them, glaring actually. Little Richie followed the boy's gaze up to the stage, just in time to see the principal angrily yank the needle from the record, producing a loud and very unsettling scratching sound.

Instantly, the room seemed like it was filled with cotton balls in a vacuum chamber. Not a sound, with the exception of the man's large wingtip shoes stomping down the few steps from the stage, and huffing toward them, like a runaway locomotive. His nostrils flared like an angry bull's as he approached the boys' table.

Suddenly, the principal violently yanked little Richie up by the armpits. He dangled helplessly, like a baby rabbit in the clutches of an eagle's talons, and the next thing he knew, he was airborne, a marionette being roughly transported through the crowd of his peers—all one million of them—without a word and to an uncertain fate. When they reached the front of the auditorium, at the base of the stage, the principal wordlessly set little Richie down, less than gently, his face an inch from the wall. The man positioned him so that his nose was making contact with the wall, then slowly made his way back toward the stage.

Little Richie's eyes blinked rapidly as he stood there before God and everybody, his nose pressed against the wall. It was cold. All of his senses were heightened, and his mind raced for an explanation.

But there was none.

An invisible dunce cap sat atop his head, along with the invisible *KICK ME* sign on his back. Tears began to stream down his cheeks.

He could smell the enamel of the freshly painted surface, and the sound of the principal's leather shoes walking away and up the wood steps to the stage was deafeningly loud.

So was the silence. He felt like he was under water.

"Now," the principal said, taking a deep breath before continuing. "When I say 'No talking,' that's what I mean, children. No talking."

In that brief, seemingly never-ending, thousand-year moment, little Richie listened intently, the words, and this twisted lesson, muffled, distorted, yet crystal clear as they etched themselves into every one of his formative brain cells. An abyss of confusion, embarrassment, and self-loathing began to set in as the music was re-cued from the beginning.

At some point, it eventually faded away, as did the room itself.

Little Richie's one takeaway from this day started to crystalize: *Talking, sharing, and expressing yourself is wrong. Internalize, at all costs. And never, ever communicate your feelings again.*

Ever.

Fade out.

Rich bolted upright, covered in sweat, and breathing like a marathon runner. With panicky eyes and deep disorientation, he looked around the dark room and over at a sleeping Tami, who angrily yanked the comforter back onto herself.

He looked back over at the picture on the nightstand, then lay back down on his side, staring into the darkness and silently wept in recognition of his own long overdue epiphany.

◆

CHAPTER 36

RICH WAS WEARING a long-sleeved *America's Funkiest Folks* hoodie, the hooded part concealing the mother of all bedheads. He emerged from his room, still in a deep fog bank, like he was nursing a worst-case red wine hangover, but he'd only had the one glass with dinner. He had no idea what time it was, but he could hear a fair amount of chaos coming from the kitchen, so he shuffled toward the sound.

Scott and Ellen were leaning against the kitchen counter, watching Kailee and Adam go at it as they played a boisterous toy boxing game called Rock 'Em Sock 'Em Robots. Scott put an arm around Rich's shoulder and handed him a cup of coffee. Ellen passed him a small plate holding a bagel with cream cheese. She gave Rich a long hug. Nobody said a word, and Rich was grateful.

After a minute or so, and a resounding clunk, the game sounds stopped, and Kailee squealed victoriously. Her red robot had delivered a sharp, fatal uppercut jab to Adam's blue robot, vaulting its head up the neck violently.

"Ha! I knocked your block off!" she declared.

"Whatever!" Adam said angrily.

"Come on! One more!" Kailee pleaded.

"Nah," Adam said as he got up from the table.

"What's the matter?" she taunted, "afraid of a girl?"

"Shut up!" he yelled.

"Adam, we don't say that," his mother said.

"She started it!" he retorted, storming off.

Kailee looked over at the adults. "Come on, Uncle Rich! Play me! I promise not to give you a black eye!" she laughed.

Rich stopped chewing his bagel.

The awkwardness of the moment was palpable.

"Kailee, how 'bout we put the game away now, okay, sweetheart?" Ellen said.

"Oh, Mom..."

"Kailee?" Ellen replied, with a *don't-push-it* tone.

"Okay," Kailee said under her breath as she grabbed the game box.

"Good morning, everyone," Jeanette said cheerfully, emerging from the hallway, still in her peach robe.

"Morning, Gram," Kailee said, as she left the room.

"Mornin', Mom," Scott and Ellen said.

"Good morning," Rich said quietly.

Jeanette surveyed the room, taking an extra moment as she looked at Rich, her mother's intuition radar always on alert. Ellen handed her a cup of coffee with extra cream, the way she liked it. Jeanette thanked Ellen, gave her a peck on the cheek, and looked up at the clock. Ten-thirty-five.

"Where's Tami, Richie? Don't tell me she's still asleep."

"Nope. Right behind you, Jeanette," Tami said, smiling at the group as she entered, still in her Looney Tunes nightshirt. Rich had bought that for her as a birthday gift years ago, at the Warner Brothers store, and he'd seen her wear it a million times, but as she stood there before them in his parents' kitchen, with all that had transpired, Rich couldn't help noticing how appropriate the graphics seemed now.

"Good morning, dear," Jeanette said, giving her a hug.

The smattering of "Mornin'" salutations was followed by a brief, yet awkward silence. Ellen handed Tami a mug. "What do you take in it?"

"Hmm? Oh, I don't drink coffee, thank you," Tami said.

"Don't drink coffee?" Jeanette asked. "Then you can't possibly be a Bryson!" she said playfully.

Rich looked down at the floor during much of this exchange.

"No, but if you have some juice, that'd be great."

Ellen set down the mug and retrieved a juice glass from the cupboard. "Apple or orange?" she asked, not very warmly.

Jeanette picked up on this nuance and watched Ellen open the fridge.

"Orange, please."

"Orange it is," Ellen said, grabbing the carton.

Rich cleared the frog from his throat.

"How'd you sleep?" he asked.

"Okay…good, I think," Tami replied.

Scott's eyes stealthily moved back and forth during the exchanges, as if watching a tennis match.

"You really have to rush back home, Richie?"

"Yeah, Mom, we do," Rich replied, pausing for a sip of coffee. "I have an early call tomorrow morning. Should only take five or six hours, if we get a jump on traffic."

"You working tomorrow too, Tami?" Ellen said, looking her in the eyes as she handed the glass to her.

Scott was watching Tami closely too.

"No. I have tomorrow off," Tami replied with a smile.

"Acting's a little slow now, is it?" Scott said, his sarcasm barely concealed.

Tami looked over to Rich, but he was looking down into the black void of his coffee.

"Uh, yeah, a little," she answered somewhat uncomfortably.

"Gives me time to work on my demo reel, though," she said with a smile. She was an excellent actress.

"Ah, good!" Scott said, exchanging glances with his sister.

A loud yawn broke the tension.

"Mornin', everyone," Len said, all dressed for the day. He was wearing a collared polo shirt and some exceedingly loud plaid slacks, which suggested he—and his new putter—had a date with the greens.

"Good morning, dear," Jeannette said, kissing him.

"Mornin', Dad," everyone else chimed in.

"Good morning, beautiful," Len said, with a hug for Tami.

Ellen, ever on point, handed him a mug of black coffee, gave him a peck and wedged another bagel into the toaster.

"What's this I hear about Rich and Tami driving back early? I was going to do some chicken on the grill after I played nine holes."

"Sorry, Dad. It's true. We have to shove off in a little bit. Work."

"Ah. Work," Len said, winking at Tami. "I remember that."

He turned to Jeanette and gave her a playful pat on the fanny. "Don't you, honey?" he laughed.

"Yes, I remember," she said, rolling her eyes.

"Don't you just love having Dad around all the time, now that he's retired, Mom?" Ellen interjected.

"No comment," she said with a chuckle.

Tami walked over to Rich and gave him a small hug.

"I think I'll take a quick shower, honey," she said.

"Okay. I will after. We're pretty much packed, except toiletries. Like to get a jump on traffic," Rich replied.

"I'll show you where the fresh towels are, dear," Jeanette said, leading Tami down the hall.

"I'm going out front," Len said, as he grabbed the new putter that was leaning against the door.

"Have fun, Dad," Scott said as he watched him leave. He waited for the sound of the door closing before looking over at Ellen. She met his gaze and nodded almost imperceptibly. The three of them were alone now.

"Hey, let's go check out Dad's roses, Rich," she said, smiling as she put an arm around his shoulder.

"Dad's roses," Rich said numbly.

"Yeah, c'mon," she said, leading him toward the slider.

"Mind if I tag along?" Scott asked, per their script. Scott gently closed the sliding glass door behind him as they exited to the backyard patio area and a whole other world entirely.

The white crisscrossed slats of the gazebo-like patio were contrasted in stunning fashion by the explosion of color that was Len's prized rose collection.

Rich breathed in the freshness, his senses immediately picking up on the subtle fragrances of the roses as well as the abundant star jasmine that filled in an entire wall of the patio. They walked by the expertly groomed rose bushes, and Rich was reminded of just how much of a rose guru his father was. There were a range of gorgeous varieties: the peace, double delights, Mr. Lincoln, and the Chrysler imperials that he cultivated, mostly for the pleasure of Jeanette, who enjoyed them so. Her favorite was the delicate, lavender-tinted angel face, which had perhaps the most subtle fragrance of them all. Rich dipped his nose into this one, knocking off a couple of fragile pedals in the process.

"Mmm…I'd forgotten how great these smell."

As he turned back, Rich noticed Ellen and Scott staring at him. "You didn't bring me out here—" he managed.

Ellen shook her head.

Rich looked over to Scott, then back to his sister.

"Oh, Richie….I know Tami's been abusing you," she said, wiping away an unplanned tear.

"Well then I guess you know all there is to know, huh?" Richie said, before directing the next comment to Scott. "Thanks, bro. Who else did you tell?"

"I had to tell her, Rich. So far, nobody else knows. But you can't keep this a secret. Not anymore."

"Not from us. Not from family," Ellen added.

"Tami's my family too. I took vows," Rich said, looking down.

Ellen came closer and gently touched his face, causing a reflex flinch. "Rich, look at me," she said, guiding his face back to hers. "I know you took vows. And, as your sister who knows you very well, I know you took them very seriously. But, Richie, the first time Tami hit you—the first time she beat you—she broke her vows. Don't you see that?"

Rich's eyes began to glisten.

Damn it.

"It's true, Rich. Tami's got you to a place where you don't even know which end is up anymore, bro," Scott said, placing a hand on his shoulder.

"We're worried about you, Rich," Ellen added, glancing over her shoulder to make sure they were still in private.

"We're just going through a rough patch is all. We'll get through this," Rich said, unconvincingly.

Scott and Ellen exchanged looks.

"It's not going to stop, Rich. That's the way it works. It's only going to get worse—that much I do know—and we're not going to stand by and allow her to further hurt, or even kill, you, bro! Do you understand that?" Scott pleaded.

"She wouldn't—"

"I'm sorry, would you listen to yourself, Richie, please," Ellen interjected.

"We've been to counseling a couple of times and—"

"And how's *that* working out for you?" Scott cut him off, trying to curb the edge in his voice before he continued. "Tami's sick, Rich. She probably needs to see a doctor."

"She might need medication, Richie," Ellen interjected.

"You don't get it!" Rich blurted out defensively, as he wiped his eyes. "She's—she won't see a doctor, okay? She won't take meds. Doesn't believe in it," he managed before the full-on sobbing started.

Scott looked at Ellen, and they engaged Rich in a group hug.

"Then we've got to get you out of there, man," Scott said, "before she kills you."

The three of them gently rocked in a sibling huddle amongst the kaleidoscopic blooms.

"We need to make a plan, Richie," Ellen said softly.

◆

CHAPTER 37

THE DRIVE BACK had been mostly uneventful, with Tami quietly going in and out of her little trances. He didn't even play any music. Several times Rich had looked over at her, only to find her with her eyes closed and that unnatural smile, the one that often was the precursor to trouble.

Other than the slow crawl through Santa Barbara, traffic had been manageable for the most part, but a little heavy, it being a Sunday. They'd grabbed Subway sandwiches on the road and only stopped once for gas, but it was dark now, and he was absolutely exhausted.

On more levels than he knew were possible.

And emotionally toast.

For six hours, pretty much all he'd thought about were Ellen's words: *We need to make a plan, Richie.*

After he'd brought in their bags, Rich ducked into the spare bedroom office and clicked on the desk lamp, illuminating his large wall calendar. There were many annotations in red, mostly work-related, with the exception of Dad's Birthday, which was now passed. Using a black ballpoint he X-ed that one out before swapping it for his trusty red Sharpie. With his finger, he moved down to the following Friday and wrote in that box, in big letters, *NEW CLIENT.*

He turned off the light, gingerly closed the door, and washed his face for what seemed like an hour before crawling in bed next to an already-sleeping Tami.

◆

CHAPTER 38

THE NEW WEEK was a busy one, with wall-to-wall shoots, which Rich was thankful for. He thought the work would keep his mind off his troubles, but the lack of sleep, paired with the recent revelations of his unraveling marriage and obsessing over the upcoming mystery *plan*—it was more than he could deal with. He had three long days on a new game show, and these were his least favorite gigs because they were so lame.

His powers of concentration were diminished, to the point where he was getting yelled at over the headsets on several occasions. The missed shots, forgotten cues, erratic zooms, this wasn't representative of his best work—far from it—and it was the first time in his professional career that his reputation was at risk. As a freelancer, you're only as good as your last shoot, and his work right now was sucking. Badly.

As much as Rich wanted to establish himself with this new show's director, his job performance all but guaranteed he wouldn't get called back now—he knew it—and all he could think about now was *Friday*. They'd wrapped production at 4:30, and Rich slinked out to his car without a word. Mike had given him a quizzical look, but thankfully hadn't grilled him.

It took a while, but Rich eventually found his slot in the dreaded

405's queue. As always, it was slow going and roughly equivalent to being the sixty-fifth frankfurter trying to find passage through a severely-congested colon at a Nathan's Hot Dog Eating Contest.

The two-hour drive gave him more than enough time to second-guess everything about his life and to stew on the toxic cocktail of guilt, shame, and doubt. As usual, the tune-master upstairs was on point, as tonight's needle-drop was something special, and seemingly dedicated to Rich: Jeff Buckley's haunting "Last Goodbye."

◆

CHAPTER 39

RICH, WITH HELP from the Atlanta Rhythm Section, belted out the final chorus of "Spooky" before switching off the ignition and retrieving the groceries from the back of the car. Thus far, the day had been relatively uneventful, and the errands therapeutic. For this he was grateful.

He entered the house, juggling several paper grocery bags and closing the front door with his foot. Tami called out as he made his way to the kitchen.

"What took so long?" she said, descending the stairs, her wet hair in a towel turban.

"Hey."

"You were gone for so long; I was beginning to worry," she said.

"Sorry, I had to go to another store to get the light mayo," he replied, retrieving items from the bag and stashing them into the fridge. "Got it though."

"Scott called," she said matter-of-factly.

Rich froze. His mind raced, and he wondered if he'd lost track of what day it was. Today was Thursday, he remembered, with relief. He finally managed an answer from the bowels of the icebox.

"Scott? Really?"

"Yeah."

"Huh," Rich said, trying to stifle any concern in his voice. "He mention anything?"

"Nothing really. Just said he'd try to catch you later."

"Mm, okay," he replied casually. *Look, ma—I'm an actor!*

"We just saw him last week," Tami added.

"Yep. So?"

"Nothing. Just seemed strange he'd call you is all. He never calls."

"Well, maybe we forgot something at my folks', who knows? I'll give him a buzz later." He closed the fridge door, then walked over to the stairwell and held up a deli-wrapped package containing two rib eyes. "Right now, I'm going to make you your favorite dinner!" he said, happy to change the subject.

"Artichokes too?" Tami asked.

"Wouldn't be your favorite dinner without 'em."

"Nope. Okay, I'm going to finish drying my hair. How long?"

"Half hour? I'll let you know," Rich said.

Tami bounded upstairs. Rich began seasoning the beautiful Michelin restaurant-worthy cuts of beef. Satisfied, he went out onto the back patio and removed the cover on the Weber, then fired it up.

When it came to cooking, he'd become quite adept at multitasking, always making sure that all the moving parts were in synchronicity. While the grill heated up, he prepped the artichokes and got them going in the microwave, a trick he'd learned from his sister. A little water in a shallow baking dish, throw in a couple heaping spoons of minced garlic, a squeeze of lemon, and—the most important part—a tight seal of plastic wrap over the 'chokes to assure a proper steaming. Half the time of the stovetop method! He set the microwave for fifteen minutes and hit the start button. Boom.

The steak fries were slid into the oven, a twelve-minute deal. Boom.

The steaks went on and Rich adjusted the heat accordingly. He looked at his watch and smiled. This would time perfectly.

He took a long pull from his Anchor Steam and thought about Scott's call. He made a note to call him after dinner, if there was an opportune moment without Tami being in earshot. This might prove tricky, as Tami had made it a point these last several months to pick up the office phone extension every time somebody called. Rich honestly couldn't remember the last time he'd had an unmonitored call with his family—or even a friend—on the home phone. And he'd come to the realization long ago that if Tami were to look at the call logs from their cell phone bill, it was anybody's guess what might set off her paranoia. Anyway…

He seared the first side for exactly four minutes and flipped the steaks over, pleased with the grill marks. He looked at his watch, took another swig of beer and lowered the heat, flipping the meat once more. He was known for his steaks, and as the gorgeous ribeyes approached perfection, he marked the moment, not entirely secure in the knowledge, but reasonably sure—at least hopeful—this was the final one he'd ever cook for her. That is, if the plan didn't go south on him.

Better make The Last Supper great.

Rich ran inside, noted the remaining time on the microwave countdown, turned off the oven, and pulled out the potatoes.

"Two minute warning!" he called up the stairs before dashing back to his grill.

Tami futzed with her hair some more, sprayed another blast of aerosol into it, then washed her hands—at length. After drying them, she looked down at her dry, prematurely wrinkled hands—hands that could have belonged to her great-grandmother.

She looked at herself in the mirror again, now dissatisfied with her choice of blouse. She foraged for a few more minutes in the walk-in closet and tried on a couple of silk numbers before settling on her choice: the green one she'd started with.

She placed her index finger and thumb delicately on the light switch, making contact ever so lightly with the toggle as she closed her eyes and silently counted to herself for several moments until she reached some pre-determined number. Once satisfied, she opened her eyes, looked up at the ceiling with her forced smile, and flicked off the bathroom light.

"Ready…GO! Awesome!" she whispered to herself before negotiating the stairs, careful to step only on the outside edges of every other step on her way to the living room. She stopped and reversed course once, going back up to the top, pausing to count and smiling to the heavens before continuing down to the landing.

Everything was all set up. The TV trays were laden with delicious offerings, and he'd warmed up the set to be ready for Tami's favorite—and his least favorite—sitcom.

The steaks were plated, as were the potatoes, and the perfectly steamed jumbo artichokes Rich had taken his time selecting from the bin at the market. These beauties were almost the size of his head. A dollop of mayo sat in small finger bowls next to the chokes.

By his calculations, it had been exactly thirty-three minutes, start to finish. As advertised! He smiled, gesturing for Tami to take her seat.

"What would you like to drink, honey?"

Tami looked at the plates before her.

"How long have the steaks been off the grill?"

"Couple of minutes. They're done just the way you like 'em—slightly pink in the middle," Rich said proudly.

"The steaks are supposed to be the last thing ready—they aren't good if they're not right off the grill," she said, a bit of annoyance and disappointment in her voice, something Rich immediately picked up on.

"They just came off two minutes ago—exactly. Is there a problem?"

"Well, I wasn't ready!" she said, her arms crossed. "The steaks aren't any good if they aren't still hot," she obsessed.

Rich was tired and now very hungry. He wasn't even going to get into a debate over his perfectly prepared meal. He'd stuck the landing, plus these steaks had cost a small fortune. He lifted a plate to verify; the heat coming off the meat was measurable and optimal. Yet for Tami, an inner voice suggested that the moment was compromised.

"It doesn't go with that," Tami whispered to herself.

"Steaks are hot. They're fine. Better than fine, in fact. They're *perfect*. They're ready," he replied, setting the plate down.

"Well, I wasn't!" Tami said, looking up from the plate with obvious displeasure, before storming upstairs in a hissy fit.

"Perfect…" Rich muttered to himself before walking over to the stairwell and calling up to Tami.

"What do you want me to do? I'm starved! You're not hungry?"

"You can put them back on the grill and bring them back in hot, and fresh, like they're supposed to be," she answered from the walk-in closet, where she was again changing her top.

"They're done! They're *optimal*. If I cook them any longer, they'll be tough, ruined," Rich said, his anger just beneath the surface.

"Figure it out, and tell me when they'll be ready!"

He grabbed the two plates and headed to the kitchen.

"Five minutes—*exactly!*" he called over his shoulder.

He relit the still-warm Weber and angrily tossed them back on. *You want hot steaks? I'll give you hot steaks.*

"Such bullshit!" he said through clenched teeth.

Four minutes and thirty seconds later, Rich emerged from the patio, holding a plate containing two blistered steaks. He re-plated them, next to the potatoes and garnishes, as before, and brought them into the living room where Tami was seated on the loveseat, behind her TV tray. He checked his composure as he set the plates down on the trays.

"Two hot steaks," he said quietly.

Tami looked at the steam coming off her steak, smiling up at the ceiling for a long moment, then back down to her plate. She touched her knife and fork for the requisite number of seconds, then lifted the utensils, poised for the cut. Another look up, then—

"Awesome!" she said to herself.

"Yeah, awesome…" Rich lied. "Go ahead and start," he said as he poured her a glass of milk and got himself a beer. He took two long pulls, almost draining the bottle before returning.

Rich sat next to Tami, reluctantly pulling his tray closer. He sawed into what had once been a game-changer piece of meat and now more resembled the remains of a boot that had been found in an arson fire.

"How's yours?" he asked, barely hiding the sarcasm.

"Great!" Tami replied.

Tami laughed along with the canned laugh track as they sat through a lame repeat episode of *Friends,* the first of many. Otherwise, they ate in silence. Rich stared blankly at the flickering images, not paying attention to any of the idiocy. Just a bunch of thirty-something slackers hanging out in a coffee shop. And a laugh track for viewers clueless enough not to know if/when something's supposed to be funny.

The Rachel character said something that elicited another big laugh from Tami.

The next episode started, and the irony of the Rembrandts' catchy opening jingle, about having each others' backs, wasn't lost on Rich this time.

Insert outro guitar riff here.

◆

CHAPTER 40

Friday morning

R ICH FINISHED BRUSHING his teeth and took his sweet time flossing. He'd been particularly distracted when he went to bed the night before, and he was religious about flossing after eating red meat.

He surveyed his work and looked thoughtfully in the mirror for a long moment. Several telltale signs of the battle remained: the remnants of his diminished shiner, a fading bruise or three, and some mostly-healed scratch marks on his torso and arms. At least the bite marks were now barely discernable.

He surveyed his scalp. Was his hair naturally thinning, or was it just from stress? *Having it yanked out by the handful doesn't help!* He put on his shirt, signed off on his hair, and went into the spare bedroom office, where he stared at the bold red lettering in the Friday square: *NEW CLIENT*.

Grabbing a bold ballpoint pen, Rich circled the date, turned off the light, and silently closed the office door. As he stood there on the small landing outside the bedrooms, he inhaled deeply. This was really happening, and he'd have to take a break from the endless second-guessing if he was going to seize the moment.

Launch Control, Houston... We are GO for launch...

He put his hand on their bedroom doorknob and slowly turned

it, quietly easing the door open enough to poke his head inside. Tami was still asleep.

"Tami," Rich whispered.

"Hmn," she groaned.

"Tami," he said again, taking his time to choose his words. "I'm leaving."

Tami stirred, then sat up groggily. She squinted at Rich's silhouette, backlit from the hallway light.

"What time'll you be home?"

"Can't say." *Truer words had never been uttered.*

Tami rubbed the sleep from her eyes. "I start my new class today; it's from three to six," she said.

"I know," Rich said, looking at her, taking in the image of his bride one last time.

"Okay, well, if you're gonna go, go! Don't just stand there staring, you're freaking me out!"

"Okay," Rich said, the finality of the moment clear now. He took a deep breath. "Goodbye," he said softly. It felt surreally weird saying that, but there it was. Like a cosmic shift was beginning to take place. It gave him a chill.

Things seemed to morph into super-slow motion as he closed the bedroom door. He paused, turned off the stairwell light and slowly padded down the stairs. "Goodbye, Tami," he whispered to himself.

Rich quietly secured the two front door locks and gently closed the screen door behind him. He took a few steps then stopped, turning to take a long look at the townhouse. The courtyard/common area was unusually peaceful at this early morning hour, on this Friday that was like any other, but unlike any other.

He slowly, methodically drew in the longest, deepest breath ever, stretching his lungs to their tolerances before letting the air—and his pent-up anxiety—leave him. He didn't notice the slight movement of the upstairs bedroom blinds as he turned and headed for the carport.

◆

CHAPTER 41

A S HE PULLED into traffic and switched on the radio, it didn't escape Rich that the Great DJ in the Sky was in fine form that morning and had cued up a dandy of a song that Rich hadn't heard in a while. The Reverend Simon seemed to preach to him personally, reminding him that there were, well, several dozen methods he could choose from to aid his escape and get the hell outta Dodge. During the second chorus, Rich customized a couple of lines; it was an embellishment he couldn't resist:

Flip a l'il switch, Rich....

Ditch the l'il witch, Rich....

That chick is a bitch, Rich....

The forty-minute trip allowed for several variations on that rhyme, making his drive a complete blur. Before he knew it, the Explorer pulled up curbside outside the baggage claim at Burbank Airport, as if on autopilot.

He looked again at his watch, feeling a sense of relief that he was on time. Another jet screamed away, rattling Rich's eardrums in the process, as the passenger door opened and Scott climbed in, wearing cargo shorts and a tee. He had no bags.

"What's up, my brotha?" he said as he climbed in.

"Hey, bro," Rich answered, leaning over to give him a hug. "I can't believe you're here."

"Well, you'd better believe it! We're doing this!" Scott smiled. A police whistle chirped, and Rich nodded at the security person waving him away from the curb. They pulled away and entered the small stream of cars.

"How hard was it getting time off?" Rich asked.

"Wasn't hard," Scott said, affixing his San Francisco Giants cap. "Told 'em it was a family emergency...and it is, right?"

Rich didn't answer, but confirmed it in his mind as they exited the airport grounds and made their way onto the congested streets of the Valley.

"You think Tami suspects anything, Rich?"

"Don't think so," Rich said.

Scott looked at him, assessing the level of doubt.

"No," Rich corrected. "She doesn't."

"Good," Scott said, patting the back of Rich's head. "Your sister wanted to come, but I waved her off."

Rich grunted his acknowledgement. It'd been quite some time since Scott had been down here, and he couldn't get over the amount of urban sprawl, graffiti, and the frigging smog. There was supposed to be a mountain range very near them but he couldn't see it. Rising up from the dirty brown streets was the dirty brown sky, which blended seamlessly. No mountains today, mister.

They drove in uncomfortable silence as they traversed North Hollywood, parts of Sherman Oaks, and eventually pulled into the public parking lot adjacent to the Van Nuys Courthouse.

Scott looked at his watch and turned toward his brother, who was deep in thought. "You're up for this, right, brother?"

"Yeah..." Rich said none too convincingly. They went inside.

It was a good thing they'd gotten there early, as they had to stand in numerous lines, behind some of the saddest looking people Rich had ever seen assembled in one place. Way worse than the DMV.

Welcome to Divorce Court.

They were all there for the same reason, he figured. Different circumstances, he hoped, but these were all people looking to divorce themselves from their own personal versions of hell. The negative energy on this floor was palpable, and all one could feel was a general sense of misery, utter hopelessness, and foreboding. But it was a necessary process.

Not unlike a root canal.

"Next," grunted the clerk, who barely looked at Rich as she shoved the forms toward him, which he collected and took to a nearby countertop to fill them out. Rich wondered if the mood of the crowd rubbed off on the staff.

When Rich got to the part where he had to choose between the boxes marked "Separation" and "Dissolution of Marriage", Scott pointed to the latter one. The brothers exchanged serious looks, prompting Rich to take a deep breath and check that box.

"I forgot my checkbook," Rich said.

"Gotcha covered, bro," Scott said, as they got back in line. The woman in front of them quietly sobbed.

After what felt like a week, they emerged from that heinous house of pain and made their way back to the car. Rich didn't even remember where they'd parked, his head was that far up his ass, but Scott directed them to the proper aisle.

"Here, I'll hold onto these," he said, grabbing the documents from Rich and putting his arm around his shoulder. "I know that was hard to do, bro, but you do know there wasn't any other way, right?"

"I guess," Rich managed.

"Okay…next order of business," Scott said as he consulted the map in his hand. U-Haul was only three miles away. "Good," he muttered with some relief.

At the facility, the yard worker finished up the wiring harness between the Explorer and a small rental trailer. He tried the blinkers. "Take 'er slow—she'll ride fine," he said, smiling at Rich. His teeth were battleship gray, and there was a lump of chew tucked inside his precancerous lower lip.

"I will," Rich said, wondering how anyone could chew that crap. "Thanks."

Scott jumped in on the passenger side and Rich took one last look at the trailer set-up before climbing behind the wheel. He looked at his watch and over to Scott, who nodded confidently and said, "You ready?"

"Ready as I'll ever be, I guess. Let's do this."

"Tally ho!" Scott hollered, cowboy style, as he thumped the outside of his door with his palm. The tires spit a few chunks of gravel as they pulled away, the little trailer bouncing noisily as they left the driveway.

"How much time you say we had?" Scott asked.

"Not long. Tami's starting some psychology class at the college—supposed to get out around six."

"Psychology." Scott had to laugh. A glance at his watch showed 2:15 and he put on his game face. "Let's hope that it does."

◆

CHAPTER 42

TAMI'S INSTRUCTOR WAS sixty-something, balding, and trying desperately to be cool with his failed attempt at the ponytail deal. He wrote the homework assignment on the white board as the twenty students copied it into their notebooks.

"We're finishing a little early today, but for next week, please read chapters one and two of the text, plus the handout," he said.

Tami, seated in the front row, finished her annotations and looked up at the clock: 5:35.

"Have a nice weekend, everybody," he said as the students gathered their belongings and filed out.

◆

The townhouse screen door was propped open, letting in countless flies, but that was the last thing on anybody's mind right now. Scott exited with a large load of Rich's clothes on hangers, draped over one arm and gripping the necks of two Fender Stratocasters in his other hand. He walked by the bored-looking civil standby police officer, who in turn looked at his watch.

"I can give you five more minutes, that's it," he said.

"Right," Scott said, making his way to the carport.

Rich came out carrying a load of his precious LP records.

Atop the stack was the iconic red *In The Court of the Crimson King* album by the aptly named King Crimson. The artwork featured an extreme close-up of a tormented character's face screaming, with an expression of extreme agony and sheer madness—probably the title character from the "21st Century Schizoid Man" track on the album. Perhaps going through a divorce, even. Whatever it was, it perfectly mirrored the anxiety and sense of urgency Rich felt, especially since the last glance at his watch had revealed it was 5:45.

"Just about there, Officer, thanks," Rich said, puffing toward the getaway chariot.

The Explorer and trailer were parked by the Dumpster and packed to capacity with boxes and miscellany. It wasn't a neat packing job by any means, but it would have to do. They had to get out of there! Now!

Scott slid the guitars atop the stack of clothes.

"Room for these?" Rich asked, trying to hand the bulky albums to his brother.

"No way. Wedge 'em in back somewhere. We're full!"

Rich went around back and stuffed them into the rear of the trailer, with barely enough room to latch the door and attach the combination lock. "I need a second to check the carport storage," he said.

"Seriously? Dude, look at the time!" Scott said.

"Haven't looked in there in a while. Just take a minute," Rich said as he removed the padlock that secured the doors of the overhead storage space and swung them open wide. What greeted him made his eyes go wide as saucers, and his jaw dropped a foot. Inside, neatly stacked—and wedged—in place, were dozens of unopened product boxes, each displaying the "As Seen On TV" logo, and he instantly recognized all of the kitchen gadgets, the home appliances, and every other worthless device he'd ever shot the infomercials for.

Just three easy payments.

"Holy shit, Tami—" Rich muttered, relocking the doors to her secret hoarder stash. "Guess that's it," he said as he returned to the car.

"Good, 'cause we're maxed," Scott replied. "Let's get outta here!"

"I'll go lock up," Rich said, out of breath.

"Make it quick!" Scott urged, glancing at his watch: 5:50.

Rich rushed back to the townhouse, past the two small neighbor kids who were watching the cool policeman from their Big Wheels.

"We're done, Officer. Thank you," Rich said. The officer cast a glance at Rich's yellowing shiner and nodded.

"Okay…good luck," he replied.

"Yep," Rich said, running inside and taking a last look around. There were conspicuous gaps in the entertainment center where things had been removed and where the rack stereo system—his pride and joy—had stood all these years.

The Lovers statuette, which had always enjoyed an honorary perch atop his stereo cabinet, was now sitting on the coffee table. Better than the floor, he figured. They'd left the place relatively tidy though, all things considered; they weren't pigs.

For a fleeting moment, he couldn't help but feel disappointed that they couldn't have retrieved more of his treasures, but he'd have to cut his losses here or risk the consequences. It was just stuff, he reminded himself, but time and space constraints meant he was leaving behind the bulk of his record collection, which especially hurt.

His sweeping survey ended with a long look at their honeymoon photo, sitting on the end table.

That's when he heard the horn beep several times.

He closed and locked the door, then sprinted to the carport like his life depended on it.

And it just might.

◆

Tami was only a couple of exits from home now, and she was jazzed about this new class of hers. She joined in Karen Carpenter's joy on the radio as they sang, "We've Only Just Begun."

◆

The heavily packed, trailer-toting Explorer labored as it entered the freeway onramp and was riding considerably lower than normal. Scott was at the wheel and he was startled when his cellphone rang. He glanced at the number and smiled.

"The package is in the open," he said in his best secret agent voice before reverting to his normal one. "Yeah, we just got outta there and we're on our way," he continued, pausing to listen to Ellen's concerns.

"Yep. It'll be way late. What? Yeah, he's okay. I'll call ya later. 'Kay," he said, and hung up. "Your sis says she loves you."

"I can't believe we're doing this," Rich mumbled.

"Well, believe it, my brother. Ask me, shoulda happened a long friggin' time ago."

"I dunno…I can't help but feel like—I feel like I'm a horrible person. For leaving," Rich muttered, looking out the window.

Scott kept his eye on the road, but his hand found Rich's knee. "Richie, listen very carefully, okay? You are not—never were, and never will be—a horrible person. Got it?"

He got no answer from Rich, who continued his blank stare outside.

"Far from it. Got it, Richie?" he asked more assertively now. "You had to get out of there, man. Tami's dangerous. She's bad mojo, bro, and she needs serious professional and medical help—which she refuses to get for God knows what reason—and she's hazardous to your health." He let that sink in before continuing. "Tami would've ended up killing you, Richie…you do know that, right?" he said, turning toward his brother long enough to punctuate his statement with a look.

"Yeah, but—"

"Wait…you did not just say, 'Yeah, but,'" Scott replied, pissed now.

"What's she going to do now? How—"

"Honestly? I don't know, Rich. Maybe she'll eventually hit rock bottom, and maybe—*maybe* then she just might get help. You tried. God knows you tried, but it's outta your hands, my man."

Rich exhaled a huge sigh and exchanged looks with Scott. They rode in silence for several minutes before Scott turned on the radio. It never failed, it seemed, as the Great DJ In the Sky offered up another opportune gem for the occasion: the opening guitar strumming by Richie Havens, from his iconic appearance at Woodstock.

"Dude!" Scott laughed, turning up the volume. "They're playing your song! Ha—perfect!"

It took a little time for Rich to get the significance, but once Mr. Havens eventually started belting out that one single word—and the title of the song—in gratuitous repetition, for several minutes, it was, like Scott said, perfect.

Scott sang along, ad nauseam, chanting at the top of his lungs, "Freedom-muh!" for the next few miles, finally getting a laugh from Rich as they zoomed down the highway and into the early stages of what would probably become the most epic sunset in the long history of earthly sunsets.

◆

Tami's car pulled into their carport and she waited for just the right break in the chorus of Karen Carpenter's lovely ballad, which she was sure had been written just for them. She turned off the radio with a ritualistic touch of the knob and an accompanying smile, if you could call it that anymore.

"Awesome!"

She retrieved her textbook from the passenger seat and proceeded past the two kids in the common area and into the house. They watched as she closed the door behind her.

Several seconds of silence went by before Tami's bloodcurdling scream bellowed from inside.

"Mommy! Mommy!" they screamed, wide-eyed and terror stricken as they abandoned their trikes and sprinted for the safety of their homes.

◆

CHAPTER 43

WITH OWL-LIKE VISION, Scott expertly navigated the Explorer along the curves of the narrow, two-lane road. Other than the light of the full moon, it was pitch dark out, but he knew these roads like the back of his hand. A couple of years back, he had volunteered to be road maintenance chief for this three-mile stretch, so he was also aware of where most of the potholes were; the few he did manage to hit jolted the trailer loudly. He made a mental note to fix them.

He looked over at his brother who had, amazingly, slept through all of them—and most of the drive—thus far. He smiled in the knowledge that Rich was safe with him at the moment and that there was a particularly nasty pothole coming around the next corner. He deliberately aimed for this one, producing a loud clunk from the trailer's axle.

"Mmn…where are we?" Rich asked groggily.

"Almost there, little brother," Scott replied, stifling a yawn as they passed an unlighted sign:

WELCOME TO BEN LOMOND

Almost there.

◆

Scott inhaled deeply now, pulling in the fresh mountain air and the scent of these giant redwoods that told him he was close to home. This was his sanctuary, his turf, and for the next two miles he couldn't help smiling as he thought about how every redwood in this swath was on his personal property.

They'd be safe from Tami up here.

She'd never find this place.

They crossed a short, one-lane bridge that spanned the tiny creek running through Scott's property, and after several more windy curves, with no visible landmarks, Rich was surprised when Scott slowed to take a sharp left onto another unmarked road. At the juncture stood the remains of a very large, gnarled redwood that, judging from its blackened top, and the many divots in its lower bark, had been the victim of both a lightning strike and many an amateur driver in these woods. Even Scott had to navigate this with extra caution, and he barely managed to clear the trailer's left taillight with very slim margins.

They slowly traversed the next half-mile on a narrow, slightly better paved, asphalt and gravel road, Scott's "driveway."

At the end of this road was a flat clearing amongst the trees. The headlights swept across the lot, revealing Scott's two-story mountain home and the detached, three-car garage/workshop. A stacked cord of firewood ran most of the length of the building along one side. The tires crunched the loose gravel, then quieted when they met the pine needle-dusted fresh tar as Scott maneuvered their train directly in front of the wooden porch. The motion-activated porch lamp switched on and Scott doused the car lights.

"We're home, sleepy head," he said, cutting the engine.

Scott stealthily grabbed Rich's pager from the center console before his brother could and glanced at the tiny display: *22 Missed Calls.*

He shook his head and mumbled to himself, "Not gonna need this up here," then to Rich, "Let's get you to bed." He pocketed the contraption, grabbed Rich's duffle bag from the rear seat, and unlocked both deadbolts.

Rich stumbled out and made his way to the porch.

"First things first: we need to rustle you up a few tequila shots, bro."

◆

CHAPTER 44

TAMI HAD PULLED an all-nighter, and it showed. It was nearly 9:00 and she was still perched on the edge of the loveseat, in yesterday's clothes, with the phone pressed against her ear.

"Mailbox is full. Please try again later," the canned voice told her.

"Motherfucker!" Tami screamed as she hurled the handset into the couch.

She stepped over the hammer and navigated the piles of vinyl records she'd methodically destroyed, and stormed upstairs. Running on adrenaline at this point, she burst into the spare room/office, surveying the room again, the empty desk, and the wall where several framed pictures were conspicuously missing. As she approached the desk, she studied the wall calendar and its most recent entry, yesterday's: *NEW CLIENT*.

Tami's gaze drifted down to the office phone, the one with all of Rich's annotated work presets.

He'd forgotten to take it! She managed a half smile.

"Yes!" Tami punched the button marked *MIKE* and listened as it rang. "Please be home," she whispered, then heard it pick up. Thankfully she was spared the visual.

"Yeah, this is Mike," he barked, the definition of unsexy as he paraded shirtless and in his briefs, in his tiny kitchen. He scratched himself as he closed the fridge.

"Mike!" Tami said, all syrupy sweetness now. "How are you?"

"Who is this?" Mike said, furrowing his brow as he readied to pour milk onto his heaping bowl of Captain Crunch with Crunch Berries.

"Oh, sorry…it's Tami! Long time no talk to!"

"Jee-zus!" he said in disgust as he watched the rancid cottage cheese-consistency dairy slop falling out and smother his favorite cereal.

"Yeah, I know," Tami replied with a laugh. "It's been way too long."

Mike tossed the bowl onto the heap of other dishes in his sink, took a pull from the open carton of orange juice, and turned his attention to the phone.

"Tami? Wow," he replied, approaching pissed. "To what do I owe the pleasure? Wait. Don't tell me," he continued. "You and Richie are finally inviting me over to your place. For the first time, like, after *how* many years? Is that it?"

"Yeah, Mike…we definitely have plans to do that—we're long overdue," Tami said unconvincingly.

Mike pantomimed a masturbatory gesture. "Really," he said with an eye roll.

"Yeah…listen, Mike, I'm…planning a little surprise for Rich, and was wondering if you knew where he's working today?"

God, she was good.

"Nuh-uh."

"No idea?"

"Nope. Haven't seen him since he came in with that shiner the other day," he said.

"Oh, yeah!" Tami laughed awkwardly.

Mike found both her, and her response, to be a bit strange. "So, what's the, uh, surprise?"

"Oh—well, I'll tell you later, Mike, okay…hey, I've got another call coming in."

"Okay. Hey, Tami, how about telling your *husband* to call his *best friend* once in a while, all right? He's breaking a major pinky-swear promise, and that's not cool."

"Okay, thanks, Mike! I'll do that! Okay, buh-bye!" she said, hanging up. "Fuck!"

Now what?

Tami paused to scan the other names on the grid of fifty-nine other presets and stabbed another button.

"I'll find you," she whispered to the dial tone.

◆

CHAPTER 45

ETHEREAL RAYS OF fresh mountain sunshine sliced their way, like laser beams through the bountiful redwoods outside the patio slider. Rich squinted hazily out at this surreal display as Scott handed him a mug of coffee.

"Good morning, merry sunshine."

Rich rubbed his face for several moments, hoping to erase the mother of all hangovers. "I am so *never* having a drink again," he groaned.

Scott chuckled as he placed a plate containing a huge omelet and breakfast potatoes in front of Rich.

"Ever. Seriously. Gawd," Rich whimpered.

"Here. Eat this. You'll feel better…eventually," Scott said.

"Where's yours?" Rich asked, surveying the table.

"Already ate an hour ago. Don't let it get cold. I'll be back in a few," Scott said over his shoulder as he exited out onto the front porch. The screen door slammed behind him. Rich picked at his eggs.

Scott grabbed a box cutter from the top drawer of his impressive tool cart and proceeded to slice the seams of several cardboard boxes. Once he had enough pieces for the job, he took a roll of duct tape from its hook on the pegboard and began taping the cardboard panels to the inside of the glass window panes, blocking any view to the inside of the garage.

Satisfied, he separated the now-empty trailer from its hitch and drove the Explorer into the garage. After closing and locking the garage door, he walked over to the blackened window and tried to peer inside. He couldn't see anything. And most importantly, neither could Tami if she ever somehow managed to find her way up here.

After re-attaching the trailer to his own Suburban's hitch this time, he drove down the hill to turn it in at the rental yard in Scott's Valley.

◆

CHAPTER 46

ELLEN MUTED THE TV, redirecting Kailee's and Adam's attention from their favorite cartoon program long enough to establish some important safety protocols.

"Okay, let's review," she said, making eye contact with them both now. "So, what do we do if Aunt Tami calls on the phone and asks where Uncle Richie is?"

"Hang up!" Adam answered.

"Well…we don't have to be rude, Adam, but what else could we do?"

"Say we don't know. And call you," Kailee said.

"Good. Very good." Ellen said. "And, what should we do if Aunt Tami shows up at the door?"

"Kick her in the balls!" Adam offered helpfully.

"Adam!" Ellen said, horrified and at the same time trying to suppress a laugh. "Where did you learn language like that?" She regrouped and directed the earlier question to Kailee.

"And if Aunt Tami shows up—?"

"Look out the little peephole, and don't answer the door," she replied.

"And call you!" Adam chimed in.

"Yes, you're both right. Good job, guys!" Ellen said, a bit more relieved.

"Now can we turn the sound back on?" Adam pleaded.

"Yes, honey," she said and restored their precious *Scooby Doo*.

The phone rang in the kitchen. "Hello?"

"Hey, sis," Scott said.

Ellen poked her head into the living room and called out to the kids, "Please turn that down a little, I'm on the phone!"

Then, back to Scott, "Hey. How is he doing?"

"Nursing a bit of a—correction: nursing a very large—hangover, but he'll be fine. He's good," Scott said, holding his cell as he drove.

"Yeah? He probably needed that."

"Yep. I got up early and intercepted God-knows-how-many of Tami's rambling voicemails on his phone."

"Lord…" Ellen sighed.

"Yeah, the poor guy. I had no idea just how far gone she really is."

"Like what? What'd she say?"

"Mostly telling him what a loser he is: *Deadbeat—dipshit—mama's boy*—her words, the usual lovey-dovey marital talk, you know? Oh, but—get this: she loves him with all her heart and wants him to come home so *he* can get the therapy *he* needs."

"Gawd…thanks for taking one for the team there."

Scott turned into the U-Haul lot and eased to a stop. "Yeah, well, it ends here, and I'm sure not gonna let Richie listen to any more of that poison she's spewing. He seriously doesn't know up from down right now, and it's plain to see that she's equal parts manipulative and insane, if you ask me."

"Wow. How did we—how did the family—not see what was going on for all this time?"

"Well-kept secret, by them both. Speaking of family, you should hear what she has to say about us!"

"I can only imagine."

"Yeah…anyway, I stashed his car. Dropping off the trailer now. Back at the house in about twenty minutes if you need me."

"Good. My kids are dialed in too. A little confused, but they know what to do. Mom's worried sick, and Dad's been calling every hour it seems—wants to be in the know and in control, y'know?"

"I know…tell them both we're just hanging out up here and things are fine."

"Okay."

Scott could sense a hesitation in Ellen's voice, and after a moment she asked the million-dollar question, "Think she'll show up there?"

"She's never been up here, and she'd have a hell of a time finding us. She might try," he added, choosing his words carefully, "but she'd definitely regret it."

Ellen could only imagine the consequences. "All right. Call me later, okay?"

"Yep. Love you."

"Love you too."

◆

CHAPTER 47

TAMI HAD SPENT every waking moment over the past several days trying to reach every one of Rich's contacts, both professional and social. Not one of the presets had yet bore fruit. There were only a scant few she hadn't yet tried, and Rich's whereabouts remained a mystery. After she eliminated those, she thought, the only ones left were his family, which she was loathe to call, but she could leave no stone unturned. Time was of the essence, and she had to get Rich back before his family programmed him against her.

That's when she dug out the printed contact list of his family from the top drawer of Rich's desk. "The List," as it was known, contained not only phone numbers, but also birthdates, anniversaries, and—most importantly—home addresses of everyone in the Bryson family.

Would Rich drive back home to his parents', she wondered. Wouldn't put it past him, she thought. Probably went to hide at Mommy and Daddy's. Or Ellen's.

Or Maybe Scott's....

"Anywhere but with you!" the voices said, interrupting her.

"Fuck you! Shut up!" she screamed at the walls. That's where the voices lived, and she was outnumbered. "Fuck you," she whispered, beyond exhausted.

She thought about the options and was somewhat familiar with most of these residences, but she'd never been to Scott's place, and she'd heard that it was remote and in a woodsy area somewhere. She wracked her brain, pausing to smile at the ceiling and muttered, "It doesn't go with that!"

Then it came to her. Of course he'd go there!

"Told you!" the voice said.

"Shut up!" she yelled, flipping off the wall.

Moments later, she jumped in the car and went to the local auto club and requested one of their TripTik annotated maps. The agent had been very accommodating and prepared a detailed, highlighted, turn-for-turn route from her home to Scott's driveway.

◆

Tami's car barreled north on 101, weaving in and out of traffic, having abandoned the courtesy of using her turn indicators hours ago. Her red-rimmed eyes alternated between the map taped to her dash and the road ahead. Ben Lomond was highlighted, and the estimated travel time had been listed as seven hours. Which to her meant more like five. *If this clown would get out of the way!*

She took a bite out of the gas station ham sandwich in her left hand and laid on the horn as she got stuck behind a station wagon that was only going five miles over the posted speed. "Move it!" she yelled, spewing breadcrumbs. Another lean on the horn only produced momentary eye contact in the man's rearview mirror.

There was a vehicle in the left lane preventing Tami from passing, so she decided to just pass on the right. She yanked the wheel and lurched along the shoulder until she was parallel with the family in the station wagon. The driver honked as Tami recklessly squeezed alongside, and he had to make a slight jog left to avoid colliding with her. His wife reached across to the backseat to make sure their young daughter was secure and glared at Tami.

Tami flipped them off, and her expression was a combination of white-hot rage and utter madness. "Up yours, asshole!" she yelled as she zoomed by.

This was the first certifiably crazy person the wide-eyed three-year-old girl had ever seen, and she would likely never forget it.

◆

Tami had never had occasion to drive roads this dark, this absolute pitch black, before. Her eyes strained as she tried to make out any identifying information beyond the reach of her headlights. It'd be nice if they had some friggin' lights along this stretch, she thought, then she saw it. The sign:

WELCOME TO BEN (friggin') *LOMOND*

She turned down the country road, past the single, one-pump filling station and past a lot with rental cabins. Then the road curved a bit with nothing for a while until she saw a bizarre collection of chainsaw-carved bears some local yokel appeared to be advertising.

Nothing seemed open and nobody was around. No mall, no fast food stores, restaurants. Not much of a town, she thought. She turned on the car's dome light to consult the map but it made it impossible to drive, so she fired up her flashlight instead. She'd checked her odometer reading when she had exited the highway, and according to the printout, there should be a left turn coming up…anytime now.

If she'd blinked, she would've missed it, but her headlights caught the edge of a poorly marked road sign that was barely legible in this soup. Yep, that was it. Her impulse was to smile, but

her facial muscles were too heavy to oblige. She made the turn and
rubbed her eyes.

Five miles and she'd be there.

You can run, but you can't hide, Rich. Not from me.

◆

That five miles might as well have been fifty, between the twists and
turns, the potholes, the black hole she was driving through, and the
fact that she hadn't slept in a couple of days. Tami almost smacked
into the beat-up tree stump on her left and had almost added to its
legion of scars, before noticing the narrow road leading up beyond
it. Had to be it. God, please be it!

Fifteen agonizing minutes later, Tami's headlights revealed a
bank of mailboxes, one of which had the right house number on it.
There weren't any houses visible, so she continued up the road for
another five minutes before coming to a clearing and a home, visible
only by its dim porch light. She doused her own lights as she entered
the gravel driveway as slowly as possible as to not alert anyone. The
full moon snuck out from behind a bank of clouds long enough to
reveal a garage structure, which she decided to park behind.

Satisfied her car wasn't visible from the main house, she cut the
engine and remembered to flip her interior dome lights to the off
position before opening her door and exiting. She'd never heard a
cacophony of crickets like these. She hoped they'd drown out the
crunching sound her feet were making as she walked around to the
garage window. She put her nose against the glass but couldn't see
squat, so she proceeded to the porch.

No sign of Rich's SUV—surely it was hidden in the garage, next
to Scott's probably.

"You think I'm a dummy, Rich?" she murmured to herself.
"Well, you've got another think coming!" she answered quickly,
before the voices had a chance to weigh in.

She'd worn her sneakers tonight, thankfully, as the wooden porch planks were a bit creaky. Stealth was needed here, and she unscrewed the hot light bulb at the far end of the porch, with help from a shop rag she'd found by the garage. *That's better.* Now it was just the dimly illuminated doorbell button, the moonlight, and the crickets. And Commando Tami.

She reached for the doorknob and gave it a slow turn. Locked. As expected. That would've been too easy.

Tami didn't want to risk the flashlight here, so she relied on the intermittent moonlight as she scanned the darkened porch. She reached up above the door and felt along the ledge for a key, then under the weathered doormat. Nada.

Other than a lame, carved bear statue to the left of the door—definitely the handiwork of the bear-carving dude in town, she thought—there was nothing. The bear stared back at her as she weighed her next move. It was a long shot, but she'd come a long way and sure as hell wasn't going to be turned away this easily. She tested the weight of the statue and managed to tip it back slightly, just enough to reveal a shiny door key! Tada!

"Thank you, Lord!" she whispered, because clearly God was on her side.

Tami inserted the key into both the deadlock and the main locks and hit pay dirt. Thankfully, they were keyed alike, and she swung the door open slowly to diminish the slight creak it produced.

Closing the door behind her, she looked around the darkened main room for any evidence of Rich. Seeing nothing, she quietly traversed the shag-carpeted floor and stopped at the stairwell leading to the floor below.

The house was as quiet as a tomb, and she took her time to silently descend the carpeted steps to the lower level. Once there, she noticed some light escaping from underneath the first closed door in the hallway. Her heart raced as she took a deep breath and reached for the doorknob.

She burst inside, throwing the door wide.

"Found you, you son of a bitch!" she said with a demented laugh.

She'd spoken too soon, and she registered alarm—and disappointment—as she stared at the gaunt, grizzled seventy-something man looking back at her. Not the son of a bitch she was looking for.

Roy, wide-eyed, sat up in his single bed, dropped his Louis L'amour book and looked like he might soil himself as he regarded the intruder.

"Who are you?" she said too loudly.

"Who the hell are *you*? That's the question," he said indignantly, removing his glasses.

Tami didn't answer. Instead her eyes darted around the room, looking for any sign of Rich. She opened the closet and looked inside.

"Where is he?"

"Where is who?!" Roy replied angrily as he jumped up and hastily threw a weathered robe over his long underwear.

"Rich! My husband! I know he's here! I'm not leaving without him!" she frothed. "Rich!" she yelled out to the house, to the woods.

Roy reached under the bed, retrieving his .22 rifle.

"Well, that's where we're in disagreement, young lady."

◆

CHAPTER 48

ELLEN REPLENISHED HER brothers' wine glasses with generous pours from a fresh bottle of her favorite Cabernet. They'd polished off the Zinfandel with dinner, which paired nicely with her lasagna.

"Thanks," Rich said.

"No more for me. Well, okay!" Scott laughed.

"Atta boy. Been saving this bottle for just the right moment. I guess this is it," Ellen said.

"How sad is that?" Rich muttered to himself.

Ellen moved from the couch to the adjoining chair—her chair, the one the kiddos were forbidden to climb on—and poured herself one. She could hardly wait to taste this one. She'd been sitting on the bottle for a decade. Scott watched as Ellen ceremoniously swirled the wine in her glass before bringing it up for closer inspection. She closed her eyes and stuck her nose deep into the glass, completely enveloping herself in the complex bouquet of this special occasion nectar.

"Oh, my goodness…come to mama." She smiled as she raised her glass to her siblings.

"To Rich, and…" Scott said, blanking.

"…the future!" Ellen chimed in, rescuing the toast.

"I don't think I have a future, but thanks just the same," Rich muttered.

"Sure you do, Richie," Ellen replied.

"Absolutely, you do. C'mon!" Scott clinked their glasses. "This too shall pass, brother. Cheers!"

They all took a sip except Rich, whose glass emptied in one big gulp. Ellen's gut reaction was to remind them that this was a hundred-and-fifty-dollar bottle, but now was not the time. After they'd drained the bottle and its twin, they exchanged hugs in the doorway.

"Thanks for a great dinner, sis," Scott said.

"That was the best meal I've ever had," Rich said, which brought a chuckle from his brother. Rich had said the exact same thing about the omelet that morning.

"Glad you enjoyed it. Richie, we'll get through this together, you'll see. Promise. I've been there, and I know it sucks, but we're on your team, and we're gonna win. Okay?" Ellen offered, along with her best hug.

"'Kay...thanks. For everything. Love you," Rich said, returning his best hug.

Ellen hugged Scott and gave him a long look. "You're sure you're good to drive?"

"Like ridin' a bike," Scott said with a smile.

She held his gaze a moment longer, assessing his level of sobriety, before touching his cheek—signaling approval.

Having been married to—and now divorced from—an alcoholic, she'd become a pretty good judge of what *too buzzed to drive* looked like, and Scott was good to go.

She walked them out to the Suburban, shivering from the evening chill and waved as they drove off.

◆

CHAPTER 49

I T WAS JUST another otherworldly-nice Ben Lomond morning. The sky was intensely blue, polluted by puffy white clouds and skyscraper-tall redwoods. ViewMaster worthy.

The rather butch Ben Lomond policewoman stepped onto the front porch and adjusted the squelch on her radio as she reached the door. She regarded the carved bear, then noticed the illuminated doorbell, which was set into what appeared to be the sphincter of a deer's behind. She shook her head. She'd seen it all up here, but this was a first. She pushed the button, hoping not to hear a fart sound, or worse. At least it was a normal sounding chime.

Scott emerged, offered the officer a cup of coffee, and they settled in on the porch, leaning against the deck railing. Seated nearby on a bench was Roy, still in his robe and fidgety.

The officer took a few moments to jot down Scott's personal information, pausing a couple of times to shake the last bit of life out of her failing ballpoint. "Sorry. You said she entered illegally?"

"That's right."

"Any signs of forced entry?"

"Nah. She found the key I had stashed under there," Scott said, nodding toward the bear.

"I see," the officer said, scribbling. "And she barged in and surprised you?" she asked, looking up from her notes.

"Not me," Rich replied. "My roommate. Roy," he added, gesturing to the man holding the trembling coffee mug.

"He lives here part time," Scott continued. "Used to work for me, needs a place to stay for a while. Nearly deaf, so he wouldn't have heard her come in. Poor guy—scared the shit out of him."

Roy hoisted himself from his chair and set his coffee on the railing. "Ain't deaf!" he barked.

"Good morning, sir," the officer said.

"And I reckon it's her 'at was scared shitless!" Roy said.

The officer stifled a smile as she added to her notes.

"I'm going to file a restraining order," Scott said.

"Mm, probably not a bad idea from the sounds of it," she replied. "Might want to change your locks too."

"Yep."

They all turned as Rich came out onto the porch clutching a coffee.

"Mornin'," he said to everyone.

"Good morning. You're the husband?" the officer asked.

"I'm afraid so," Rich replied with an embarrassed nod.

The officer studied Rich for a moment. It had mostly healed, but there was still the telltale yellow to his shiner. "Would you consider your wife to be dangerous, sir?" she asked.

Rich stared down into his mug.

"Sir, has your wife ever threatened you with harm or exhibited violent behavior?" the officer pressed gently.

Rich looked up and met her eyes. He took his time before answering, "Yes, ma'am, she has."

The officer nodded her head slightly, closing her pad. "Believe it or not," she said to Rich, sensitively yet matter-of-factly, "you're not the only one."

Rich looked at her blankly, not sure if he was hearing her correctly. Of course he's the only one. He's a man.

"It's not as widely reported—far from it—but of the domestic violence reports I've seen, several have involved female-on-male violence," she continued to the group.

Rich's brow furrowed. "Seriously? Wait, there's others?" he said, dumbfounded. "And here I thought I had a lock on that demographic," he added, his voice trailing off.

"It's sad, but it's true. Domestic violence—spousal abuse—is an equal opportunity offender. Most guys don't report it, mostly from embarrassment. That's why you don't hear about it much at all really," the officer said before adding, "You were smart to get out when you did, sir."

Rich looked at his feet, doing his best to process this and absorbing the enormity of the fact that he wasn't the only male human on this planet who was going through their own personal version of this nightmare. Scott put a comforting hand on Rich's shoulder.

"I've seen these situations turn out badly. Real badly," the officer offered. "I know it's hard to comprehend right now, but you shouldn't feel guilty for leaving. Not at all."

Rich looked at his feet and nodded slightly. "That'll be a hard one to get my head around," Rich replied.

"I can imagine so, but you will. You will."

"Anything else you need from us, officer?" Scott asked.

"No. That's all," she replied.

"Thanks for coming out," Scott said.

"Yes, thank you, ma'am…Officer," Rich said softly.

"No problem. My report will be filed today. And now that we have a description of both her and her car, we'll keep an eye out," she said as she started down the steps. Then she paused and turned back to them. "If she's half as smart as you say she is, she probably made a hasty exit out of town and won't be back," she said. "But watch your back, just the same."

"We will," Scott said.

They watched the officer's vehicle descend the drive, and Scott squeezed Rich's shoulder.

"C'mon, bro. Let's get some breakfast. Believe me, you're gonna need it today."

◆

CHAPTER 50

A FTER A FEAST that would satiate any lumberjack, Scott set his favorite iron skillet aside and put the other dishes in the sink to soak. The scramble he'd concocted was comprised of six eggs, a pinch of fresh spinach leaves, some wild boar sausage from his most recent bow hunt, chopped onions, minced garlic, and a little shredded Monterey Jack all mixed together with his famous red breakfast potatoes. Add to that a full pot of freshly ground French Roast, some local cider, half a loaf of sourdough, and the best orange marmalade around from the little bakery he'd stopped at in Scotts Valley. It was tasty and would definitely hold them for a while on this, Rich's first day of school.

Rich followed his brother into the garage, which was impressive both for its organization as well as its vast collection of implements. It was like nothing he'd ever seen, actually, like a modern tool museum.

Scott pointed to a pair of well-worn work boots next to the door. "Shake 'em out good before you put 'em on," he said.

"Shake them out? What for?" Rich asked.

Scott took the other pair and shook them hard, then turned them upside down. Out dropped a tiny black scorpion, which he crunched in its tracks. "That's what for, little brother," he said, laughing at the look of horror on Rich's face.

Rich banged his boots together, shaking them violently, then repeating the process several times before slipping them on.

Scorpions?! *Are we in Arizona?*

He followed Scott over to the far wall, where the heavy artillery was stored. Scott selected his favorite of the three chainsaws and grabbed two sturdy pair of work gloves from the tool bench. He tossed a pair to Rich.

"Here, put these on. And these," he added, handing Rich some protective goggles and a hard hat, which Rich studied before donning.

Scott led them out to the driveway clearing and looked up at the tree line facing his front porch. He pointed to a dying madrone that was leaning perilously in their direction.

"That one. She's gotta go. Before it takes out my roof," he said. Scott carried his implements over to the base of the madrone and did some mental calculations. It would be tight, and he'd have to plan the cut angle perfectly in order to avoid demolishing either his garage roof or his porch overhang.

Rich pressed down on his hard hat as he stared upward through the goggles. Yep, it sure looked pretty dead. Probably tall enough to hit the property too, he imagined. He was ready to ask a question about the tree when the deafening scream of the chainsaw interrupted his thoughts, making him jump. He looked over at Scott, who was waving him over to a place of safety.

He was only too happy to comply, running to the safe zone.

Rich watched with wonder and pride at his brother's abilities. He could never live this remote mountain lifestyle; of this he was sure. Scorpions, chainsaws, killer trees, and the like were outside of his realm of understanding, and it was all black magic to him. He had a healthy respect for Scott, and he looked up to him for that.

Scott made several small cuts, stopping each time to study the desired trajectory before slicing deeper into the malignant tree's trunk. The tree was starting to lean a little more now, and it was close to the moment of truth. There was no acceptable margin of error.

"She's gonna go, Richie! Stay back where you are!" Scott yelled over to him, waiting for Rich's thumbs-up gesture before delivering the deathblow. One last cut produced a sharp, cracking sound. Scott cut power to the saw and jumped back from the stump as the madrone began its dive. Her diseased branches scraped their way through those of the healthy neighboring trees, and both men held their breath as they watched them plummet down, until it all landed with a thunderous crash.

Scott removed his goggles and surveyed his work. She'd cleared the porch overhang by four feet, and the same from the garage. The proud surgeon smiled.

"Wow!" Rich said, looking at the felled giant. "Looks like you've done this before," he laughed.

"Yeah. Couple of times," Scott said, walking away.

"That was so cool," Rich said to himself.

"Glad you think so, brother," Scott said, handing him an axe. "'Cause we've got a lot of firewood to chop," he added, nodding to the impressively stacked woodpile, "and stack." He smiled.

"Isn't that why God invented Presto-Logs?" Rich replied, looking at the foreign chopping implement in his hand.

Scott began chain sawing the tree into smaller, manageable pieces—about fifteen inches in length—so as to fit his rustic, free-standing fireplace. Rich grabbed one of the pieces, stood it atop the old redwood stump, and took a big swing, missing it completely. Scott laughed to himself as he watched his brother take his hacks. *Best way to learn.*

He was going to make a mountain man out of Rich yet. If nothing else, this should take his mind off Whistle-Britches—Scott's new nickname for Tami—for the time being.

◆

Three hours passed, and by 11:00, the day had turned into a scorcher. Scott delivered another wheelbarrow full of firewood to Rich, who was stacking it neatly, like puzzle pieces. Rich had long ago ditched the flannel work shirt and stopped to wipe the sweat from his brow.

"Not bad for a first-timer, Rich!"

"Glad you approve," he said, almost collapsing. "How much more?"

"Last of it right here," Scott said, dumping the load at his feet.

"Thank God!" Rich said.

"When you're done put the tarp over it and cinch it down. The bricks go on top. I'll rustle up some lunch."

"You'd better, or I'm filing a grievance against this sweatshop!"

They shared a tired laugh, and Scott proceeded inside.

◆

CHAPTER 51

THE TWO LUMBERJACKS polished off their foot-long hoagies, the entire large bag of barbecue chips, and a large can of pork and beans. Rich had been in charge of heating those up, and he took pause upon opening the can to find that ever-enticing, floating globule of fatty tissue they dare called "pork." Rich didn't know if it was pig scrotum or snout, but whatever it was he carefully scooped it off the top and tossed it down the disposal. Technically not kosher, sure, but not pork by any stretch of the imagination.

They also polished off three beers each. It was Coors, so it was almost like drinking water after their hard work. Scott let out a belch that could probably be heard down the hill in Scotts Valley.

Rich picked up his cellphone and looked at the display. Zero bars of reception.

"Would you stop looking at that damn thing? I told you, you're not gonna get reception up here, plus you don't need to be listening to any more of her psycho rant bullshit," Scott said, crumpling the beer can.

"Okay, but if I were to rig a couple of sticks to my phone, where'd be the best place to go dousing for a signal up here? Gotta check for work calls, man…I'm dyin'," Rich said, not hiding his frustration.

"About a half mile down the road, down by the mailboxes. You can get a signal there usually."

Rich nodded, licking the barbeque chip residue off his fingers.

"You tell anyone you were leaving? Where you were going?" Scott asked.

"No. No way," Rich said.

"Good. Don't. I'll shoot that varmint myself next time she tries showin' up here."

His chores for the day were done and Scott popped the tab on his fourth Coors. He turned to Rich. "Look, I can loan you some money while you're looking for work up here."

"Thanks, but I'm not exactly sure what kind of work I can get filming for the Firewood Channel," Rich replied. "Sorry. Didn't mean it to come out that way. I appreciate it. Everything, man."

"I know," Scott said. "Still…think about it."

"I will. Thanks for lunch," Rich said, getting up from the table. "Wish me luck."

Scott took a gulp and nodded. "Yep. And don't forget to check the mail while you're down there." Rich nodded and left. Scott stared out at his redwoods.

His babies.

◆

The hike to the mailboxes wasn't terrible; it was all downhill, after all. But it'd all be uphill on the way back. Rich tried not to think about that and instead focused his attention on the phone's display, and its *zero freaking bars!*

As he lumbered down the hill, he wondered just how much work he'd lost since he'd been up here. Work calls had been pouring in, he'd been working a lot, started on some new shows, and now nobody—except his family—knew where he was. This sucked royally.

This concerned him on many levels: not only was his career at stake, but the bills would continue to stack up, like so much firewood. His and Tami's.

Despite what the police officer had told him, Rich still couldn't help but feel guilty for leaving Tami. He'd taken his marriage vows very seriously, and now he felt like pond scum for leaving his wife so suddenly. She was troubled, that was for sure, and he wondered if Tami had enough food to eat. Was she okay? Did he make a huge mistake? Should he go back? Every possible doubt crossed his mind over the course of that half mile, and he felt like an absolutely horrible person.

Then, as he approached the mailboxes, he witnessed a small miracle: two bars of reception on his display! "Praise Jeezus," Rich said as he saw his display indicate a gazillion missed voicemails. He sat down on a nearby log and listened to each, deleting several. The messages from Tami alternated between sugary and venomous, and her mood, and state of mind, could turn on a dime during any given one. She recited her epiphany mantra during several of them, and now that he was removed from it, he noticed just how truly bizarre it—and she—sounded. *Delete, delete, delete.*

The next message made him pause, listen, and smile.

He hung up and hurriedly punched in the numbers. He prayed they picked up. *Please. Please. Please. Please.*

"Yes, hi, this is Rich Bryson, returning a call to Kenny," he said, trying not to sound too excited. "Yes, I'll hold." He offered up another silent prayer as he waited, then the familiar voice came on the line.

"Kenny! Hey! Yeah, it's me, Rich," he said, a broad smile finding his face for the first time in quite a while. "No. I'm out of town, just got your message," he said, apologetically. "Did you already call my home number?"

As he listened to Kenny's reply, the color drained from his face.

"You did, huh? Did you leave a message?" he asked, terrified of the answer. "Mmm…okay," he said softly. *Crap!*

"No worries. Yeah. So, where? Mm-hmm. Tacoma? Hell, yes, I'm available!" As Rich listened to the details he also thanked his lucky stars for the work. "Yeah, very cool, Kenny! Say, if it's all the same, do you think you could fly me out of San Jose this time? Yeah…yeah, long story," he replied.

◆

CHAPTER 52

TAMI PUT ON one of her best performances as she wound down her phone call with the Seattle-based company that had hired the production crew. "Yes, I know that hotel and the school's location," she lied, "and I appreciate your help so much. This will be a great article and great press for your awesome organization. I'll be sure to send you a copy of the article once our paper's published it. Perfect! Okay, bye-bye!"

Tami hung up Rich's business phone and thrust a celebratory fist in the air. "Yes!!!"

Her next call was to Alaska Airlines. She should have enough on her MasterCard, she thought. If not, she had two Visas. Hopefully one of them would still work.

It was going to be tough waiting these next few weeks, but she'd continue to work his phones in the event she could locate him sooner. At least she had something for now. Surely he missed her.

See you soon, Rich! Soon we'll be back together!

◆

CHAPTER 53

FOR THE BETTER part of a month, Rich tried to do damage control from his hidden bunker. Going underground was career suicide, but was necessary, and he couldn't risk telling a single one of his contacts where he was now holed up. *Gawd! Shoot me now!*

On your best day, it was hard enough being a freelancer, working in a town flooded with other freelancer talent—your competition—all trying to grab the same gigs, work the same shows, win the same clients, impress the same directors and, sometimes, even steal others' clients. Rich didn't play that portion of the game; he didn't have to. But you were only as good as your last job, and if you've been out of the loop for any length of time, or, as in his case, if you've wholly vanished from the face of the frickin' earth, well, good luck getting back in the loop.

He'd worked so hard for so many years on so many shoots and had clawed his way toward the top of his profession. Rich's career and stellar reputation as the Human Tripod were now at risk of extinction. Trying to find work up here, doing what he had been doing—and what he was truly good at—was proving to be impossible, and that sad reality had begun to set in. And it was depressing as hell.

It had also been a hassle changing his address to a personal mailbox at the local grocery store in Scotts Valley, but that was the price of doing business. Some of his bills were beginning to arrive here now, and he was damned if he knew how he was going to pay them, now that he was forcibly removed from his reliable income stream. He'd changed his bank account over to the little one-teller micro branch, also in the grocery store. This must be what it felt like to be in the Witness Protection Program, he thought, and he didn't like it one bit.

He'd managed to squeak out a few mortgage payments with the small remaining balance in his account. Wouldn't want Tami being thrown out in the street after all, would we? Sheesh... Rich had been able to take a couple of stealthy two-day jobs in enemy territory here and there, but they involved a whole day of driving each way, and he'd had to pony up for a motel stay each time, plus gas, plus food, not to mention that he had to drive right by his old freeway exit to get there. Passing right by his neighborhood, that was the scary part. It fed his paranoia to think that at any moment Tami might recognize his vehicle, and the rest, well...oy.

On the few gigs he'd had down there, he'd innocently asked the client, without tipping them off, if they'd called his home number, and two of them had said no. One of them replied in the affirmative, adding that Tami had grilled them for information, but they hadn't obliged, and that she'd been rather unpleasant as a result. That information wasn't much of a shocker, but he felt compelled to apologize for her behavior and did so without elaborating further.

Before he'd left for the airport, Rich hired a local process server. He took a deep breath as he thought about all of this, but decided to let those concerns go by the wayside, for now, as he looked out his window of the regional jet, on his way to the Tacoma gig he'd set up with Kenny.

Down below, one of his favorite views: the Three Sisters volcanoes in Oregon. It was because of these that he always asked for a window seat on his flights north. They were awesome to behold, these snow-covered bumps on the landscape. He wondered if there might be an eruption in the foreseeable future. Who knows? He sighed. If so, perhaps they should rename the one that spews most "Mount Tami."

He smiled as he crunched the last pretzel from the teeny-tiny snack bag and settled back in his seat. It was going to be great to see his cohorts and to be working again.

◆

CHAPTER 54

KENNY, THE PRODUCER/DIRECTOR/FELLOW camera guy who had hired Rich, was an amiable teddy bear of a man, really, and his crew enjoyed working for him. He'd assembled his usual suspects again; he was very loyal that way. Twenty years of production experience had taught him to always plan for the dreaded X-factor, whether it be equipment malfunctions, weather problems, or missed flights. There was reliability and comfort in having the same crew guys for these gigs. Not to mention copious amounts of fun to be had, especially working in a town known for its microbrew.

He'd had the travel person schedule all of the flights to have as close to coinciding arrival times as possible, thus avoiding unnecessary cab fares and the like. Also, having all hands meet at the baggage claim carousel assured that all of the thirty-five cases of gear and luggage were wrangled quickly, efficiently, and equitably.

Rich's flight was the last to arrive, just a scant twenty minutes later than the rest of the crew, who had flown out of Orange County. He'd received a text telling him which baggage claim area to meet at. When Rich arrived, pulling his single wheeled case, he noticed that the lion's share of the gear had come off the carousel already and was being carefully stacked on a couple of flat dollies by two baggage handlers. Rich gave each crew guy a quick bro-hug and went about wrangling the remaining Anvil cases from the carousel. These were particularly heavy due to the many batteries they contained, and he couldn't help but wonder if the guys had saved these ones for him. *Nah!*

Three large tripod tubes were the last of the oversized items to come off, and when all of the luggage tags were tallied against the piles of gear, Kenny directed the baggage guys to the curb where two large Suburbans and two minivans were just pulling up. Kenny coordinated the vehicles' arrivals by walkie talkie, which each vehicle driver also had.

Kenny's crew had done a million of these shoots together over the past decade and by now it was a well-oiled machine. He peeled off several bills from the wad in his pocket, thanked and tipped the two porters, and the video crew began loading the gear. This part was always a bit tricky, as they had seven crew guys to fit in the vehicles along with the gear, plus their personal luggage. And only a few minutes to do it, with the airport security hustling them along.

Rich helped Kenny stuff the three tripod tubes into the rear SUV, and then the delicate electronics, which were piled atop the rest of the gear. The three video cameras were always carried in padded, zippered carryon cases, along with a battery, so they would pass Security's scrutiny, and they would assuredly arrive in good working order. Suitcases went in the minivans, along with the guys.

Kenny would only begin to relax a little once the crew was checked in, the cameras were safely stowed up in his room, the batteries were all on chargers, and, most importantly, he had a couple of Seattle's finest amber ales in his belly.

He could almost taste them.

Kenny did a walkie check with each driver, and they were on their way to the hotel, like a presidential motorcade, but without the escort. And perhaps an escort would've been advisable.

Rich found himself sandwiched between two larger guys in the rearmost seat of one of the minivans. He didn't mind; he was just happy to be there, and he smiled all the way to the hotel.

◆

CHAPTER 55

I F TAMI WAS consistent about one thing, it was that she always managed to run late. Always. And she was again, right now, as she awkwardly brought her suitcase out through the front door and watched it tumble down the steps to the common area pavement.

"Shit," she mumbled as she jammed her key into the deadbolt lock. She might miss her flight! Before she could turn around, she heard a man's voice.

"Tami? Tami Bryson?"

She turned around to find a moderately attractive Hispanic man standing in the common area. He was wearing slacks and a sport coat, along with a smile. He seemed to know her.

"Hi...do I know you?" She smiled.

"Tami Bryson, right?" he said like an old friend.

"Yes, I'm Tami. I'm sorry, have we worked together?" She righted her suitcase and tried to figure out where.

He took a step closer, reached into his breast pocket and produced an envelope, which he handed to her.

"Um, what's this?"

"Tami Bryson, you've been served," he said, the smile gone now, and he walked away.

"Oh, yeah?! Well, fuck *you*, too, motherfucker!" she screamed after him, throwing the envelope down. "And fuck you, Rich," she muttered through clenched teeth as she hurried toward the carport.

She wasn't going to miss this flight!

◆

CHAPTER 56

I T WAS ONE of Tacoma's most popular pizza/brew pubs, and the crew—eight of them—were assembled around a large table littered with appetizers: wings, stuffed jalapeños, potato skins, the whole nine. Kenny traditionally bought the first round of drinks, and this was no exception.

They were currently enjoying their third round of some new-to-them local microbrews, recommended by their twenty-something, much-tattooed, ear gauge-wearing, tragically-hip server. Rich had to give the guy points for steering them toward some fine brews, though. He was surprised to find his palate morphing toward the India pale ales, with their hoppy-yet-not-too-bitter flavors and smooth, almost-grapefruity notes. The taste was complex—not unlike his life now—and not for everybody, but somehow he found it pleasing.

Kenny took a swig from his frosty amber and wiped the head from his mustache. The rest of the guys were yucking it up at the other side of the table, which gave Kenny and Rich a chance to catch up.

"Richie, we've missed you, brother. Glad you could join us!" he said, and he meant it.

"Believe me, Kenny, it's good to be here. Thanks for the call, man…" Rich replied, his voice trailing off.

"Of course, my man, of course," Kenny said. After a slightly awkward pause, he tested the waters. "Very sorry to hear about you and the missus," he said. "How long's it been, Richie?"

"Filed and been separated—trying to get divorced—several months now, I guess. Kinda losing track of time, to be honest. Been living underground since I left LA."

"Wow. Huh…so, how's work?"

"Ha!" Richie laughed louder than he'd intended to. "Funny you should ask," he said, taking a pull of ale.

"Do tell," Kenny said, resting his hand on Rich's shoulder. "Only if you want to, though."

Rich shook his head and set down his glass. "I've been out of the loop for so long now; nobody knows where I am—I can't tell anybody—and I can't work in LA for fear she'll show up. And it's been really hard—understatement—to reinvent myself up north. Between trying to keep payments up on the house, sending her money when I can, car payments—mine and hers—and now attorney fees to the tune of three hundred fifty bucks an hour, I'm hemorrhaging, man. Sucks."

"Ouch, that's rough, dude," Kenny said softly, gesturing to their server to bring two more.

"Seriously, Kenny, I appreciate your bringing me along on this," Rich said, looking at him earnestly.

"Dude, you'll always be on my "A" team. You can count on that, okay, Rich?"

"Yeah," he replied with a half-smile, and they clinked glasses.

◆

She'd never seen the Three Sisters before, and they were an intriguing sight with the white slopes beginning to turn slightly pink from the coming sunset. Tami turned from the window.

"Awesome!" she said quietly to herself.

The man in the next seat put his book down and turned to her. "I'm sorry, did you say something?" he asked.

"Oh, no. I didn't," she replied, returning to the window.

The man shrugged and went back to his novel.

"*It doesn't go with that!*" the voices said.

◆

CHAPTER 57

KENNY'S TEAM, ALL eight of them, was now standing in the lobby of the motel. It'd been a fun dinner, judging from how goofy they were being as they stood there waiting for their fearless leader to announce the morning call time.

The crew guys were all in their early-to-mid-forties. There were three sound guys: Greg, Mark, and Nick. The camera department consisted of Kenny, Billy, and Rich. One production assistant/Jill of all trades: Jill (duh), and the client, Mary. As clients went, Mary was the coolest, and could truly become one of the guys on these gigs.

"Five fifteen, out the door, gentlemen!" Kenny said.

"Ahem…" Mary cleared her throat teasingly.

"And ladies!" Dave corrected.

Mary laughed at this, also at knowing that her call time would be an hour later, at the location. She was the client, after all.

Nick, the lone Hispanic in the bunch, was also known to be the most vocal. "Five fifteen! Fuckin' A!"

"Nick…" Kenny began, as if correcting his child.

"Sorry, man, but that's way early," Nick said.

"First day's load-in, gear check, cable runs…nothing new here, guys," Kenny said, digging out his key. "Wheels up, 5:15…goodnight, everybody!" he said.

A couple of groans from the guys, but everybody verbally confirmed the call time before heading for the elevators. They arrived at the third floor and said their goodnights. Rich's room was down the hall a ways, directly across from Nick's, near the ice machine. Rich was so tired, he didn't think he'd hear anything tonight.

"Fuckin' A," said Nick, belching as he closed his door.

"Yep." Rich nodded and put his card key into the door slot. The flashing green light welcomed him inside. It'd been a while since he'd worked with Kenny and the gang, and he wasn't accustomed to consuming this many adult beverages with his evening meal. These guys even topped his brother. He hoped he wouldn't regret it in the morning.

After changing into jammies, he brushed his teeth and dialed the lobby, requesting a 4:30 wake-up. Man, it'd been a while since he had one of those, he thought.

Once Rich flicked off the light, he fell into a deep, coma-like sleep within minutes.

◆

CHAPTER 58

THE PHONE WAS surreally loud when it rang, jolting Rich from whatever dream he was having. Was he dreaming now? He looked over at the clock radio display, which read 11:40. *What the hell?!* He fumbled in the dark until his hand clumsily found the receiver and he raised it to his ear.

"Emm...hello?" he mumbled groggily.

Silence.

He was about to hang up, when he heard a familiar voice answer.

"Hi, Rich," she said.

Rich's eyes blinked rapidly, and he was instantly, fully awake.

"Rich, it's me," she said, a combination of seductive and sing-songy. "It's Tami!"

Rich jolted upright in his bed, his eyes widened, and he could almost see in the dark now—like a cat. His heart began to race. This was not happening. Definitely a nightmare. He slapped his face to wake from it.

"Rich?"

"Tami?" he managed through the alarm bells in his head.

"Yes! I'm here!" Tami said.

Rich shook his head to clear the cobwebs. Obviously he'd heard incorrectly. "What? Wait...you're where?"

"I'm here, silly. At the hotel. I'm in the lobby!" she said, winking at the night desk clerk who allowed her use of the guest phone. He paid little attention as he busied himself with his guest folios.

Rich flipped the lamp's switch and squinted in pain as the bright light stabbed his eyes. He said nothing.

"I wanted to surprise you!" she said through his handset.

He rubbed his face and looked at the clock.

"Tami, do you know what time it is? I—"

"I know it's late, I'm sorry…I got the last flight in," she said. She had expected more of a response from him. She looked over at the desk clerk and lowered her voice to a whisper before continuing. "So, what room are you in? The guy at the desk wouldn't give that out for some reason. I mean, we're married…"

This wasn't happening!

Rich put the receiver to his other ear, hoping this was just a bad connection. But it wasn't. "Look, Tami. I'm not going to give you my room number. I have a very early call and have to get up in a few hours, and you—"

"Come on. I just want to say hi. What's your room number?" she said too sweetly.

"Tami. You aren't hearing me. I have to get to sleep. This isn't right, and you know it," Rich said with a bit more resolve.

"You do remember what tomorrow is, don't you, Rich?" she asked.

It was late, he was probably still a little buzzed, and his psycho wife was stalking him. He wracked his brain and couldn't for the life of him think what tomorrow was. "Monday," he ventured.

"It's my birthday, silly," she admonished playfully.

"Mm…happy birthday, Tami," he said, exhausted by both the hour and the conversation.

"I thought we could spend some time together, talk about things—"

"Tami! Are you serious? I'm hanging up. How about we talk about this…another time? Or, better—"

"If not tonight, Rich, when? I'm here now, honey," she pleaded.

He regurgitated a desperate response in hopes of ending the conversation.

"How about tomorrow evening, after I get done?"

"What time do you get done?"

"I don't know…four or five, probably," he said weakly.

"You'll call me tomorrow after work?"

"Yes," he lied. "Tomorrow."

"Okay, honey…I can't wait to see you. I—"

Rich hung up the phone and jumped out of bed. He doused the light and paced in the darkened room. "Fuck!" he whispered to himself, in full panic mode now. He went back over to the nightstand and pulled out the phonebook, grabbed a book light from his duffle, and began rifling through the dimly-lit pages until he came to the listings for hotels. He jotted a couple of notes on the memo pad and began repacking his clothes.

As he padded over to the bathroom for his toiletries, he heard the unmistakable ping of the elevator chime, which froze him in his tracks. He darted over to the bed and switched off the book light, casting the room into pitch dark again. He stood by the door, listening, and trying to regulate his breathing.

A few moments went by before he heard the sound of a wheeled suitcase coming his way. He jammed his eye against the peephole and prayed that it was some other late arrival. Anybody. *Anybody but Tami. Please.*

The sound stopped, somewhere down the hall, and he saw no movement. He was about to turn away from the door when he heard the sound of the wheels resume, louder now, coming closer…closer. Then they stopped.

Right outside his door.

And there she was, looking at her key card, standing right outside his door.

Jeeeeee-zus!

Rich stopped breathing and kept his eyeball glued to the peephole. And just as quickly, she went out of view. The next sound he heard was that of a key card slipping into the door lock of the room next door. The door opened, the case was wheeled inside, and the door closed, then locked.

He placed his ear against the adjoining wall and could hear her settling in. She was here, and if he could hear her, she could hear him!

"Okay, okay, okay, okay," he whispered to himself, trying not to hyperventilate. He padded silently back and forth, trying to think.

He silently placed the rest of his belongings into his suitcase and set the alarm function on his wristwatch: 4:00. He unplugged the room phone's jack.

He didn't know if he could, but he'd have to try to get a couple hours' sleep if he wanted to survive this deal.

◆

CHAPTER 59

RICH HAD CHOSEN the room's sofa, on the far side of the room, on which to crash for the few hours still available to him. He'd purposely fallen asleep with his left wrist under his head in order to hear the chirp of the watch's alarm, which was now sounding: *Chirp. Chirp. Chirp.* Deafeningly loud, he thought, as he stabbed the tiny buttons until it finally stopped. He prayed Tami hadn't heard that.

Despite being sleep deprived and having consumed several beers before bed, he awoke with a clear head. He couldn't remember thinking with such clarity, actually, as this was adrenaline-infused survival mode kicking in, and there was no margin for error in this scenario. What did they call this? Fight or flight? He was too tired to fight, and he'd been there, done that—and got the tee shirt.

He skipped his shower as to not risk further noise, and after splashing cold water on his face and brushing his teeth, he threw his toiletries in his bag and slowly, agonizingly zipped his case and carried it to the door.

He turned the brass door handle slowly, silently, and peeked out into the hall. He looked both directions, then grabbed his *DO NOT DISTURB* sign and gently placed it on the door handle to Tami's room. He hoped that would buy him a little time.

Once outside, he took his time closing his door, exacting all of the care a bomb technician would take to defuse an explosive, until it finally, gently…clicked.

The suitcase was quite heavy, but he elected to schlep it versus risking a squeaky wheel. As the elevator doors closed, he took his first breath in several minutes, and looked at his watch: 5:01.

At the lobby, he wheeled his case past the desk and was headed for the glass doors when the clerk's voice called after him. "Sir?"

"Yes?" Rich replied, turning toward the bubbly-for-this-hour blonde teen manning the morning desk.

"Good morning. Are you checking out?" she asked, smiling.

"Me? No…I mean, not yet. I'm just…taking this to the car."

"Oh, okay. Everything going well with your stay so far?" she asked.

"Oh, yeah. Perfect! Thanks," Rich said. *Perfect.* He returned the smile and headed outside.

It was still dark and it took Rich a couple of minutes to get oriented, but he found Kenny's Suburban. He parked his suitcase on the far side of the vehicle and sat down on the planter box nearby. He chewed his cuticles almost to the bone before the lobby's sliding doors opened and the crew guys began pouring out. Some were carrying boom poles and mixers, one a parabolic microphone, like those dish mics you see on the sidelines at the football games. Kenny was utilizing the hotel's luggage dolly to wheel out the three cameras, battery case, and the field monitor to his vehicle.

"Good morning, handsome," he said once he saw Rich.

"Hey…" Rich replied weakly, his nervousness evident.

Then Kenny noticed Rich's suitcase.

"Don't care for the movie channels here, huh?" Kenny said kiddingly as he unlocked the doors. He knew an explanation would be forthcoming, but time dictated he multitask while waiting for one. The other guys had split off and were heading to the other SUV and the minivans.

Kenny placed the delicate electronics on the rear seat, and seat-belted them in. If they made car safety seats designed for cameras, Kenny would be first in line. "Hop in," he said.

Rich wheeled his case to the rear and threw it in, atop the Anvil cases. They drove off. The Starbucks was a little over three miles away, per Kenny's location scout.

Once they were on a straight piece of road, Kenny took a longer look at his passenger, trying to assess the level of Rich's concerns. "So...talk to me, Rich."

Rich stopped chewing his fingernail long enough to ramble a run-on answer. "It's Tami, she found me and flew here and checked in and called and I—"

"Whoa...slow down a second, buddy; I haven't had my coffee yet...Tami...that's your wife, right?" Kenny asked, his eyes searching among the row of darkened signs for the Starbucks.

"Yes,"

"And you say she's where?"

"She's here, Kenny."

"Here..." Kenny replied, still not quite up to speed.

"She's at the hotel, Kenny! *Our* hotel—in the room next to mine! Tami's *here!*"

Kenny looked over at his panicked passenger. Then he turned his gaze back to the road and began twisting his mustache. It was something Kenny did when he was thinking or panicking. He began processing this new information, and the gears were spinning more quickly now. That explained the suitcase.

"Wow...okay...you're sure..." he said as he looked over at Rich, whose look told him that he was rock solid with his intel.

"All right," Kenny began and then paused, "let me think."

"I'm sorry, Kenny. I had no idea she could find me up here."

"No. Don't apologize." He took a few moments before he asked, "You mentioned before that she's violent?"

"Sometimes," Rich replied. "Yeah."

They rode in silence for a full minute while Kenny began working out his threat assessment. He thought back to some of the things Rich had shared with him over dinner.

"And you say she's…" He paused, choosing his next words carefully. "You said she hears voices, and acts irrationally?"

"Off and on. Yeah," Rich replied.

Kenny was at risk of twisting off his last whisker.

There were a lot of variables in play and several moving parts to consider. From a sheer safety standpoint, there were a few important unknowns. Kenny wondered just how unhinged this woman truly was. Might she come to the school location looking for Rich? Was there a chance she might have a weapon with her?

He pulled out his phone and called Jill, the production assistant, keeping his explanation generic for the moment, but instructing her to book a room at another hotel across town, and to put the reservation under his brother's name. Yes, he'd explain later. He also told her to check Rich out of their existing hotel and to talk to no one if asked about it.

Kenny's next call was to the client, Mary, and he went into just enough detail to get her up to speed. They both agreed that, out of fairness and safety, the school had to be notified and, if needed, they'd have to arrange additional security personnel.

Kenny called the crew minivan and told Mark that he and Rich would meet them at the location instead of Starbucks. "And bring us a couple of large coffees, please."

"Venti?" Mark asked him.

"What?"

"Do you want venti, grande, or tall?" Mark said, seeking clarification.

Kenny wasn't at all well versed in the bullshit *Starbucks-speak*, and his reply came out a little sharper than intended. "Just…please get us two of the biggest, blackest coffees they have—I don't have time for a friggin' French lesson right now, okay?"

"It's Italian, actually, but okay," Mark risked. When he hung up he turned to the guys and said, "Kenny's being a bitch."

Rich numbly listened as his boss went about calling the shots and coordinating damage control. He'd always valued Kenny as a friend and admired him as a production colleague, but now he was witnessing another side to him, and he likened it to a military commander making life and death calls, while protecting his troops under enemy fire.

And all before having his first sip of coffee.

Rich shook his head as he heard all of the emergency arrangements that were being put into play because of him and his situation. And it wasn't just his situation any longer; it was all of theirs.

He didn't know how he felt; it was a toxic cocktail of numbness, sleep deprivation, utter embarrassment, acute panic, and a general feeling of disbelief. His thoughts drifted. He closed his eyes for a moment, and flashed back to a couple months before...

◆

CHAPTER 60

THERE HAD BEEN a couple of close calls since he left LA, but Rich hadn't seen Tami since then, except for that weird Christmastime incident at his folks'.

Rich and Scott had been immersed in a competitive domino game called Chicken Foot at their parents' house on Christmas Eve. Len had served his legendary eggnog and the four of them were enjoying a festive evening together after an amazing turkey meal. It had been a perfect evening, and Rich basked in the warmth of family.

At one point in the game, there was a soft knock on the front door, and Rich, being closest, had gone to answer it.

As the porch light was off, it wasn't until he'd opened both the main door and the metal security one, that he saw the familiar silhouette standing on the porch, and it sent a blizzard of frost down his spine. The sound of her voice completed his paralysis, and—just like that—whatever reserve of power he thought he'd had was instantaneously drained and transferred to the other party. In that invisible moment his sails slackened, while hers began to billow. His shoulders sank, while hers appeared to broaden with newfound strength and resolve. She seemed to be in a celebratory—even victorious—mood, perhaps as she'd certainly come a long way. She'd found him.

"Awesome!" Rich heard her whisper to herself.

His heart raced, but his feet were cement blocks, and he was rendered both immobile and mute.

"Hi!" she said with a laugh.

"Richie? Who's at the door, dear?" Jeannette called from the other room.

He couldn't answer his own mother. The sole thoughts going through Rich's otherwise-inert mind were self-loathing and questioning how he could have been so stupid.

"May I come in?" Tami said, smiling as she squeezed by the mannequin holding the door. She caressed his hand before walking into the dining room, where the other three jaws must have dropped as well. Rich closed the door and shuffled in. His face broadcast the end of the world.

"Merry Christmas," Tami said breezily, as if she were the guest of honor they'd all been waiting for. Rich found himself wondering if she'd rehearsed this scene many times, it seemed to come so easy to her. She removed her coat and set her purse down next to Scott's chair.

"Oh…uh, yes, merry—" Len's awkward attempt at politeness was quickly interrupted in less polite fashion.

"What are you doing here?" Scott asked.

"Hello, Scott. Jeanette, Len," she said, fake-smiling at each before continuing. "Well, I miss—and love—my husband," she replied, almost as if it should've been painfully obvious, and put her arm around Rich's waist. It felt like a Burmese python had just sidled up next to him. She gave him a kiss on the cheek, which Rich received like an acid attack. He took a step to the side.

"Anyway…merry Christmas! Mind if I join in?" Tami said as she pulled up a chair for herself.

For what must have been close to an hour, but felt more like eternal damnation, the game play was forced, as was the limited conversation that took place.

Rich's eyes must have looked like saucers as they darted back and forth between his family members. His mother's expression was blank, but her eyes were full of concern. At one point she managed to silently mouth the words "I'm sorry" to Rich.

His dad offered Tami an eggnog, which she politely declined. He intercepted his mother giving his dad a stern "Don't encourage her" look, which he apparently received loud and clear.

Scott had always had the best poker face in the family, and Rich recognized the unusually friendly show his brother now began to put on for their uninvited guest. As Scott excused himself to go to the restroom, smiling to Tami as he got up, Rich observed him stealthily grabbing the purse at his feet in the process.

Game play resumed, and after a few minutes Scott returned to the table. He suggested a coffee break and invited Tami outside to chat for a moment. Tami got up, seeming to take this as a friendly—even loving—gesture, grabbed her coat and proceeded outside into the cool night air, Scott following close behind. Once she had cleared the threshold, Scott closed the heavy, metal security screen door behind her and locked its dual locks.

Tami obviously heard the solid *clank* of the door latch, if the surprised expression on her face was any indication, and turned to find Scott still standing inside, looking at her through the robust metal screen.

"Aren't you coming outside?" Tami laughed.

"No, Tami, I'm not. Your purse is in your car. Just leave, please, and don't come back. Rich doesn't want you here, and neither do we," he said coolly.

"What the hell? Yes, he does!" she cried, closing the distance. She tried the door but it was very securely locked. Scott shook his head. "Don't make me call the cops, Tami."

"Rich!" she yelled past him, into the house. "Rich! Let me in, honey! It's Christmas! It's Christmas, baby!"

"Shut UP!!" Tami screamed to seemingly nobody. Scott shook his head as watched her argue with herself.

"Absolutely crackers," Scott mumbled.

Rich could feel the commotion outside unnerving everyone, as well as the swiftness with his mother hastened to get Dad's nitro pills from the kitchen cupboard. She shook out two pills and helped him get them to the right place. She handed him a small glass of water as a chaser and started to cry softly, while Rich tried to comfort them both.

Scott closed the main door and dialed a number. Tami continued to pound on the screen for several minutes, intermittently ringing the doorbell and yelling obscenities at the Bryson collective until the flashing red lights announced a police car in the driveway.

Tami had been resistant, and the officers had to escort her off the property, following her vehicle until she had exited the security gate and was headed down the dark road.

Twenty minutes later, she had apparently snuck past the security gate on foot, for her car was nowhere in sight, and walked the mile to the Bryson home for a second wave. She rang the bell repeatedly, pounded on the door furiously, and yelled like a freaking maniac.

The next time the officers responded, they escorted her the three miles to the edge of town and instructed her, in no uncertain terms, that she was not to return.

Merry Christmas....

Since then, the voicemails she'd left him over that span had run the whole spectrum, and it concerned Rich, and saddened him to no end, that her state of mind had deteriorated so far. Sometimes, in the course of the same phone call, she could seemingly shapeshift between sanity and utter madness effortlessly, then end the call sweetly, asking him to come home to get the help he needed, so they could live happily ever after together like they were destined to. Or, she could end with a vitriolic tirade of venomous spew and hang up after screaming bloody murder. He never knew which version of Tami he was going to get.

During one such voicemail, Rich had even heard, through the receiver, a knock on the door interrupting her scream fest, only to overhear police officers checking, at the request of her neighbors, to see if she was okay. Rich now longed for the day when he could finally, triumphantly shout from the rooftop, "Not my monkey, not my circus!"

He'd walked on eggshells too long…

Regardless, guilt still hung over Rich's head, like the darkest of clouds, and it consumed him. Even though he had been forced to leave, he felt compelled to do what he thought was right under the circumstances. He'd send Tami money orders when he could, hoping she'd be taking care of herself. But after scraping together the mortgage payments, paying the friggin' homeowners' association dues, holding off the creditors seeking payment on both of their cars and credit card bills, he couldn't any longer. Especially now that his divorce attorney had burned through his third retainer, and there was seemingly no end in sight to any of it.

No end in sight.

◆

CHAPTER 61

RICH WAS JARRED back into the present as the Suburban stopped suddenly.

"Wait here, Rich," Kenny said as he jumped out and walked briskly toward the school's office. Rich quickly reoriented himself and did as instructed, even locking the doors, as he surveyed all of the mirrors for anybody even remotely resembling his stalker.

Shoot me frickin' now.

After a few minutes, the other crew guys' vehicles arrived, parking in the adjacent spaces. Kenny had been watching for them and immediately jumped out, striding to each of the vehicles to give a very pithy update on the day's scenario and the revised game plan. Today wasn't going to be a normal day. Not by a long shot.

Rich saw the guys glance over toward Kenny's SUV as he sat there. He could only imagine what was being said. As the meeting seemed to be adjourning, they began to pile out of their rigs, and Mark handed two big-ass coffees to Kenny, who brought one over to Rich.

"Here, you're gonna want this," Kenny said. "The guys will bring in the gear. Just go inside, start building the cameras, and stay out of sight. Room twelve."

"You sure? I can help with—"

"It'll be okay, Rich. Just get inside, please."

Rich strapped one camera bag over each shoulder and proceeded through the gate and into the brick building.

Kenny did another walkie check and a visual sweep of the area before heading inside.

◆

For the next twenty minutes, it was a steady stream of heavy gear being schlepped inside, some by manual labor, and a few loads, like the heavy battery cases, benefited from a loaned audio-visual cart, courtesy of the school custodian.

Rich wasn't accustomed to being excluded from the load-in, and he felt more than a little awkward about that. But Kenny had instructed him to remain inside the building and instead to work on assembling the tripods, running the cables, etc., so as to not risk exposure.

Just in case a certain uninvited party were to show up.

Rich adjusted the legs on the three Sachtler carbon fiber tripods to the proper height, placing each upon a three-wheeled dolly, then installing the cameras atop them. As he busied himself with the cable runs, setting up the monitors and a myriad of production gear, the rest of the guys brought in the remaining Anvil cases. Rich tried to avoid eye contact as much as he could, but they were going to be working together all day (he hoped!), so this couldn't go on forever.

"Hinkey!" Nick said loudly to break the ice.

"Yeah." Rich chuckled awkwardly.

Kenny's walkie beeped to life and he set his coffee down to answer. "Go for Kenny," he said into it.

"Yeah, this is Officer Porter, checking in on the northern perimeter, street side. No sightings to report at this time."

"Okay, thank you, sir," Kenny said. "Please continue to be vigilant, and let's report in every ten minutes, over."

"Roger that. Out."

A moment later, another voice called in.

"Officer Barone reporting in from the southwestern perimeter. Same here, no sightings as yet, over."

"Roger that. Thanks, guys," Ken said into the walkie, inhaling his entire gonzo coffee (with espresso add shot) with all the gusto of his favorite amber ale. He looked at his watch and turned to the crew. "We get kiddos in forty-five minutes, guys. Keep building. I'll be back in a few."

Thirty minutes went by quickly, as Kenny conferred with his security personnel, the administrative team, and even the elderly janitor, a former Marine, who said he was up for any challenge.

He'd done two tours in 'Nam.

Kenny jogged back to Room Twelve and surveyed the completed equipment setup, then switched gears.

"Okay, guys, gather 'round. Here's the deal," Kenny said.

The guys all abandoned the gear and huddled around their fearless leader.

"Hinkey!" Nick said again, hoping to break the chill.

"Not the time, Nick," Kenny said.

The wholesome looking, fiftyish school principal walked in and Kenny nodded to her as he spoke to the group. The crew and she had made their introductions earlier.

She was sharply dressed in a suit, with heels, for the occasion of having a Hollywood video crew on site. Things had changed a bit, and she hadn't planned on an intruder alert today. She longed for her comfy sneakers now.

"Okay, she—Tami—obviously knows where we're staying, so she probably knows where we're working. This confirms what Rich told me, about her being very resourceful."

Rich nodded solemnly.

"She packing?" Nick asked.

"Packing?" Kenny said.

"Y'know. Is she armed?"

"Not likely, according to Rich, but we can't rule anything out. She's highly unstable, and we aren't going to take any chances," Kenny replied. "She may be on the petite side, but do not underestimate her. Is everybody clear?" He surveyed the crew, and each nodded to confirm their understanding. Kenny turned to the administrator. "I'm sorry for this development and for any inconvenience. This has never happened in the ten years we've been doing these training videos."

"No need to apologize. We've practiced for this type of thing. My staff knows what to do in a lock-down situation, and we've had a drill for the students," she said. Both her and Kenny's game-faces were seemingly set in stone, like they were auditioning for spots on Mount Rushmore.

"Lockdown?" Nick mouthed silently, his brow furrowed as he looked at his crewmates.

Kenny's walkie squawked to life. "Go for Kenny."

Outside, a long line of cars was jockeying for position to safely drop off their precious cargo. Parents and children hugged goodbye, backpacks were strapped on, and two yellow-vested teachers assisted in the orderly dispatching of vehicles from the lot. A Tacoma police department cruiser was parked about fifty yards back, and its two occupants kept a watchful eye for anyone resembling the description they'd been provided.

Teachers ushered children into their classrooms quickly, quietly, locking doors behind them. The campus bell rang, indicating school had begun. The metal gates at the school's entrance were now closed, and a large padlock secured it.

After the flurry of cars had left the lot and the kids were safely inside, the custodian stretched a chain across the driveway's two entrances.

The rather portly vice principal, Lanie Miller, wasn't used to this much stress, nor physical activity. She too had dressed for the occasion of having a crew from Hollywood visit the school, and she was uncomfortably squeezed into the suit she hadn't tried on since her father's funeral two years before. It fit like a lumpy sausage casing, but it was all that she had, and she made a mental note to buy a new one during the spring break. She cringed at the thought of being buried in this thing.

Lanie took a deep breath as she surveyed the now-quiet scene where she stood out front, her mental checklist's last boxes being filled in. She raised her walkie. "Entrance secured," she said, a bit out of breath.

"Roger that," her co-administrator replied.

Even though the potential threat had not presented itself yet, she still reminded herself: *This is not a drill.*

◆

CHAPTER 62

IT WAS 2:35 when Tami emerged from her long, hot, afternoon shower. She wrapped the generous bath towel around herself, used another for a turban, and began tweezing her eyebrows. A green silk blouse, one of Rich's favorites, was hung on a nearby hanger. She stopped to smile at her reflection.

"Happy birthday, Tami! Love you!" she said, before punctuating it with an OCD moment. "Awesome!"

◆

It was a typical second-grade classroom except for the three broadcast video cameras, three boom poles, the parabolic microphone and virtual spaghetti of cables on the floor, and a film crew hovering over the kids.

The kids had just completed a lesson—and a "take"—and Kenny walked to the front of the class, standing next to Miss McMahon, their teacher. She was a twenty-something newbie and foxy for a teacher. The crew guys, save Rich, had been staring at her lasciviously all day.

"Hey, you guys! Guess what?" Kenny said in his best kid-friendly voice. It was like he was hosting his own kiddie show. "You guys did a great job for us today!"

"Yes, children," Miss McMahon chimed in. "You behaved very responsibly. And I'm proud of the way you all handled the *drill* and the indoor recesses today." She winked at Kenny, and he returned it.

A little boy at a front desk raised his hand.

"Yes, Timmy?" she said.

"Does that mean we get popsicles tomorrow?" Timmy asked hopefully.

"I think that sounds like a good idea, Timmy!" Miss McMahon said with a smile. "What do you think, class?"

"Yay!!" the entire class erupted like they'd just won a trip to Disneyland.

Kenny reached into his pocket and dug a twenty out of his wallet. "For popsicles. Please, it's the least we can do," he said, handing the cash to Miss McMahon.

Kenny waited for the kids to have their moment, then asked them, "And you know what else? Who can guess what I'm going to say now?"

A darling, pigtailed seven year old in the back raised her hand shyly and Kenny pointed to her. Her perfect smile revealed two missing teeth, which just made her that much cuter.

"That's a wrap!" she said very excitedly.

"That's right!" Kenny said. "Let's all say it together. Ready? One...two...three!"

"That's a wrap!" everybody squealed.

Even the crew guys chimed in on that part, because those were their three favorite words in the world. The children all laughed, excited to briefly experience Hollywood for a day. The crew guys guarded the gear as the kids rose from their seats, several of them delivering hugs. A couple of kids started putting their chairs atop their desks.

"Watch out for the cables, children, and don't worry about putting your chairs on top of your desks today. We'll do that later. Don't forget your homework folders," Miss McMahon said as the chaotic end of the day's routine was in motion.

Greg walked over and retrieved the teacher's wireless microphone and belt pack as she oversaw the exodus. Kenny turned on his radio and keyed the microphone as he left the room. "Security, this is Kenny…"

The kids continued filing out, each getting high-fives from Miss McMahon. Nick, the crew perv, watched her out of the corner of his eye as he slowly wrapped an audio cable. A Van Halen tune was playing in his head: "Hot For Teacher." "Hinkey!" he blurted, like someone with Tourette's.

Kenny popped his head back in and gave a thumbs up. "Guys, good job. Weird day, I know. Just head-wrap cameras, they're going back to my room. No interviews today. Rich, so far so good, but stay inside. Guys, protect the quarterback!" And he was gone.

The strike was always quicker than the set-up, especially when the lion's share of the gear would stay at the school for the next day's shoot. The crew was always highly motivated to get back to the hotel and regroup for a fun meal out somewhere, so the wrap only took twenty minutes. It was muscle memory.

The guys carried the three camera cases to the vans and came back in to retrieve Rich. They surrounded him, like a protective shield, as they walked outside.

"Protect the quarterback!" Nick laughed.

"Why do I suddenly feel like a mob informant?" Rich had to chuckle.

Once Rich was safely secured in the passenger seat of Kenny's SUV, the guys piled into the minivans, and Greg closed the side door. "Elvis has left the building!" he said into an imaginary sleeve mic, which got belly laughs from the guys.

Kenny watched the vans leave, then climbed into the Suburban and closed the door. It was eerily quiet now, and even the police cruiser had left the scene. He turned to Rich and smiled. "Well, that was interesting," he said as he turned the ignition key and checked his mirrors.

"Welcome to my world, Kenny, sheesh. Man, I can't tell you how much I appreciate how cool you've been with all of this. Sorry to get you involved."

"Don't worry about it, Rich. We've got your back. Important thing now is to get you checked in at your new digs," he said, pulling from the lot.

They'd driven several miles in silence, each internally replaying the day's experience, when Rich noticed a music store ahead. "Kenny. Hey, would you mind if we stopped there for a couple of minutes? It's Tami's birthday today. I know...weird request, especially now."

"No worries, my friend," Kenny said as he pulled to the curb. "I'll hang here with the cameras."

"Thanks! Be right back!" Rich said as he hopped out. He prayed they had what he was looking for.

Ten minutes later he emerged with a bag and an expression of—almost—*hope*. Good fortune had once again smiled: the store had delivered for him!

◆

It was only another two miles before they entered the parking lot of another budget three-star motel: the Vagabond. Appropriate, Rich thought as Kenny pulled up to the registration entrance.

"Be right back," Kenny said.

While he waited, Rich inventoried the vehicle's cluttered console until he found a Sharpie and began playing with the contents of the shopping bag on his lap. With some effort, he opened the clamshell packaging and extracted the piece of ancient technology he'd found in the bargain bin: a Sony Walkman cassette player. He installed the AA batteries, removed the cassette tape from its case and cued Side A to the third song. After testing it with the headphones, he put everything back in its packaging, with the exception of the tape case, which he put in his pocket for later disposal.

With the Sharpie, Rich wrote *Happy Birthday, Tami* on the outside of the festive-enough gift box, and replaced it in the bag.

A few minutes later, Kenny emerged and popped the SUV's cargo door. Rich got out and retrieved his suitcase. Kenny handed him a card key.

"It's not fancy, but any port in the storm, right? It's on my credit card. Your new name is Craig Weisberg. My brother gives his blessing," Kenny said, patting Rich on the shoulder.

"Thanks, Kenny."

"You can buy me a beer—hell, you can buy me three beers—at dinner!" Kenny laughed as he climbed back into the Suburban. "We'll keep an eye out at our hotel. Rest up; we'll call you about dinner. And if she calls, for God's sake, don't answer!"

"Okay. Oh, hey, Kenny. One more favor, if you don't mind?"

"Name it, Rich."

"Think you can get this to Tami, somehow? Birthday gift." He shrugged.

Kenny took the bag. "If she's still around, probably," he said, as he looked at the now gift-wrapped box in the bag. "You're a class act, Rich." Kenny laughed and pulled away, giving a thumbs-up out the window.

"Yeah," Rich said as he returned the thumbs up and wheeled his case inside.

He exited the third floor elevator, and his senses were immediately assaulted on two fronts: the pungent smell of somebody's nasty delivery pizza and the horrid carpet pattern he had to navigate until he reached his new room. Inside, he found it to be very basic—the property's three-star rating seemed generous—but at the same time, he couldn't be happier. Hey, if Tami wasn't part of the package, he'd gladly leave a glowing, five-star review.

As he plopped his suitcase atop the neighboring queen bed, he felt a peace that comes with feeling safe.

At least relatively.

For now anyway.

For the first time that day, he powered up his phone and looked at its display. There were seventeen messages. He turned on the ringer and placed it on the nightstand. Right now, all he knew was that Craig Weisberg needed to close his eyes for a few minutes. And figure out the next phase.

◆

CHAPTER 63

THE CREW GUYS, with camera bags in tow, poured out of the hotel elevator when it reached their floor.

"Elvis has left the building!" Nick laughed as the guys retrieved their card keys and approached their rooms.

The room directly across from Nick's opened and Tami stepped into the hall. She was wearing her silk blouse, an attractive skirt, three-inch heels, and was in full Hollywood make-up and hair mode.

"Hey, guys!" she said with a megawatt smile.

Nick recognized her, and he smiled back, only because she was a babe. But he knew she was bonkers. The guys all stopped in their tracks and exchanged looks.

Tami didn't see her husband amongst them. "Where's Rich?"

Nick looked over at the other guys, then back to Tami. "I guess you didn't hear…"

The corners of Tami's smile flickered momentarily. "Hear what?" she said.

"Oh, uh, Rich…he flew back early," Nick said.

"Ha!" she said, not appreciating the joke right now. "No, really. Where is he? Where's Rich?" she demanded.

Nick looked back at her with a blank expression. Her smile

immediately vanished, and Nick couldn't help but notice that her attractiveness had as well, in the blink of an eye.

"I just told you. He flew back this morning. Didn't say why—he just split. Went back home. Emergency, I guess," Nick said.

Tami searched his face, then the others'. They gave her nothing back, only a couple of nods, a shrug.

"He left this for you though," Nick said, producing the shopping bag Kenny had given him moments earlier in the lobby. "Happy birthday, right?" Nick smiled as he handed it to her.

Tami snatched the bag from his hands and began pounding like a maniac on the door next to hers. "Rich! Open the door!" she yelled.

The guys disappeared into their respective rooms, including Nick, who watched Tami from his peephole.

"Honey, it's me...Tami," she said to the door with a softer tone now. "Please open up and let me in, Honey."

Nick shook his head as he watched, from the safety of his own room, this manic incident playing out. She banged her fist against the metal door until she winced in pain.

Two doors down, another occupant peered out at the hallway disturbance. "What's going on here?" the middle-aged man asked.

"None of your fucking business, old man! Go back inside!" Tami yelled back at him. The pounding continued. "Rich, open up, you piece of shit!" she screamed.

The man closed, locked, and chained his door.

"¡Ella es una locura!" Nick muttered to himself as he continued watching the tirade for several minutes.

Tami then grabbed her gift bag and went into her room, slamming the door behind her.

"Richie, you poor devil," he whispered.

◆

CHAPTER 64

THE RINGING JOLTED him awake, and for a few moments Rich didn't know if it was Tuesday or Christmas. He looked at the display and answered it without speaking.

"Richie...dude, pick up," Nick said.

"Nick? What's going on? Is everything okay?" Rich asked, sitting up now.

"Dude. She just left!"

"Wait—what do you mean? Just left?"

"Yeah. I told her you split, dude. She didn't believe it at first, but I just saw her jamming out of the hotel. She had her shit, and the taxi just left, man!"

"She's gone? You're sure?" Rich asked anxiously.

"Dude, she bought it! She's headed to the airport, dude!"

Rich took a minute to process this before responding. He went to the bathroom and splashed some water on his face, having put the phone on speaker. "Wow. Okay...and you gave her the bag?" he asked.

"Yeah, man. She had it in her hand when she climbed in the taxi, dude," Nick confirmed.

"Cool...wow, thanks, Nick...really," Rich said, taking a deep breath. He regarded himself in the mirror as he puckered his lips and allowed himself a controlled release, deliberately expelling a long-contained hurricane of stress from his ballooned cheeks. The effect was not unlike a puffer fish blowing out a hundred birthday candles.

"Still there, Rich?"

"Yeah, yeah, I'm here. Just processing this."

He quickly dried his face with a coarse towel, retrieved the handset, and made his way back to the bed, plopping down hard. He felt completely and utterly drained. This on-the-lam stuff was exhausting.

"Richie, look…hope you don't mind me sayin', but that's some seriously bad mojo you're hooked up with, dude," Nick said.

"You have no idea, man," Rich replied with another sigh.

"Oh, and one more thing," Nick said, lying back on his bed now, all comfy in his skivvies. "You're buying me dinner tonight," he laughed.

"Count on it, man," Rich said.

"Okay," Nick said as he perused the adult movie list with the remote. Within easy reach was a bottle of the hotel's finest complimentary hand lotion.

"Hey, I'll catch you at dinner, Richie."

"Okay, brother."

"'Cause right now, I'm gonna whack it!" Nick crowed maniacally.

Rich cringed as he stabbed at the phone's End Call button. That was a visual he didn't need, and he couldn't hang up fast enough.

He shook his head as it returned to the pillow.

It had been a day…

◆

CHAPTER 65

TAMI WISHED SHE could have extended her stay another night or two, to confirm whether or not what she'd been told was true, but all of her credit cards had declined her. That, plus the fact that she had to get back to her new housemate: her eight week-old kitten, Bubba.

She was also royally peeved that she'd come so far, had been so close, and let him slip through her fingers.

She sighed as she stared out her window of the regional jet as she once again passed over the Three Sisters. This wasn't the way her birthday was supposed to have been celebrated, and she hadn't had so much as a phone call from Rich since their conversation the night before. How could he be so heartless?

Then she remembered the gift bag between her feet. She reached down and set it atop her lap, which caught the attention of the four-year-old girl seated next to her. The girl stopped playing with her new Barbie long enough to smile broadly and announce to Tami, "Today's my birthday!"

Tami's smile was strained, but she tapped into her reserve acting skills to appear happy for the youngster. "Happy birthday."

The girl turned her attention back to her doll, and Tami reached into the bag, looking for a card. She pulled out the pieces of white tissue and inventoried the bag. There wasn't a card. Must've fallen out, she thought, disappointed.

Further exploration netted a wrapped box with Rich's salutation written on it. As she read it, her fingers drummed the lid for a long moment, and she looked up and away, toward the illuminated reading lamp.

"It doesn't go with that," she whispered.

The young girl found this odd and gave her a quizzical look, but the lady only acknowledged it with a half-smile, so she shrugged and returned to the task at hand: remedying Barbie's wardrobe calamity.

Tami stuffed the empty bag under her seat and opened the box's lid. Inside was the Walkman and headphones. She examined the player and could see through the tiny plastic window on its door that there appeared to be a cassette tape already installed, though she couldn't make out what it was. She didn't open it to check, as she didn't want to spoil the surprise. *He must've made me an audio Happy birthday message.* The slightest of smiles found her face as she settled in.

Tami adjusted the comfort of the headphones, trying not to mess up her hair in the process. Everything was plugged in and ready.

"Ready, go!" she whispered a little too loudly and a little too weirdly, prompting another glance from the girl, as well as from the young woman across the aisle, the child's mother.

"You doing okay, Honey?" she whispered to her daughter. The little girl nodded hesitantly.

Tami smiled, reclined her seat a few degrees, and closed her eyes. Maybe Rich might redeem himself here with something mushy. A musical memory from their wedding day, perhaps? That had to be it!

Her finger hovered over the controls for several seconds as she finished counting to herself. Then, with great ceremony, she pushed the play button and listened for what she hoped would be Rich's voice wishing her a happy birthday, telling her how much he missed her, and apologizing for not calling like her like he'd promised.

Instead, what she heard was an odd instrumental intro to a song she wasn't familiar with. It started out with what sounded like an almost tribal electronic drum riff, then a very brief bass guitar lick, and what came next was a strange, almost Indian-sounding instrument she couldn't quite recognize.

A sitar.

Tami's musical tastes had never shown much appreciation for rock, per se. Other than, perhaps, the Beach Boys, she was more into show tunes, ballads, and the like. So far, this seemed like an odd romantic song choice, and she couldn't for the life of her figure out Rich's intention yet, but after a few bars of the weird instrument, came a brief vocal of somebody yelling, "Hey!"

That got her attention.

Maybe she'd eventually recognize it. *Give it a chance.* So far, it was just a little strange, but she let it play on. The sitar intro continued for the better part of a minute before a rather unconventional-sounding male voice began singing—if you could even call it that, she thought, but she went with it:

> *Don't come around here no more*
> *Don't come around here no more*
> *Whatever you're looking for*
> *Hey! Don't come around here no more*
> *I've given up. I've given up*
> *I've given up on waiting any longer*
> *I've given up, on this love getting stronger*
> *I don't feel you anymore*
> *You darken my door*
> *Whatever you're looking for*
> *Hey, don't come around here no more*
>
> *I've given up. I've given up*
> *I've given up, you tangle my emotions*
> *I've given up, honey please admit it's over*

Don't come around here no more
Don't come around here no more

Whatever you're looking for
Hey, don't come around here no more
Stop walking down my street
Who did you expect to meet?
Whatever you're looking for

Hey, don't come around here no more...

As the tape played, and with each new line, Tom Petty's lyrics—and Rich's choice of song—relentlessly slashed her to shreds. Her shoulders heaved as she listened to its message, until near the end—during Mike Campbell's punched-up guitar solo—when she finally pulled off the headphones and fumbled to yank out the offending tape. Tears streamed down her face now, and her young seatmate stared at her with equal parts concern and horror.

◆

CHAPTER 66

RICH DUG DEEP in his effort to appear to share in the humor his tablemates were enjoying—after all, it had been a far from typical day. Plus, they were on their third round. But as he nursed his twenty-two ounce Moose Drool, his thoughts were up at 30,000 feet, imagining Tami's reaction to his "gift."

Had she opened it? Did she play it?

As was his oversensitive-at-times way, Rich was second guessing himself, wondering if perhaps the song's message was too cold, too blunt, too *mean* even. He took another pull on his beer and then thought about all of the conversations they'd had these past months—hell, *years!*—where he tried to communicate what he was feeling—and not feeling—and how it had all been ignored, even trampled over.

Yes, he thought while nodding to himself. Passing the song along to Tami had been a necessary step birthed of his own countless attempts to put into words what he finally, after all he had been subjected to, realized needed to be said. He made a mental note to write a few words of gratitude to Mr. Tom Petty one day, for such a brilliant and succinct message. Like Tom and the rest of the boys in the band, Rich was, as of now, officially and literally, a *heartbreaker*. He just prayed that maybe, somehow, this time she might get it.

Happy Birthday, Tami…

Rich stared, alone in his thoughts, down into depths of his choco-laty-brown ale.

Kenny watched his crew, even shared in a few laughs, but, as he twisted his mustache, he kept a close eye on Rich, as he knew him well enough to see how conflicted he was. Especially now.

He signaled the server for another round for his horses and began silently calculating what the next morning's call-time would be. He'd try to give the guys an extra hour of sleep tonight, especially since the gear was already on site and built. They still had three more production days here and, thankfully, the wheels hadn't completely come off.

Years from now, they'd all remember this one.

◆

The rest of the week had gone smoothly for the shoot.

There were no longer any threats to necessitate another lock-down at the school, and there had been no other unforeseen variables, which made Kenny a happy man. Kenny had gleaned, from his conversation with the client in Seattle, that Tami had posed as a journalist interested in doing a story about the video crew working in an educational setting and that she had been quite convincing in her role. They'd been only too happy to provide her with dates, locations, and any other information she requested. Kenny and the client agreed to new protocols that would be put in place to prevent any future scenarios such as this.

As the crew buttoned up the last of the cases and finished load-ing the gear into the vehicles, it was time to scurry to the airport and run the gauntlet with the thirty-odd pieces of baggage. It was always a stress fest for Kenny and a bit of a hassle to coordinate the return of the numerous rental vehicles; checking all of the equipment for the return flight also always cost a lot of dough. Knowing that, Rich chose to say his goodbyes to Kenny now, before the ensuing airport chaos. Richie would be flying home alone, and nobody really knew when they'd all be reassembled. Kenny and Rich locked in a long bear hug.

"'Til next time, Richie. And there will be a next time, count on it!"

As Rich held Kenny's gaze, his immeasurable appreciation was clearly communicated. Words failed him, but he punctuated it with a simple, "Thanks, Skipper," and threw his bag into the awaiting cab. He rolled down the window and flashed the peace sign, which Kenny returned, as they pulled away.

Rich's flight home found him in a trancelike state. He'd replayed the week's events over and over in his mind and eventually surrendered it to God.

He was physically, mentally, emotionally, even spiritually exhausted now, and he wasn't even aware of the inflight snack that had been placed on the seatback tray in front of him. He'd stared blankly out the window for nearly two hours, searching every single cloud for that fabled silver lining.

Rich finally nodded off, only to be wakened by the flight attendant two minutes later as she asked him to return his seatback and tray table to their upright positions in preparation for landing.

◆

CHAPTER 67

OVER THE COURSE of the next couple of years, what was left of Rich's career managed to complete its final, painful, agonizing death spiral and eventually slam into the ground. And the crater was huge.

As his hasty exodus had necessitated his going underground without notice or explanation, his carefully cultivated and painstakingly-nurtured client list eventually gave up on trying to book his services or even find out what had happened to him. In the Hollywood media arena, where Rich had long enjoyed being a prince, the next freelancer on the list would now be getting his gigs, and there would be no getting back into that loop. Not now. He had flatlined, and there was no defibrillator that would bring him back.

As to what happened to Richie, there were rumors, sure, but, other than the handful of crew guys he'd rendezvoused with on Kenny's now-annual gigs, nobody really seemed to know his whereabouts, his story, or even if he was still alive.

All they knew was that he wasn't available. *Next!*

And so, it was slow death in the sun, career wise, for Rich, and his once considerable skills had all but atrophied now. Along with that, any creative spark, and self-esteem, had been snuffed out, and the combination of these factors was beyond depressing for him to deal with now.

But all that was taking a backseat to what was consuming him even more at the moment: impending financial ruin. That would surely manifest itself as rigor mortis. At this point, he hoped it would be quick, but he knew it wouldn't.

Before Tami (BT, as he now referred to it), he had been proud of his eight hundred-plus credit score. Going into the marriage, he'd had everything paid off, a platinum credit rating, and zero debt. *BT.*

But at this point, three years of divorce court hell had sealed the deal, and bankruptcy was assured.

Tami had all but squatted in the townhouse all this time, with Rich trying to keep things up financially, but you could only get so much blood out of a turnip, or whatever the saying was. And this turnip had bled out.

Rich had long ago given up on even trying to do the math, but his $350 per hour divorce attorney was probably enjoying his new yacht by now, after Tami managed to stretch things out and manipulate the court, until the judge had had enough of her shenanigans and finally slammed the gavel one final time.

But it was too little, too late. The damage was done. Or, as Scott, the family poet, had put it so eloquently, *The shit's out of the donkey.*

◆

Rich had surrendered the Explorer a while back due to inability to keep up with the payments, and the mandated short sale of the townhouse was what he was now faced with. That is, unless it was foreclosed upon first.

He absorbed the full weight of all this as he took a seat on the stump, adjacent to the mailboxes, down the hill from his brother's place. His hair was a little longer now and more sun-bleached, and he was a leaner version of himself. Stress on this level was not for wimps and a diet he wouldn't recommend to anyone.

He held the phone to his right ear—the good one—and closed his eyes. "Listen, Tami. How much clearer can I make this?" he said, not trying to hide the agitation in his voice. That agitation was the new normal every time he had to deal with her, and he hated it. Through his trials, which were many, he was beginning to find his voice, and it sometimes surprised him to hear himself.

"They're foreclosing on us next week!" Tami cried.

"You sound surprised, Tami. Really. Are you surprised? Huh?" Rich said, incredulous. "And you're telling me this because you expect me to do something about it—now?"

"Rich—"

"No. No, wait. You might remember that I've been removed—*forcibly*, by the way—from my income stream for, what…God knows how long. I've literally lost track. There's nothing left, Tami. Nada! Zippo! Zilch! Okay? Are you beginning to get a clearer picture of this situation now? Please, I'm begging you, understand that!" he said, quaking with rage now. Rich closed his eyes. He could visualize what Tami must look like at this very moment.

And he was right: The blinds were drawn. Tami looked like she hadn't bathed in a week. Her oily hair hung flat and she was dressed in baggy sweats and a tattered tee. Next to her sat an enormous stack, many months' worth, of unopened, overdue bills and legal notices.

"And I'm going to lose my car," she sobbed.

"Well, you're preachin' to the choir there, toots." He picked up a rock and threw it at a discarded beer can across the road. "I don't know what to tell you, Tami. Sorry about your car, but…that's all I've got," Rich said as he looked around for another rock. Not finding one, he unclipped the now-worthless pager from his belt and threw it instead, knocking over the can with this second attempt. He felt no need to retrieve it. Not anymore.

"I'm driving an old beater of my sister's right now, Tami. Things are tough all over, okay?" he said, pausing when he heard a warning beep. He looked at the blinking battery light. "Look, Tami. I'm about to lose my battery here. Have them fax the foreclosure documents to my sister's and we'll be done. There's nothing left to haggle over—there's nothing left, period. You've got *everything*. *That's* the last piece of the puzzle. We're—" he began, then paused, looking at the rapidly blinking icon that had become a metaphor for their life together.

"—We're *done*."

"But what about—?"

"Good bye, Tami. I wish you well. I honestly do—"

The phone went dead.

"*FUUUCK!!*" Tami screamed at the top of her lungs, throwing the handset violently over her shoulder.

The loud shattering sound startled her, and she turned to see the most horrible sight imaginable. The phone she'd so angrily hurled had completely obliterated the Lovers statuette on the coffee table. The figures' heads—hers and Rich's—were severed now, and the toppled piece had broken into several, irreparable bits of gold plaster and dust.

"*NOOOOOOOOOOOOOOOOO!!!!*" she bellowed.

And this is what it had taken.

This.

Tami stared at the carnage. This pile of broken pieces and dust that had once represented her true hope of a lasting love now served up one last, impossible-to-deny nugget of truth: it was completely and utterly shattered, and now, so was she. *Shadoobie...*

She gathered her knees under her chin in the fetal position, and thus began a long series of the deepest and most primal sobs ever to emanate from a living creature.

This final thing, this absolutely shocking, point-of-no-return cause/effect action is what it had taken, and now—in this split-second moment in time—it could be argued that Tami had officially, and unequivocally, hit that ultimate low point that therapists clinically refer to. This is where the elevator operator would probably say, after the ding: "You've now reached Rock Bottom. Please be careful as you step out."

Bubba jumped up on the loveseat next to her, but the deep abyss that was Tami's pain made her unaware of his presence. It also made her oblivious to the knocking sound on the screen door.

After a few moments, John and Carol Matthews knocked again, then looked at each other. The blinds were closed and they thought they'd heard a whimpering sound coming from inside.

Carol nodded, and Tami's father opened the screen door and began to knock more robustly.

"Tami!"

◆

CHAPTER 68

FOR RICH, THE next twenty-four months proved to be a full-time process of soul-searching, processing the trauma in hopes of one day understanding it, second-guessing himself, identity rebuilding, self-esteem repair, and several failed attempts at rebranding himself and his career. The emotional wounds had definitely taken their toll, and it remained to be seen how long they would linger. His credit hemorrhage would last a decade, but what could you do?

The physical wounds had healed, thankfully, with the exception of his threshold of hearing in his left ear, which had once suffered an open-palmed slap to the side of his face and apparent damage to his eardrum.

At the time of impact—on one of those many special evenings at home, in that hellish cage-fight arena that was his living room—the force of Tami's blow had felt akin to being a guppy in a bucket of water and having a lit cherry bomb dropped into it.

Rich's ear rarely rang anymore, but the damage had clearly been done, resulting in him sometimes having to ask people to repeat themselves for the first time in his relatively young life. He hated that, but he had come to accept it, along with all of the other life changes that came with crawling from the wreckage and living to tell about it. Considering the alternative, he was thankful in many ways.

Rich's parents still remained friends with Tami's—Christmas card friends, anyway—and the most recent Matthews family letter and photo card were absent any mention or representation of the fact that they still had a daughter. That's because they really didn't.

After Tami bottomed out, they'd helped her find an apartment, assisted her with move-in expenses and physically moved her but, subsequent to that, she had completely estranged herself from her family. Their Christmas letter boasted about the progress of their dream home project, a self-designed and lavish-for-the-area beach property south of Ensenada they had been slowly chipping away at for the better part of a decade. Also, they touted some of David's recent successes in his acting career, including his first minor speaking role in a recent feature film. Rich was sure that this is what had been the final straw in any attempt at family, or mental health, reparations.

It was no surprise to Rich, but it turned out that Tami had not been a good renter. Having skipped on her final rent on two different apartments, this explained a phone call Rich had received from a detective asking for her whereabouts. Rich was unable to offer any information, having not heard from her since…since.

As Tami had only left a trail of personal mailbox rental addresses in her wake, she had effectively become a ghost. Tami's privacy paranoia all but assured that personal information, addresses included, would never find their way into any database. Owing to her previous prohibition on Rich ever buying the longed-for Macintosh when they were married, there wasn't a single reference of her to be found on that new technology grid everybody was talking about, that up-and-coming computer network they were calling the *information superhighway*, or something like that.

Rich still didn't own a computer—he sometimes wondered if he was the last human on Earth to not be plugged in—but it remained on his "someday" list, right after getting a more reliable set of wheels.

And a life.

His studio apartment was humble, certainly, but fine for now, and this arguably sketchy neighborhood was only about half an hour from any of his family. So there was that.

◆

An upcoming gig with Kenny was on the horizon, and he thanked his lucky stars for the work. He'd never been to La Junta, Colorado, and it would be great to be with the guys again. And that week's pay would last him a month now, even longer if he didn't spend too much on a car. If there was one positive thing about bankruptcy, he thought, it was being able to say, "Look, ma! No bills!" But there was no pride in that, and it still sucked, big time.

Len and Jeanette had asked about Tami a couple of times when they'd spoken on the phone with her parents, but Carol's voice would trail off when she explained that they hadn't heard from her and that they really didn't even know what she was doing, or where she was living anymore.

Sometimes, Rich wondered if she was even still alive, but somehow he knew she had to be. She might be severely unbalanced, but she was a tenacious survivor and had toughness in spades. She was out there somewhere.

That fact had troubled him in almost every waking and sleeping moment all this time since the divorce, but with each passing day he was now starting to find it a little easier to relax in response to the sound of a car pulling up out front. And the nights when he'd awaken drenched in sweat, and with his heart pounding like a jack-hammer, those were becoming fewer and farther between now too.

He didn't know how long it would take, but he would eventually be made whole again. That's what the therapist told him, and he just had to believe in that light at the end of the tunnel, even if there wasn't even a glimpse of it yet.

Faith, they called it.

He'd have to check the Lost & Found for that.

◆

The sweet sound of a mockingbird interrupted his train of thought, and for this too he was grateful.

Rich leaned over and scooped up a floundering honeybee from the surface of the water and paddled his float over to the edge of the apartment's pool, where he gingerly placed the soggy little guy in the shade of a plastic table. He hopped off his inflatable and climbed out and toweled himself off before settling into the strapped monstrosity that was the cheap lounge chair—one of only two operable ones to be found at this modest complex's pool area.

Rich took a pull from his stubby bottle of Red Stripe, then laid back and closed his eyes, waiting for the sun to do its part in wicking up the remaining water droplets. The mockingbird seemed to be particularly gifted, and its solid repertoire brought a slight curl of a smile to Rich. He was momentarily transported back to his old Shangri-La, his former oasis of sanity.

It had to be close to 2:00, he thought, based on the sun's position overhead. That meant he could probably relax for another couple of hours before he had to shower and get ready for the barbeque with his folks. He made a mental reminder to pick up the requested four large coleslaws from KFC on the way.

Rich leaned back and smiled, as he was pretty sure that his dear, well-intentioned mother—God bless her—would likely be inviting the "darling redhead" from church today, but he wasn't sure how interested he was in being set up, or even if he wanted to consider any kind of relationship for the time being. Let alone the horror of dating again. Oy…

He wondered how long it would take before he would be ready for all of that, if ever, but had pretty much resigned it to when the time was right, he'd know it.

The most contact he'd had with the opposite sex since he'd left Tami was saying a shy "hello" in the lobby to the cute, brown-eyed girl who'd just moved in upstairs. She had smiled back, sure, but she was way out of his league, he thought. Oh, well. Perhaps someday this damaged-goods guy might feel date-worthy again. He wasn't going to hold his breath, though.

Let Go, Let God. These were becoming his new operative words.

Rich closed his eyes, lulled by the operatic chirps wafting from the treetops, then slipped on his wireless FM headset. *Let's see what that Great DJ In The Sky has in store for me today.*

As he settled back, he flipped on the power. "Ha!" he laughed out loud as the opening guitar strains of Van Morrison's "Brown Eyed Girl" filled his head in high fidelity. It never failed! He went with it. Rich had always been a fan of Mr. Morrison, but never as much as right this moment.

The telltale, borderline-goofy grin on his face was probably the widest it'd been in several years, and as the song faded out, three minutes later, he slowly became aware of the fact that a shadow seemed to have come between him and his personal sunshine.

He flinched.

He opened his eyes and squinted up at the silhouette standing over him. He was completely unprepared for what he saw there—probably not unlike what the Native Americans in Oregon must've experienced when they emerged from the woods and first witnessed the impossibly beautiful spectacle of Klamath's Crater Lake. Legend had it, he'd heard, they'd found the lake so surreally beautiful that they felt they'd be struck blind if they so much as looked at it.

This was on that level, and he was momentarily taken aback by the most stunning visual he had ever experienced: the quintessential, most exquisite pair of big brown eyes God had ever created. And they were smiling down on him!

Her smile hit him like a thunderbolt, and her face was perfectly framed by a back-lit, shoulder-length perm of tight chestnut curls.

Oh, and the galaxy of freckles!

This surely must be a dream.

If it wasn't, he was surely toast.

He peeled off his headset and returned the smile. He tried to find his breath again. It was slow in coming.

"I'm sorry to bother you—you looked so peaceful—but...is this lounger taken?" the Most Beautiful Girl in the World asked.

"Hi. Uh, it's no bother. And, no, it's not. Please," he offered and not nearly as awkwardly as he would've thought. He got up and moved the tiny plastic table so that they could share it between them.

"Thanks a lot," she said. "The other ones are all broken." She extended her hand, "My name's Rebecca. I just moved in upstairs."

The girl from the lobby. No frickin' way!

He pinched himself.

"Rich. Well, Richie's what most people call me. Nice to meet you, Rebecca," he said, returning the handshake.

"Richie. That's sweet. I'll bet your mom still calls you that." She smiled again, further melting him in into his lounger. He shrugged and nodded. "I like that. My dad calls me Beckers, so don't feel embarrassed," she laughed. "Terms of endearment."

For the better part of the next hour, Richie found himself having what was probably the most comfortable, natural, and thoroughly enjoyable conversation he'd had in, quite possibly, his entire life.

He went with it.

"Can you believe that mockingbird? That's my favorite sound in the whole world," Beckers had interjected at one point in the conversation.

That's when he knew.

This gift from the heavens also had great taste in music, a close relationship with her family—what a concept!—and she had just completely gotten over a rather unhealthy relationship, though she was "in a really good place now."

She loved beer, barbeque, and no, she didn't have plans tonight!

After his shower, he'd called his mom and asked her to please, politely, cancel the darling redhead.

Because he was bringing a new friend.

And, no, Mom, I won't forget the coleslaw.

◆

CHAPTER 69

R ICH'S FAMILY WAS immediately taken with his new friend, and she with them. Despite initial reservations of this possibly being too soon for their brother, both Scott and Ellen warmly welcomed Rebecca into the fold. The group had assembled at a long table on the lattice-covered patio, surrounded by a surreal display of Len's prized varietal roses. It turned out Rebecca knew a thing or two about the blooms.

"And your double-delights are beautiful, Mr. Bryson. My father's are nice, but yours are—*amazing,*" Rebecca remarked.

"Thank you, dear—and please call me Len." He smiled warmly. *She's a keeper, Rich.*

The family meal was centered around their patriarch's inimitable barbecue chicken, and nobody even noticed the missing coleslaw (ahem), as everyone instead marveled over the undeniable spark of long-overdue, and well-deserved, joy exhibited in Rich, for the first time in—well, forever.

Rebecca, they learned, belonged to a family much like theirs: healthy, happy, humble…and loyal to a fault, which was evident in the way she presented herself and reacted to others. She'd been raised well, you could tell, which went a long way.

As the meal progressed, Jeanette enjoyed her role as the quiet observer, her specialty. She couldn't help but notice Rebecca's mannerisms, her natural smile, her eyes' sparkle, the way her curls danced when she laughed, and how comfortable she was in her own skin. And—most importantly—how she looked at Richie, with warmth, a glow, and genuine kindness.

That's what Richie needed, that's what her son truly deserved.

Throughout the evening, Rich would pause to glance from face to face, searching each and assessing the family's reactions to his invited guest. The feeling seemed to be unanimously in favor, which comforted him to no end. The reaction when his mother met his eye said it all as she gave him a smile and a private wink of approval, both of which he returned.

There are moments in this life, sometimes, when you just *know* something. It may not be attributable to anything you can put your finger on, necessarily, but still—you seem to have come into irrefutable knowledge.

Jeanette's intuition had always been strong, and her faith unwavering, through the good times—which were many—and any, and all, personal and family trials. She considered her relationship with the Almighty to be a strong one and she trusted it completely. Comfortable in that knowledge—and unbeknownst to anyone else sitting there—she sent up a silent prayer right there from the dinner table, that this angel might be the one.

Little did she know that in that moment, Rich, whose faith had long ago gone missing in action, was testing the connection again, subconsciously thrusting that big, cobweb-covered, Frankenstein's lab-esque, breaker switch to the ON position, and sending up that very same request.

Amen.

He went with it.

◆

CHAPTER 70

OVER THE COURSE of the next several months, Richie and Beckers' friendship began to bloom, slowly yet steadily, and undeniably. They didn't want to risk screwing anything up.

Admittedly, when they'd first met, neither had been looking to be in a relationship, as both had experienced considerable pain in their previous ones. She now knew Rich's story, and he hers.

He'd expressed his sense of dread, shame and guilt for the way his marriage had played out and she fully affirmed his decision to leave and reminded him in a nonjudgmental way that caught him off guard: "You *absolutely* did everything you possibly could, Richie. At that point...it's not your circus, not your—"

"Monkey," he interjected quietly, letting that nugget fully sink in.

As for Beckers' situation, it had taken a year for her fiancée to show his true colors, but his narcissistic ways had raised their ugly head, and his constant putdowns became too much to handle on top of his infidelities.

Through sharing, with a great deal of mutual sensitivity and trust they both found it to be a very safe place, and their individual communication skills strengthened each other and the collective. Good therapy and good mojo this.

Born of a mutual like and respect for each other, they treaded lightly as they got to know one another on that basis, and waited a full two months before they'd found themselves on an actual date, a trip to a Santa Cruz karaoke bar—her idea.

In the car—by himself—was one thing, but singing in front of other humans was more than a little outside of Rich's comfort zone. After hearing her knock it out of the park on a cover version of Susan Tedeschi's "Angel From Montgomery," Rich eventually found the requisite courage—buoyed also by a couple of strong margaritas— and surprised everyone, especially himself, with a very respectable and unintentionally amusing turn on Billy Idol's "White Wedding."

Where'd that come from?

Poolside hangouts, family time—his then hers— the occasional movie night, and, a mutual favorite, garage sales and monthly swap meets, had provided ample opportunity to get to know each other, test the waters and plumb the possibilities.

And the possibilities seemed to be increasingly many.

Everybody saw it—how they looked at each other, the knowing smiles, the way they held each other's hand at every opportunity— and Ellen's kids had recently taken to singing the age-old teasing rhyme when the family would get together: *"Rich and Becky, sittin' in the tree, K-I-S-S-I-N-G…first comes—"*

"Okay, guys…that's enough," Uncle Rich would say with a chuckle, and a wink to his partner.

He always cut them off there. Thus far, anyway.

But probably not for long…

He'd go with it.

◆

ABOUT THE AUTHOR

Jafe Danbury hails from the trenches of the Hollywood production scene, where he spent decades as a camera operator, director of photography, and director. He has also worked as a teacher and is a decorated U.S. Navy veteran.

He enjoys noodling on the guitar, long road trips, likes his bacon crispy, and loves a good dive bar—especially if it happens to have a twenty-two-foot shuffleboard table. He prefers a leisurely walk to running, unless being chased by a clown with a chainsaw.

Jafe and his lovely bride currently reside in central California and are working on their exit plan. Their children consist of several rescue dogs and a couple of cockatoos. *The Other Cheek* is his first novel.

AUTHOR'S NOTES

The Other Cheek takes place in the early nineteen nineties, a time before most of us had the luxury of the internet. It was a time before the existence of many things we take for granted today: smart phones, social media, search engines, shared information and online links to helpful informational resources.

Thankfully, all of these things are in existence now, and help is readily available if you—or a friend, or loved one—are subjected to domestic abuse.

If you happen to be going through any form of domestic abuse, please seek out the proper local resources in your area. Get to a safe place, physically, emotionally, and spiritually.

The National Domestic Violence HOTLINE is an excellent resource. A link to their site is listed below.

Good luck, blessings your way, and listen for the mockingbird...

~ Jafe Danbury

The National Domestic Violence HOTLINE

www.thehotline.org

CPSIA information can be obtained
at www.ICGtesting.com
Printed in the USA
LVHW091706120520
655458LV00004B/1024